# YOUR
# ONE &
# ONLY

# YOUR ONE & ONLY

Adrianne Finlay

*Houghton Mifflin Harcourt*
Boston   New York

For information about permission to reproduce selections from this book, write to trade.permissions@hmhco.com or to Permissions, Houghton Mifflin Harcourt Publishing Company, 3 Park Avenue, 19th Floor, New York, New York 10016.

hmhco.com

The text was set in Sabon LT Std.

The Library of Congress Cataloging-in-Publication Data is on file.
ISBN 978-0-544-99147-7

Printed in the United States of America
DOC 10 9 8 7 6 5 4 3 2 1
4500695901

*For Jeremy*

# YOUR
# ONE &
# ONLY

*Chapter One*

# ALTHEA

Althea-310 waited for class to begin, sitting in a neat row with her nine sisters. They'd spent the morning on their floor of the Althea dorm twisting bright ribbons into their hair, and all ten of them had a different color winding through otherwise identical dark curls. Althea-310 had chosen lavender. Althea-316 had wanted lavender, so they'd agreed to draw sticks, but Althea-316 still scowled three seats away with her blue ribbon, even though it had all been fair and she didn't have any reason to sulk like that. As the sisters casually communed while waiting for class to start and their emotions mingled together, Althea-316's resentment threaded through them all like a faraway hum. A Gen-290 Althea had admonished them for inviting the conflict into their group, but Althea-310 overheard the older woman comment a few moments later how she'd secretly laughed about it all.

"They should use white, like our generation did," she'd said. "It'd be so much simpler. I guess it's something Altheas have to learn on their own. I just thought the Gen-310s would have it figured out by the time they were fifteen. We certainly knew better."

Althea-310 didn't care what Altheas were supposed to learn. She liked the way the silky colors fell down her sisters' backs, a rainbow in an otherwise boring classroom. Anyway, she felt pretty. Lavender really was nicer than blue.

The sisters' nine faces all turned in Althea's direction as they sensed the pride coming from her, and Althea-311 gave a small shake of her head, a silent warning. Althea clasped her hands together and focused on tamping the feeling down. It would only make things worse with Althea-316, and there were other things to worry about today besides ribbons.

Vispera's town council had told the class there would be a test. They were to expect a visitor, someone who was part of a new research experiment that would make the three communities better. Though Althea had a hard time imagining that Vispera, or even the other two communities, could be any better than they were now.

A Gen-290 Samuel walked in brusquely and put his books on the desk up front. It was Samuel-299, who wasn't actually a teacher, but a Council member and also a doctor at the clinic. So the experiment to make the community better was something medical. That was odd, however, since genetic modification meant that, in three hundred years, no one in Vispera had ever had so much as a cold.

The Samuel's gaze passed quickly over the ten Carson brothers in the back, their feet spread lazily in front of them, taking up as much room as possible. The younger versions of himself, the Gen-310 Samuels, filled the middle row. Then he took in the front row of Altheas, their posture straight and hands folded on their desks. He shook his head at the different colored ribbons in their hair, smiling absently.

"You Altheas," he said. "Always up to something." He fiddled with his books, acting strangely nervous for a Samuel. "I know the Council talked to you some about what we're doing today," he said, perching on the edge of the desk. "You need to meet someone. He's going to be part of our class from now on, part of our community, and if things go well, you'll see a lot more of him. Now, understand, you'll find him . . . different. But I expect you all to behave and be polite."

Althea had no idea who the Samuel would want them to meet. And what about the test? Althea had spent last night with her friend Nyla-313 quizzing each other on history, so a medical test would be a disaster.

Althea liked working with Nyla-313. Nyla was learning in the labs how to engineer clever little oranges spliced with wild seeds so they tasted of cinnamon, and she would bring her experiments to Althea for their study sessions. Also, the Nylas never teased Althea about the scar on her wrist, and Nyla-313 often told her she shouldn't bother hiding it. But while Althea enjoyed the colored ribbons, she didn't like her scar. When it wasn't covered, the eyes of those in the community landed on the smooth line of white skin circling her wrist, and she hated how they'd inevitably say, "Oh, Althea-310," as if all they needed to know about her was that she was the sister born with the defect, the one who'd needed a replacement hand grown separately in a limb tank. She used to wonder why she hadn't been eliminated once it was discovered. It must have been apparent while she floated in the tanks, months before she was born. But it would have shown up too late to start creating another Althea. It had happened before, usually through accidental death, that a model's generation had only nine people instead of ten, but it caused a lot of discontent, even some disruption. That must have been the reason she hadn't been eliminated.

Now all the studying they'd done would be for nothing. This was all very unusual; they never strayed from the curriculum. Maybe Samuel-299 had brought in someone from one of the other communities, maybe from Copan or even all the way from Crooked Falls. Maybe even an Althea. Althea had always wondered how the Altheas in Crooked Falls might be different. Was their penmanship as elegant as the Vispera Altheas'? Did they cut their hair shoulder-length, like the Altheas in Copan? Maybe there was another Althea out there who was born with a defective right hand and also had a scar like the one around her wrist.

But it couldn't be an Althea from Crooked Falls, of course. The Samuel had said *him*. It was probably just another Samuel, then. Althea sighed, realizing the ribbons were probably going to be the only real excitement of the day.

Samuel-299 paused at the door before stepping out, his brow creased, his voice plaintive. "Remember, just . . . be kind."

When Samuel-299 returned, a boy entered behind him. On seeing him, the row of Samuels collectively sucked in a breath. A Carson huffed an incredulous laugh. Every Althea reached a trembling hand for the hand of the sister next to her until their fingers wove together in an unbroken sequence. Althea communed with them, feeling their emotions as she felt her own. Every sister and brother communed in small, subtle ways all the time when they were close together, as did everyone in Vispera, but in moments of stress or fear, it was important to seek a strengthened connection through touch. Her sisters' collective

4

effort to calm one another coursed through her like liquid. It was warm, seeming to fill her limbs. She exhaled as, little by little, the shared anxiety eased.

The boy fidgeted miserably. He ran his fingers through his hair, then pushed his hands into his pockets. Althea tried to figure out his age. She thought he was probably fifteen, like the rest of them. He looked scared, but no one stroked him or tried to comfort him, no one held his hand to commune, not like the brothers and sisters did for one another.

His eyes glanced from student to student, quick and nervous. He looked like he might be somewhat intelligent, but it was hard to tell. *Even if he is,* she thought, *he's still so strange. He's not one of us. Not at all.* He was like no one else.

Althea had seen so many faces. She'd seen all the nine faces of the nine models of *Homo factus,* at all different ages. She'd seen these faces in Vispera as well as on a school trip to Copan. They were the same faces she'd see in Crooked Falls as well. There was nothing beyond the walls of the communities but an empty, overgrown wasteland left by a long gone civilization. The faces in the three communities were the only faces that existed anywhere in the whole world, the only ones that had existed for over three hundred years.

The picture on the wall on the far side of the classroom showed these nine faces in a painting an early Inga had rendered based on a photo of the Original Nine. They were the human scientists who'd founded Vispera, using their genes to create the nine models. They stood on the steps of what was now Remembrance Hall in two rows, serious and self-assured. Their hands rested on one another's shoulders, and they gazed out at the students in the classroom as if glimpsing the future, hopeful and confident about the new world they were building. The same painting hung in every classroom, and the very first version resided in Remembrance Hall.

There were the Samuels, with their dark skin, even darker eyes, and their sharp, angular jaws. They radiated compassion in their thoughtful expressions, which helped when they treated a scraped knee or broken bone. Every model had a specified set of skills and a role within the community, and the Samuels were the doctors, nurses, and caretakers. The Altheas were historians, of course, which meant they kept records and preserved the history of Vispera.

The Nylas, the scientists, had eyes as dark as the Samuels', but with a life and humor in them that the Samuels didn't have. The Nylas' eyes reminded Althea of a black stone on the shore, still wet from salt water and shining with hidden colors. The Ingas, the community's artists, were tall and broad shouldered, as imposing as statues, but with light, creamy brown hair that would start turning white in their fortieth year, at about the same age the Carsons' faces softened and widened, right along with their waists. Not like they were now, in class. As young men the Carsons were sleek and flat-stomached. Though whatever age the Carsons were, they always strode through the town Commons like it belonged to them. They were the engineers, and they thought that made them more important than the other models.

The Hassans, the ecologists, carried themselves gracefully, like leaves floating over rippling river water, and their small, agile fingers could tinker with a threshing machine so adeptly you'd think they were talking to it and telling it in which direction to move. The Hassans were the complete opposite of the Viktors with their brooding foreheads and hulking shoulders. The Viktors were the philosophers, which meant they were always ready to lay a thick hand on the arm of anyone who broke even the smallest rule. They kept the community safe and regulated.

The Meis and the Kates were a study in contrast, too. Althea admired the Meis' sense of style, which went far beyond colored ribbons. As theologians, they loved the rituals of the community and always knew how to put the final touches on a ceremony, something that would keep it familiar and comforting, while still offering a new element, like when they hung a glittering chandelier from a balsa tree. They had delicate limbs, and always dressed with careful thought and precision, never forgetting to include something shiny in their matching dresses. If they wore a ribbon in their perfectly straight hair, it would always be something shimmering. The mathematician Kates, on the other hand, shunned anything sparkly, preferring instead their serious, demure outfits that went along with their turned-down mouths and sloped brown eyes that always made them look somehow disapproving. Or at least that's how they often looked at the Altheas, who were too unpredictable to ever please the Kates, especially the older ones.

These were the faces Althea knew. She'd known them her entire life, and knew them at every age, and in every mood. Sure, sometimes an accident or slight genetic nuance would alter a familiar face—the tiny freckle on Inga-313's ear, or the little indentation on Viktor-318's collarbone from when he broke it in a wrestling match. And of course, Althea's own scarred wrist. These faces were her whole world. They *were* the whole world.

She'd never seen a face like this boy's.

And his *eyes*. Something was wrong with them. The eyes of the nine models were all brown, though they varied in the range of shades. This boy's were almost colorless, watery and cold, an odd bluish-gray. How could eyes be gray?

Althea shook herself, shivering at the ghostly translucent color, but at the same time realizing it was not simply what he looked like that was disturbing. She also *felt* nothing from him. It certainly looked as though he was nervous in front of the class, but the only indications of fear were what she could *see*— his shuffling feet and shaky hands, the way he blinked nervously. Emotions that strong should have been radiating off him like a fever, infecting the whole class. Instead, he was isolated, a solitary figment as cold as the stone wall that surrounded the town.

Everyone in class was rustling and shifting in their chairs. They felt the bone-chilling detachment from the boy as well.

"What's wrong with its face?" Carson-315 asked.

Althea had wondered the same thing, but couldn't imagine asking the question herself. The boy's ears brightened red, which meant he had heard and understood Carson-315.

"Nothing's *wrong* with his face," Samuel-299 said. "He's simply different."

"Different from what?" a Samuel asked, Samuel-317.

"From the nine models." Samuel-299 nodded to the painting on the wall. "He's human, like they were."

"So he's not *Homo factus,*" a Carson said, grimacing.

"No. Like I said, he's human—*Homo sapiens.*"

"Where are his brothers?" Althea-316 asked.

"He has no brothers—he's alone."

*Alone.* The word struck Althea's ears, its awful power tightening her chest. She leaned back, trying to put distance between herself and the strangeness of this boy.

"Why would we bother making a human? What good is it?" Carson-317 said.

Samuel-299 rubbed his mouth as if realizing this situation —whatever it was—should be going better. He took a breath. "The Council has been conducting an experiment. Humans were a great people. It's because of them that life continued through us."

Althea noticed that the Samuel hadn't actually answered the question. He hadn't said what the Council's experiment was for. He was hiding something.

"They couldn't have been that great," Samuel-314 said. "I mean, they're dead."

The Carsons cracked up at that. Carson-310 slapped Samuel-310 on the shoulder, and then all the Carsons copied the same action nine more times, right down the row of Samuels. Samuel-299 watched them mimic each other, one by one, a strange look on his face.

"They're extinct," Samuel-299 finally said. "Humans reproduced genetic lines that shouldn't have been allowed to continue. Their mistakes are what caused the Slow Plague."

It was hard to imagine what it was like when humans covered the planet. Althea pictured a world overrun by an unrestrained population, reproducing like animals, their genes mingling unpredictably and disastrously. The communities now were entirely regulated and controlled. Her people maintained the same three communities with populations that never rose above nine hundred. There were ten generations of each of the nine models, and a new generation born every decade. But before Vispera, every face was unique, and there were millions of them. To Althea, it sounded horrible, like thousands of insects crawling in a thousand directions.

A Carson nodded his chin at the boy. "So is he going to get sick and die like they did?"

The strange boy looked up at Samuel-299 as if waiting for him to say something that would make the others stop looking at him with suspicious glints in their eyes, like they didn't know whether they should laugh at him or actually be angry that he was contaminating their classroom. The Samuel rested a hand on the boy's shoulder and said, "He's healthy so far. His lack of abnormality is one of the reasons we chose his genetic material from the Sample Room."

The boy's shoulders turned in, deflating under the Samuel's hand. Althea thought perhaps he wasn't happy with the way the Samuel was talking about him.

"All of you," Samuel-299 said, "come from the Originals who lived here back when the humans called it Costa Rica. Our genetic lines are refined and perfected. Where humans relied on natural selection, we have technology and science. That's what makes us fundamentally singular from humans. We have no mutations, no genetic outliers, no mistakes or abnormalities. We all work together, communing and cooperating. Jack, on the other hand . . . genetically, his cells were never altered. He's an exact copy of a human boy who lived in the twenty-first century. And that makes him different. But while he may be different in some ways, in many other ways he's just like you."

"Does it talk?" Carson-312 said.

"Yes." Samuel-299 pierced Carson-312 with a stare. "*He* talks." Samuel-299 turned to the boy, hovering over him, his body rigid and impatient. "Go ahead, say hello. Introduce yourself."

They waited while the boy shuffled his feet.

"My name . . . my name is . . ." He spoke uncertainly, but then stopped as if making a decision. He straightened his shoulders to stand with more assurance. "I'm Jack."

One of Althea's sisters giggled. "*Jack?*" she said. "That's not a name. There's not even a number after it. What generation is he supposed to be?"

"Maybe he's Jack Zero," a Samuel said, and everyone laughed.

"Hey, Jack!" one of the boys called. Almost immediately a chorus of calls followed, with the name being shouted by everyone in the classroom. They shouted as if testing the name out, though the more it was said, the more they took delight in jeering at the boy. His name did sound strange, Althea had to admit. Foreign and unfamiliar. Her fingers slid unconsciously to her wrist. She didn't join in the shouting.

"Please, everyone," Samuel-299 said. "That's enough."

Jack's chest rose and fell, and then rose again.

"Sam," the boy said, which was odd, because he was talking to Samuel-299. Nobody called any of the Samuels *Sam*. It seemed disrespectful, though Althea couldn't say why exactly.

Samuel-299 looked at him sharply. "Jack? Are you all right?"

Jack wiped his nose with the back of his hand. His breath wheezed. Carson-318 snorted laughter, repeating the name Jack, mimicking the concerned way Samuel-299 had said it, though the man was too focused to hear.

"Is it an attack?"

The boy nodded. Althea couldn't figure out what the problem

was. He seemed to be having trouble breathing. Sensing something wrong, the class went silent until the only sound in the room was the whistle of air being sucked into the boy's lungs. As she watched him struggle to breathe, the seconds moved so slowly that Althea imagined for a moment she could see them shimmering the air like heat.

Jack fumbled in his pocket, producing a plastic tube gripped in his palm. Samuel-299 touched his back.

"It's okay," he said to Jack. "Calm down."

Jack put the tube in his mouth, pressed down, and sucked in. It looked like something he'd done many times before. A tension seemed to release from Samuel-299 as Jack's breathing eased.

"What was that?" a younger Samuel asked.

Samuel-299's eyes closed briefly before he looked up, reluctant to talk about what had just happened. "He uses that device, an inhaler, for a condition called asthma. It makes it hard for him to breathe sometimes, that's all."

"That's all?" Carson-317 said, distaste showing on his face. "He's sick. What if we catch it?"

"You can't catch it."

"You said he wasn't abnormal. That looked pretty abnormal to me," Carson-314 said.

"He's not abnormal. He's human, and in humans a certain amount of abnormality is, well . . . normal."

The Carsons looked disgusted at the Samuel's response.

Samuel-299 braced his hands on the desk and seemed to come to a decision. "You know, let's continue this after lunch, shall we?"

"It's too early for lunch," someone said.

"Nevertheless, we'll have a break," Samuel-299 said dryly.

"Everyone should go outside. Maybe you can all get to know Jack a little better."

As Althea stood with the others, her pencil bag fell from her desk, spilling its contents. Her sisters were already at the door, so she quickly bent to gather her things. She found herself at eye level with the top of her desk, and there was Jack right in front of her, holding out one of her pencils. She froze, and then realized it was rude to stare at him. Still he waited, his hand steady and patient. She reached to take the pencil, and her sleeve rode up to reveal the scar.

One of the Carsons strode past. "Need a hand?" he snickered, as if proud of a joke she'd heard a million times before.

Althea grabbed the pencil and tugged her sleeve down. Her eyes met Jack's, and his head tilted questioningly. Up close, his eyes startled her yet again with their pale gray.

Altheas were an observant model, so even though Jack seemed unable to commune, Althea could see in his face that he was curious, and also lonely. The other eight models relied exclusively on communing to understand the emotions of others. They would never notice the way his eyes dipped down to her hand holding the pencil, or the way he sucked his lip against his teeth.

He gave her a tentative smile. Two of his bottom teeth overlapped just a tiny bit, a distracting imperfection none of her own people had. A carved bead hung at the base of his neck on a leather string. As with everything else about the boy, this was strange too. None of the four boys in the community wore necklaces.

"Thank you," she murmured, clutching the pencil and allowing herself to smile back.

A remaining Carson bumped into her, and then a sister returned to grab her arm and hurry her along with the rest of them. When she glanced back, she saw Jack still watching her.

Outside, the students milled about the schoolyard, unsure of what to do. The brick school was on the edge of town, bordered on one side by the stone wall that surrounded Vispera, safeguarding it from the jungle outside, the wild animals and poisonous plants. Jack leaned against the wall, his arms crossed over his chest. Everyone else had clustered as far from him as possible, their feet kicking up dust from the rust-colored gravel of the yard.

The usual games and sports didn't feel right. Activities were supposed to happen after lunch, and Jack was making everyone nervous. Althea saw her own worry mirrored in the faces of her sisters. They huddled together, their hands lightly touching hair and arms and backs. The Carsons and Samuels were in their own clusters, and then the Carsons all laughed simultaneously. They passed the Altheas and sauntered toward Jack, who pushed himself away from the wall as they came near.

Carson-312 smirked. "That's Samuel-299 who brought you, isn't it? He's on the Council." He looked Jack up and down. "What'd the Council do, make a hairless monkey? Isn't that all a human is, a bald monkey?"

"You're humans, too," Jack said. "You're clones of the Originals, and they were human."

The Samuels crowded Althea and her sisters as they gathered to watch while keeping a safe distance from Jack.

Carson-312 smirked, then casually picked up a handful of gravel from the ground, jostling it in his palm as he moved closer to Jack. "He's not very smart, is he? He just called us *clones*."

Jack licked his lips uncertainly. "Isn't that what you are?"

A young Samuel came forward. "Don't you know anything? We don't say *clone*. We're *Homo factus*." He straightened as if proud of the title. "We're the self-made man."

"You," Carson-317 said, looking Jack up and down, "you're just some defective experiment of the Council. You're an accident."

The boy couldn't be an accident. The Council didn't make mistakes.

"I'm not an accident," Jack said, clearly wishing he could offer more of a rationale for his existence.

"Yeah?" said another Carson. "So you want to tell us what we need a monkey-boy for, then?"

Althea could tell that Jack was trying. He wanted the other boys, and the Altheas too, to accept him. The Carsons especially were being mean, but Jack looked hopeful, as if somehow things would still be okay. Althea kept quiet. The Altheas weren't involved in this, and there was something wrong with the boy, something much worse than a replaced hand. Whatever *asthma* really was, it was obviously a disease her people had spent generations eradicating. Her people didn't suffer from disease. That Jack had a thing like asthma was terrifying. Despite what the Samuel said, human illness was contagious. It was what had killed them all. It was better to keep her distance, as the rest of her sisters were doing.

Jack's eyes flickered between the Carsons. He looked to the Samuels for help, searching for a friendly face. While they wouldn't join in with the Carsons, not with an elder Samuel right inside, they also wouldn't try to stop them. A few of Althea's sisters chewed their nails.

Carson-312 flicked a pebble at Jack's shoulder. "Well,

monkey-boy?" he said. "If you're not an accident, what the hell are you?"

"I . . . I don't . . ." Jack struggled, not knowing what answer to give.

"You're not one of us," Carson-311 said.

Carson-312 flicked another pebble, hitting Jack's arm. "You don't belong here."

A third pebble immediately followed, this one striking his shoulder again. Jack backed away, his tongue pressing his teeth. The boys sniggered, and now the Samuels joined in. More of the Carsons took up handfuls of gravel.

Jack closed his eyes and pulled an unsteady breath into his chest. "Stop it," he said, his voice thin and strained. His fingers reached into his pocket, seeking the inhaler he'd used inside. It was the asthma again. The Samuel had called it an attack, as if the boy's own body were assaulting him just as much as the Carsons seemed ready to do. Althea shuddered. Jack finally got the inhaler out but then dropped it in the dirt. He fell to his knees, his hands scrambling for it frantically, panic etched on his face.

All ten Carsons grinned at once.

Althea's sisters stood like her, watching. They were feeling what she was — fear, and also disgust. Carsons were confrontational. They were engineers, but also leaders. They liked being in charge, even in Vispera, where the only hierarchy was age and decisions were made by consensus. Still, the community celebrated the Carsons' sense of leadership as much as it did the Nylas' work in the labs or the Ingas' paintings. The community taught the young people that they should think of the differences in the models as the various organs of the body, each with its own role, but working together for the good of the whole.

This, however, was the bad side of the Carsons.

As much as Althea didn't like what the Carsons and Samuels were doing, it was painfully clear to everyone that Jack wasn't *Homo factus*. He did mostly look like all of them, but that only made the blankness they felt from him more terrible. Everyone's emotions were so strong. In one moment of communing, Althea could most palpably feel her sisters' sick fear. Under that, she sensed the uneasy, excited tension of the Samuels, and then the current of gleeful anger emanating from the Carsons. Like everyone else, she felt nothing from the boy. As if he were an animal. As if he were dead.

Jack's shoulders hunched forward. Another Carson threw a pebble at his forehead. The pebbles weren't large enough to cause more than a brief sting, but Jack's eyes darted from face to face as if he feared what might come next.

Althea peered toward the window of their classroom. Where was the Samuel? And then she saw him. He was watching the students through a window. He was frowning and taking notes. Why didn't he do something?

It occurred to her then that this was the test the Council had planned. It wasn't on history or science, or anything they'd studied for. The test was how they acted today, with this boy the Council had thrust upon them. And perhaps they were watching Jack as well, to see how he would fit in. But surely Samuel-299 wouldn't let things go too far. Althea didn't like the sneers growing on the Carsons' faces.

"Look at you," Carson-312 said, taking a step forward. "You

think you're not an accident? You're so defective you can't even breathe right."

Jack flinched as another pebble hit him. He clutched the retrieved inhaler close to his chest, and the students closed in.

Althea didn't know what to do. Her sisters didn't know what to do. They met each other's eyes, silently communing with the same feeling. This had to stop.

Althea-313 said, far too softly, "Quit it, you guys."

It was as if she'd said nothing. The boys paid no attention.

The Carsons continued throwing the pebbles while Carson-318 tore a narrow switch from a nearby patch of brush and handed it to Carson-312, who whipped it back and forth, testing its heft. It hissed as it cut the air. Standing over Jack, Carson-312 snapped it against Jack's arm, leaving a thin welt. The brothers continued to jeer and gather more pebbles. Carson-312 swung again, striking Jack's back.

Althea couldn't see Jack's face, but his limbs tightened with each snap of the switch, and she saw his shivering, barely contained control. There was a rigidity in his muscles, like his entire body was a spring straining for release.

He was using all his will to hold himself back. He was still hoping they'd stop.

It was too much to watch. Althea broke away from her sisters and grabbed Carson-312's arm as it rose up again. His elbow hit her eye, and she fell to the ground. Her sisters ran to her, closing her in their protective circle, touching her face.

Althea cupped her aching eye. Her sisters held their own eyes, feeling the burgeoning pain themselves. Carson-312 hadn't even paused, had probably hardly noticed her near him. The whip slashed across Jack's back until specks of red dotted the fabric of his shirt like a string of beads. Carson-312 licked his lips and aimed for those lines of red, a glint in his eye. *He's enjoying it,* Althea thought. Seeing Jack recoil at the targeted strikes, Carson-312 quickened his swings. Breathless with exertion, he muttered, "Go back to whatever lab they've been keeping you in, *human.* You don't belong here."

As the switch came down once again, Jack's hand shot out and caught it. It sliced into the flesh of his palm as he yanked it from Carson-312. He launched himself off the wall, a yell wrenched from his throat, and flew at Carson-312 faster than Althea thought possible. Jack tackled him to the ground and straddled his chest, striking him over and over. The other Carsons didn't dare touch him, even to protect their own brother. They'd never seen such fury.

Jack slammed his fist into Carson-312's face, and blood poured from his nose. Jack's wild hits landed again and again. The Carson brothers began to collapse on the ground, moaning and clutching their heads, the sound and pain of the blows echoing in their own skulls. One of Althea's sisters clutched her stomach, and at the same time, Althea felt sick too, all the Altheas did.

The class looked on in horror as Jack pummeled Carson-312 until his face was swollen and bloody. Only a few moments had passed, but to Althea it felt like an eternity before Samuel-299 finally ran outside. He hauled Jack off Carson-312. Jack fought, heedless and wild, as Samuel-299 dragged him across the yard and through the school doors.

The class stood silent and motionless, like a held breath, the only sound in the yard Carson-312's wet, snuffling moans. Althea felt everyone's anger and alarm slowly recede like a tide.

The Carsons gathered around Carson-312, ghosts of his pain stirring in their own bodies.

A couple of them pressed their white shirts to Carson-312's face, and the cotton bloomed red. Eventually, the Samuels came and took Carson-312 away to the clinic. By the time the students filed back into the school, Jack was nowhere to be seen, and a Hassan was at the front of the room.

Once more the faces in the painting of the Original Nine stared down at Althea and the rest of the class, their expressions as placid and confident as ever, as if nothing at all had happened.

## Chapter Two

# JACK

TWO YEARS LATER

J ack sat in the grass on the steep side of the hill, knocking a ball against the side of the white-boarded cottage. He heard Sam's heavy breathing from climbing the steep rise, and he didn't need to turn around to know he'd find the man standing over him, wearing his white lab coat and disapproving frown.

"You shouldn't be here," Sam finally said.

"I should be dead," Jack said. Although if he thought about it, that wasn't really true. It wasn't that he should be dead, but that he should never have been born. He should be extinct, like all the other humans.

High on the slope, Jack could see the entire wall encircling the town, six feet high and broad enough to walk on; a double-winged gate of wrought iron faced Blue River. Within, the school sat on one end, where the Gen-320 children played in the gravel-covered yard, the same one where, two years ago, he'd attacked the Carson; next to that was the cluster of labs where the clones conducted their experiments and grew the new

Gens in their tanks. On the other end stood the stout line of nine dorms, one building for every model, a separate room inside for every Gen, each with its own row of ten beds. In the middle of the dorms was the dining hall, a circular, two-story building of limestone quarried from the distant cliffs. All the clones gathered there for meals at wooden banquet tables, at least when they weren't outside celebrating one of their seemingly incessant rituals. In the center of everything stood Remembrance Hall and the Commons, an expanse of lawn around a large kapok tree where the clones held their ceremonies and parties. Sometimes Jack watched at night from a distance while they danced and lights twinkled in the lanky branches of the huge tree.

Beyond the wall at the foot of the cottage's hill, the lawn dipped down to the banks of Blue River, which flowed north until it disappeared, swallowed by dense jungle. On the far side, fields of corn, barley, and wild rice, dotted by the lingering shadow of summer clouds, stretched all the way to the Novomundo Mountains. *Novomundo,* the New World Mountains. They'd been named by scientists, years before Jack was born, and the world they'd made was no longer new.

Jack had spent his whole life isolated from the clones his own age, and when he'd finally been allowed to join them, it'd been a disaster. The Council never let him go back to school. Now he spent his days living in the tiny bedroom they'd built for him in the labs, occasionally performing some task in the clinic for Sam, like rolling bandages or folding linens. They would never let him forget what had happened, or that it had all been his fault.

Jack hadn't spoken for several moments, so Sam sighed and sat next to him in the grass. He watched Jack throw the ball. Again and again, he caught and threw, and Sam waited.

If that's how Sam wanted this to go, that was fine. Jack plucked the ball out of the air once more.

For some reason, Sam couldn't catch a ball if his life depended on it. Jack had tried to figure out why Sam had such a hard time. He simply couldn't get the rhythms down, and he missed every throw. Inga-296 had given Jack the ball when he was little. Jack couldn't remember exactly when, but he must have been about five years old.

"It's called a *baseball*," she'd said, "Young people from your time, they played with it." She held it out, smiling. "Who knows, maybe your original did."

Jack had looked up a description of *baseball* in one of the books that filled the little cottage he and Sam and Inga-296 had shared back then, before Sam brought Jack to live in the labs in town. Before she died. The book said you needed nine people to make a team, so now he just tossed the ball at the side of the house. If the clones ever wanted to play, even with their lousy coordination, they already had their nine models. They wouldn't include him.

Sam stopped watching the ball. He frowned at Jack while Jack ignored him, each trying to outlast the other. Sam finally heaved a breath and gave in.

"I've been looking everywhere for you," he said. "It's not safe outside the wall. You need to come home."

"This is my home." Jack felt familiar resentment welling in his veins.

"This hasn't been your home for years. Your home is in Vispera."

Jack tossed the ball. "You should have told me."

"My brother told you."

23

"*You* should have told me. You act like you're all the same person, but you're not. You're different from them."

Sam bristled. "I'm not different from them. They're Samuels, and I'm a Samuel."

"They're Samuels. You're Sam. Don't send them to me thinking I can't tell the difference. They don't care about me. They wouldn't care if I died."

"I don't think that's true."

Jack knew Sam didn't really believe they'd care, but he let the man lie to him.

"I'm sorry, Jack. The Council won't budge."

"You're on the Council. Did you even try?"

"Of course I did."

"It's that fat Carson, isn't it? He thinks I'm a freak, and the others listen to him."

"It's all of them. They think it'd be disruptive."

It wasn't fair. He was turning seventeen, just like the Gen-310s, and he should be in the Declaration with them. He'd had as much of an education sitting in the labs as they had at school. More, he'd guess. It was just like last year, when they wouldn't let him participate in the Gen's first Pairing Ceremony. He'd wanted to, desperately, but the Council had said no, citing that disastrous day at the school.

That night, when everyone had Paired for the first time except him, he'd watched their celebration hidden in the branches of a tall tree. They'd danced and eaten colorful foods he'd never seen before. The girls wore gauzy dresses, and the boys wore the ceremonial robes tied with leather belts, and in the evening they'd all chosen their partner for the first Pairing and then spent the rest of the evening laughing together and talking. Jack wasn't even allowed to sit at the table with the Gens in the Commons for their meal. Sam would bring him potatoes and carrots from the dining halls, or rice and lentils, and sometimes Sam would stay and eat with him, but mostly he was alone. For Jack, those nights were the worst. And it would all happen again tonight after the Declaration. They would eat and dance and laugh, they would Declare and let the community know what apprenticeship they'd chosen, and then they'd Pair in the evening.

The laughter of the children in the schoolyard carried up the hill on a breeze. Usually they romped on climbing ropes, swings, and slides that the Ingas had made for them, but today they played a game. The children stood in a row with their fisted hands extended, while a single girl walked down the line and cupped their hands in her own one by one. Jack had seen this game before. Sam had told him it was called Button. One child would hold a button in his hand, and the rest would pretend they also had a button. The finder had to guess who actually had it. When Jack had first seen it, he'd thought the point of the game was to keep the secret of having the button, but he'd been wrong. He slowly figured out that the child wanted to be found out. If they played the game well, everyone would know where the button was. It was a way for them to practice communing, not just with their siblings, which seemed to come easily to them, but with the other children in their Gen.

The laughter stopped as abruptly as it'd started, and even from a distance Jack could tell that smiles had spread across their faces as if they'd all heard the same joke at the same time, though nothing had been said. There were no words in this game. Another eruption of laughter ran through the group in eerie unison.

Sam had once tried to describe communing to Jack. He'd had difficulty finding the right words, like describing colors to someone who'd never seen them. He said communing was like a *murmuring,* a sort of whisper of emotions passing from one clone to another when they touched or were close. They didn't know each other's thoughts, but they sensed each other's feelings.

Jack couldn't commune, of course. He could never play their strange, silent games, and maybe they'd never let him participate in their rituals and ceremonies. But why shouldn't he be in the Declaration? It only happened once, and then they could send him back to his room in the labs and forget again that he ever existed. What harm would it do to let him be part of the community in this small way? He hadn't asked to exist. He'd heard the Council talk. They called him an experiment, like one of their genetically modified cows. They called him a de-extinction project, and maybe they called him an accident, but they had *created* him.

Earlier that morning, the jagged cliffs in the distance had been covered in gray mist, now burned away. They'd looked like prehistoric beasts hiding under the earth. Jack wondered, as he always did, what lay beyond those hills.

"I could leave," Jack said. "Grab supplies, go to the jungle. Nobody would care anyway."

"You can't leave."

"Why not?"

"Because," Sam said, puffing out his cheeks, "you would die in the jungle. You can't survive out there alone. I've kept you safe here because Inga-296 asked me to. I'm not going to stop now. She said we needed you."

"That's a joke, Sam. No one here needs me."

Sam's eyes lingered on the baseball that had fallen idle in Jack's hands. "I know you come here because of the Inga. I know you miss her."

Jack touched the bead around his neck. He was surprised Sam had mentioned her. Inga-296 had called herself Jack's mother, even though mothers didn't exist in Vispera. Jack hadn't cried about her in years, not since he was little, because early on he'd sensed too keenly Sam's discomfort with Jack's emotions at losing her. It was one of the many things that kept Jack apart from everyone else. The clones didn't miss anyone. They saw themselves as the countless iterations that they were. A part of a whole. Replaceable. But Inga, his mother, had been different from anyone else in Vispera. She'd been different from the other Ingas. She had loved him.

"Of course I miss her. She was my mother."

"Yes, your mother." Jack noticed how the word *mother* rolled in Sam's mouth, foreign and strange. Not unpleasant, just something to work his tongue around, like a sour candy. "I didn't agree with her using that term, but she'd taken charge of the experiment, so I didn't argue. Now I think perhaps I should have." Sam spoke more to himself than to Jack. "And maybe it was a mistake for her to give you all those books."

Sam was talking about the *human* books. The ones Sam never read. Jack had learned about humans by reading those books, and one of the things he'd learned was how, even though the humans couldn't commune, they still cared about each other.

Maybe it would never be enough to *tell* Sam how he felt and Sam was capable of caring about someone only if emotions emanated from them like a cloud of reeking smoke.

Deep down, even Jack sometimes wished his mother hadn't given him the books. According to Sam, she'd been the one who wanted to raise him in the cottage on the edge of the jungle, outside the walls of Vispera. She'd wanted to raise him the way his original might have been, the way a human boy would have been raised in human times—with a home, parents, with human books and games and his own bedroom instead of a line of beds in a dorm. She'd raised him to give him some sense of who he was as a human, when really all he wanted was to be like everyone else and have friends his own age. Sometimes he resented all the ways his mother had made him different. And then, in the process, she'd made herself different too, and that had ended in the worst possible way.

"I'm sorry you won't be part of the ceremony, Jack. But listen, I do have good news. The Council has agreed to let you have an apprenticeship. We'll meet with you after the ceremony, and they'll let you Declare."

"Declare an apprenticeship?" Jack hadn't considered this possibility that they might let him have a job in town, serve some useful purpose. He stood. "I'll show them my music," he said, thinking of the instrument Sam had given him years ago that was tucked away in the lab.

*It's a guitar,* Sam had said back then. *At least, that's what the catalogue in the Tunnels called it.* As a child, Jack had built a crude wooden box with strings pulled across the top, trying to mimic the sound of the human recordings his mother had given him. Once Sam had figured out what he was trying to do, he'd brought Jack the guitar from the Tunnels. From the beginning, Jack had been entranced.

"I can tell them how it works," Jack said. "I'll explain the history and play for them."

"That's a bad idea," Sam said, eyeing him worriedly. "They won't understand. I don't even understand it, and I've been listening to you play for years."

Jack had learned a long time ago that the guitar mystified the clones. He played it sometimes in his room during the day as the lab workers outside the door peered into their microscopes. They'd cast him sideways glances, grumbling under their breaths, but the resonant sounds and the strings under his fingers soothed him. Sometimes playing his guitar was the only thing that made him feel sane, the only thing that made him feel like he could keep trying for another day.

In the beginning, watching Sam's reaction to the sound, it had taken a while before Jack understood. The clones actually couldn't hear the music. No, that wasn't right. They could hear it, but they couldn't *hear* it. They called it noise and compared it to the drone of insects outside in the forest. Once or twice, as if they felt like they should research the question, the clones in the lab had asked him why he sat on his bed for hours, making that racket on a hollow piece of wood. How could he explain that, from the first time he'd held an instrument and strummed his fingers over it, he'd felt the pulse of the strings like it was his own beating heart?

When Jack realized the clones couldn't hear music, he'd grasped for the first time how different he was from them. He'd always known they communed with each other and he couldn't, but somehow, their inability to hear music made him feel even more of an outsider. He'd put the guitar away then. But now, with an apprenticeship, it could be different.

"Don't you see?" Jack said. "I'll teach them, really help them understand. I'll show the Council what I can contribute to the community."

"No, I've already thought about this. You'll Declare an apprenticeship in the clinic, work with me. You'll learn medicine, something useful."

"The clinic?" Jack said.

"Of course." Sam stood, done with the conversation. "Just be ready. You'll talk to the Council tomorrow, after the ceremony's done."

Jack chewed the inside of his lip, thinking.

"Don't look so worried. This is a good thing. And I'll be there to help. It'll all be fine."

Sam walked down the hill, back toward town. Jack's gaze followed the man's path until he reached the school, where something had happened in the children's game. They'd clustered together, their hands resting on each other's shoulders, and seemed to collectively sigh into each other as if they were one body. Then, just like that, they broke apart and ran across the field, as sudden and synchronized as a flight of birds.

The next day, Jack sat in the chairs facing the outdoor stage in the Commons, waiting for the ceremony to end so he could make his presentation to the Council.

The Gen-310s had each Declared already. The Meis would apprentice in the kitchens, working on the menus for the dining hall and telling the Hassans, who had Declared as livestock managers and field planners, what food they would need and what to cook. The Viktors, as always, were order keepers. They'd never Declared anything else. The Carsons would work with the Kates and Nylas in the labs, monitoring the tanks, researching genetics, and preparing for the next Gen to be born in three years. The Samuels, as always, Declared as doctors. The Ingas would be designers, keeping the open spaces in town manicured and beautiful, and the dorms comfortable and clean. The Altheas Declared as record keepers.

They carried on with the ceremony as if everyone didn't already know what the models would Declare, as if the community hadn't gone through the exact same motions of the Declaration every ten years. Samuels never worked in the kitchens, as far as Jack knew. But it didn't matter. Every ten years, they played out the ritual.

With the Declaration over, the Gen was performing the dance now. Jack would speak with the Council when it was done. His guitar lay next to him on the ground, and he tapped his foot nervously. He'd thought about making graphs and charts, but had decided in the end to just play for them, and talk to them about the history of music, about how it was a vestige of human history. For some reason, it had been forgotten, but they could get it back again. Jack would help. He had a skill, an ability, and it wasn't new or strange. It was old, had been around for millennia. It was simply waiting to be picked up and dusted off.

Sam still thought he was going to Declare to work in the clinic. He wouldn't be happy about this, but Jack didn't want to work in the clinic. He had to show them that they didn't need to be afraid or repulsed, or think he was strange for offering something like music to them. It could make them better. *He* could make them better by giving them back something they'd lost.

Jack wiped damp hands across his pants. He felt the inhaler tucked in his pocket and took a deep breath in and out, searching for any telltale signs that his lungs were going to betray him. He watched the dance. The Gen-310s traded partners and moved silently across the stage, their performance punctuated only by the sound of their tapping, shuffling feet and the birds in the distant trees.

The clones had many dances. The Pairing dance, for one, and the dances for the Binding Ceremony, or the Yielding Ceremony. The one being performed now wasn't particular for the Declaration, it was simply a dance of contentment, meant to express a kind of pleasure or happiness that things were as they should be, and as the Original Nine intended. The Carsons grasped the Altheas and moved in quick, sure steps, holding the girls' hands with a certain confident authority.

Jack pushed down his dislike for the Carsons. He had to learn. He had to get along with them if the Council was finally going to allow him to have a real purpose in the community. He'd made a mistake when he was fifteen, fighting with the Carson-312, and the Carsons had spent the past two years making sure he didn't forget it. They taunted him, tripped him on his way through town, or acted as if he was invisible, knocking into him as they walked past.

They weren't all like that, though.

Jack searched through the ten Altheas, looking for the 310. The Altheas were graceful as they danced. They moved with a fluid ease that left their dresses flowing behind their legs like birds' wings. They were pretty, with their long dark hair and smooth limbs. He liked the way their mouths turned down in a flat, serious line when they were thinking hard about something.

He always remembered Althea-310 from that day at school. She'd been the only clone that whole day who'd looked at him and smiled. He'd search for her anytime he walked through town. He'd see her, sometimes with one of the Nylas, or he'd pick her out from her group of sisters by searching for the scar on her wrist. She never spoke to him. He'd tried a few times to talk to her, but she always scurried off or was pulled away by her sisters. There were times, though, he was sure of it, when he caught her staring at him, and there was something in her eyes. It wasn't pity. It was something else, something better. Like maybe she understood him.

The Altheas' long sleeves covered their arms and the scar that would be on her wrist, and as they swirled together in the dance, it was impossible to tell which one was her.

Jack kept watching, though, and as he did, his foot tapped to their movements. It was a struggle for them, learning these dances. It reminded Jack of Sam trying to figure out the rhythm of catching and throwing a baseball. None of it came naturally to them, and their only hope of learning the intricate moves was through rote practice, memorization, or careful counting in their heads. Dances for the clones were an exercise in mathematics as much as anything. Jack never let on how different it was for him, the way he could hear music in his head pulsing steadily in time to the steps.

He picked up his guitar, getting ready for the end of the dance and to speak to the Council. He was second-guessing whether he should actually play for them. They wouldn't enjoy the music, after all. Maybe he would just show them the instrument and introduce the concept. He would Declare as a teacher, perhaps, rather than a musician, but he would teach them music.

His fingers brushed the strings absently as his eyes lingered on the dark hair of the Altheas all spinning with the other clones. The pad of his palm thumped lightly against the wood, and he strummed the strings again. Slowly, he picked up the movement of the dance, and without thinking about it at all, he plucked the strings in time until a soft melody only he could hear synced with the dance.

It was several moments before he realized a hush had spread across the crowd, and the dance he'd been lost in came to a confused, disjointed halt. A Mei bumped into a Carson, who had stopped suddenly. They all stared at him. Not just the Gen-310s onstage, but the entire audience of all the other Gens in Vispera. The 290s, 280s, the old 240s at the food table, even the little 320s. And the line of Council members, seated in the front row, who'd twisted around to see what was going on. And they weren't just staring. They were glaring, their eyes cold and resentful. The last reverberations of the guitar faded away as his fingers stilled, and the echo was loud enough for him to understand that he'd been playing much louder than he intended. They'd heard him. He hadn't meant to play at all. He'd assaulted their ears with a noise that to them sounded like no more than wasps droning in the roof of a barn, and he'd done it without thinking. He'd just ruined everything.

It was such a stupid mistake.

Jack saw Sam in the line of Council members. The man met Jack's gaze, and the only thing Jack could see in his eyes was disappointment. Jack's throat burned.

*They could hear it if they tried.*

The rebellious thought crept its way into his mind, and he forced it away. That kind of thinking wasn't going to help.

His mother, at the end, had heard it. Her eyes had shone with the understanding. It was right before she'd run away, taking him with her, that she'd first heard it.

Carson-312 jumped down from the stage, a furious crease between his eyebrows. Jack could tell it was the 312 by the patch in his eyebrow where the hair had never grown back after Jack's fist had split his skin. Before Jack could stop him, he'd wrenched the guitar away.

"What's wrong with you? Why are you even here?" Carson said, raising the instrument out of Jack's reach.

It stung that Carson's questions were the same ones Jack asked himself every day.

"Give it back," Jack said.

Adrenaline pulsed through him, but he tamped it down. The Council, and Sam, were watching. Jack refused to give them a reason to punish him. After that day in school, they'd locked him in the labs for a long time. He wouldn't let them lock him away again. He knew they'd spent days back then discussing whether they were going to let their experiment continue. Jack had been too scared to ask Sam what terminating their de-extinction project would mean for him. He clenched his fists against his side and stayed seated, waiting.

"Give it back," Jack repeated.

Carson's eyebrows rose with Jack's words, and Jack realized he'd made yet another mistake. He shouldn't have let Carson see how much the guitar meant to him. Carson grinned and moved closer. Jack stood and backed away until his legs hit the chairs behind him. Maybe if he played nice, Carson would quit squeezing the neck of his guitar, knocking the strings out of tune.

The Declaration was in disarray. Most of the remaining Gen-

310s were still onstage, though the dance had ended. The audience had begun to disperse, not really clear on what was happening and confused by the interruption caused by Jack. A small cluster nearby still watched the two boys, including the Council members. Jack was on display. They wanted to see how this confrontation would play out, and Jack would bear the brunt of anything that went wrong.

"Are they letting you Declare, monkey-boy?" Carson said, bumping the guitar against his hand. "What are you Declaring as, town freak?"

"I'm Declaring as a teacher," Jack said, his gaze flicking from Carson to the guitar.

Carson pulled at one of the strings. It gave a sharp twang. "What's that got to do with this thing? I mean, does it do something?"

"Give it back, and I'll show you."

"Why, so you can attack me with it? We all know you're violent. Do you think I'm stupid?"

"I don't know. Are you?"

Carson tilted his head, that cool grin widening. In the corner of his eye, Jack saw Sam stand from his seat, but the man didn't move forward or speak.

Jack shook his head. He was clearly the stupid one, insulting a Carson in front of everybody. Why couldn't he just keep his mouth shut?

"Listen," he said, taking a breath, his voice low. "It's nothing. It plays music, that's all. Just . . . give it back, okay?"

"Okay," Carson said. "Come get it."

The onlookers murmured when Jack reached for the guitar and Carson brusquely pulled it away.

He drew Jack close, and Jack felt the other boy's breath as he snarled, "You want to hit me, don't you?"

Jack pressed his lips together, stifling the desire to do just that. It was exactly what Carson wanted, for Jack to lose control in front of everyone.

"It's okay," Carson said, pushing Jack back and suddenly feigning friendliness. "I'll give it back, for real this time. But listen, tell me what it's called first."

"Why?"

"Don't be so suspicious. I really want to know."

"It's a guitar," Jack said curtly. "It's called a guitar."

Jack watched Carson while, as if in slow motion, he dropped the guitar on the ground at Jack's feet.

"You shouldn't have ruined our dance, monkey-boy. Say goodbye to your guitar." And with that, Carson smashed his foot into the base of the instrument, splintering the wood into fragments. Jack yelled incoherently as Carson crushed the remnants with the heel of his shoe.

The Council was watching. Sam was watching. The Altheas' brown eyes were on him, too. The Meis, the Hassans, all of them were watching now. None of that mattered as the anger exploded in Jack's chest. He rushed at Carson. Immediately, two Viktors and a Hassan grabbed his arms. They must have been behind him the whole time, waiting for him to do exactly this. Before he had a chance to connect with Carson or even realize what was happening, he was on his back, the breath knocked out of him. They pinned his hands, then hauled him up again. His limbs shook with unreleased energy.

"Good job, teacher," Carson said, his mouth twitching up. "I think we learned everything we need to know from you."

One of the Viktors twisted Jack's arm, steering him away from the snickering Carson and the stage.

"Sam!" Jack called into the crowd. "Sam, where are you?"

Jack searched across the Commons. Countless dark heads mingled in the crowd, at least twenty different Samuels, any of which could have been Sam. It was impossible to tell. Sam had abandoned him. Again.

The Viktors escorted him back to his room in the labs, locking the door behind them. The usual punishment for bad behavior.

Jack had grown a lot in the past two years. He was taller than the Viktors, taller in fact than all the models. He was stronger than them, too. There were times Jack would look at them and be struck by how delicate the clones were. Thin and narrow-chested. It didn't matter, however. They controlled every situation, every move he made.

When Sam came by that night and unlocked the door, Jack wanted to scream at him, tackle him to the ground and hit him the way he'd wanted to hit Carson, hit him until that desolate expression left his face. Instead he said, "You left," and hated the sorry plea in his voice. "You just left."

Sam sat in a chair, crossing his ankle over his knee. Jack's room in the labs was nothing like his room in the cottage. It was a small, sectioned-off corner of the building, with linoleum floors and white-tiled walls. It was as sterile as the larger sections, where banks of fluorescent lights swung over rows of marble-topped desks fitted with gas spigots and sinks. He had a narrow bed, a small chair and desk, and a doored-off bathroom. The lab workers could see him through the small window in the door that led out into the hall. They didn't bother him much. He sometimes watched them working in the daytime, and then at night the bright lights were turned off, and everything was silent and dark.

"I'm sorry," Sam said with a heavy sigh.

"They locked me in. You told me after last time they wouldn't do that again."

"Not everything is in my control."

"You're afraid of them. You're afraid of the Council."

"I'm *on* the Council. I have to consider the needs of the community. I can't just worry about one boy."

"What am I even doing here? I can't figure out the point of your experiment. Why the hell was I born, Sam?"

"You have so much potential, Jack, but you certainly weren't born so you could disrupt the entire community."

Jack's heart sank even as pinpricks of anger pierced him. "My mother, she used to call you my father."

"The Inga wanted to give you something human. Fathers are something humans had. I never had one—none of us do. I've done the best I could."

Sam used to read to him, before Inga died. Not from the novels that Jack liked, the ones Sam called *human,* but from the histories, his physiology books, and the books that had taught him to be a doctor. The clones didn't get sick, but he'd read to Jack about setting a limb and treating a concussion or infected wound. When they'd all lived in the cottage, Jack remembered Sam sitting in the creased leather chair studying textbooks and psych manuals, discussing with Inga how humans lived their day-to-day lives. Occasionally Sam would see something in the books and then abruptly declare some new activity, like reading aloud together or throwing a ball outside. Jack still remembered Sam dressed in his lab coat and black shoes, chasing after the balls Jack threw.

"It must have been tough, pretending to care for the sake of your experiment." Jack heard the venom in his own voice. "Acting human, like some kind of animal."

"I care about you, Jack. More . . . more than I should. It *has* been difficult. My brothers don't understand. It's put distance between us, and you don't know how hard that's been."

"So what now?"

"The Council will meet about what happened. I don't know what their decision will be for your apprenticeship. Why did you have to bring the *guitar*, Jack? What were you thinking?"

"You're not even going to stick up for me, are you? You'll abandon me like always. Like you did today."

"I have to do what's best for Vispera."

"So go, Sam. Go away and leave me alone."

"Please, listen—"

Jack didn't want to be mad anymore. Instead his voice was almost gentle when he said, "You can stop trying to be a father. You're not very good at it, and I don't need one anymore."

Jack thought he saw something in Sam's eyes, but he turned away too quickly to see what it was. He looked up only when the lab door closed and the sound of the latch, this time unlocked, rang through the room.

Later that night, Jack lay sleepless on his bed in the dark, his eyes sore and his head aching. Light from flickering lanterns outside shone through the tiny window above the bed, mottling the floor of his room. Distant voices floated in with the pattering of rain over the wide jungle trees.

With the Declaration over, the Gen would be holding their monthly Pairing Ceremony now. He could picture the girls in the circle of the Commons, each choosing her partner. In his mind he saw a girl with dark curls walking down the path to the Pairing tents, teasing and playful, hand in hand with a boy who couldn't possibly grasp how much it meant for her to take him in her arms, their bodies lost in a pile of quilts and tapestries.

Jack curled into himself, burying his head under a pillow in an effort to block out the soft laughter of the strolling couples outside.

*Chapter Three*

# ALTHEA

Althea-310 gazed out the window of Remembrance Hall. She was only a few weeks into her apprenticeship, and she was already forgetting to pay attention to the minutes she was taking of the Council meeting. Remembrance Hall was the oldest building in all three communities. It was the very building where the Original Nine had lived and slept, before there were dorms. Inside the meeting room, mahogany walls framed tall windows that looked out on the Commons. Althea sat at a desk in the corner while the nine members of the Council, one representative for each model, sat at a long table, the gold badge of the Council, embroidered with the words *Harmony, Affinity, Kinship,* sewn into their clothes.

In contrast to the hushed voices and shuffling papers in the meeting room, the Commons outside was a flurry of activity. The Gen-310s would have their Pairing Ceremony tonight, and all day the four boys and four of the five girls would hardly be able to concentrate on their apprenticeships as they looked forward to the coming celebration. One of the girls always hosted, and this month was the Meis' turn to sit out the Pairing and instead plan the décor and menu for the evening. They'd already converged to hang lanterns and garlands from the kapok tree in the center of the Commons, and they'd encircled the huge trunk with lighted, colored stones, a new decoration they'd created that Althea knew they were particularly proud of.

Altheas tended to choose Hassans at the Pairing Ceremonies. Since the Gen-310s had turned sixteen and celebrated their first Pairing a year ago, the Altheas had chosen the Hassans half the time. Althea-310 turned her attention back to the meeting, but she studied the Samuel at the conference table while her fingers flew over the letter machine, recording a conversation about the rice mills. Perhaps the Altheas could choose the Samuels tonight. They were pleasant, and more decisive than the Hassans, who tended to be timid.

Althea shook her head. It was impossible. The Kates had already made it known that they were choosing the Samuels, and Althea's sisters had made a specific decision for this month's Pairing. The Gen-290 Altheas had had a long discussion with them about how conspicuous it'd become that the Gen-310 Altheas never chose the Carsons at a Pairing.

"I don't understand why your generation seems to have a problem with the Carsons," Althea-298 had said. "The rest of the Altheas are fine with them. You've hurt their feelings. It's causing problems."

If the others in Vispera sensed a lack of harmony between the Gen-310 Carsons and Altheas, then Althea and her sisters were obliged to seek a resolution. It was the way things were always done in Vispera. As a result, they had agreed to choose the Carsons tonight, and there was no way around it. Althea had to go along or risk upsetting her sisters, all the older Altheas, and really, the entire Pairing Ceremony itself. She sighed, returning her full attention to keeping the record.

Carson-292's voice picked up and droned through the meeting hall. They were discussing the amniotic tanks.

"The timers on the tanks are missing," he said. "They disappeared, and they're not the first thing to disappear from the labs either, but they are the most critical. The next generation will be born soon. If we don't find the timers, how will we control the oxygen levels in the amniotic tanks? We have to get to the bottom of this."

"We're as interested as you in figuring it out, Carson." The Inga sat at the head of the table, presiding over the Council meeting. "We're all aware of what's at stake, and we're working on the problem."

Althea noted the gray hair at the Inga's temples and realized she'd recorded the wrong Gen. In the end, which individual Inga was acting on the Council made little difference. Council members were chosen with a Gen communing and deciding by consensus who should represent the models in a given month. Those selected were usually the most adept at weaving through communing currents and picking out slight intimations of difference, swirling eddies of dissent and divergence. Though everyone was capable of serving on the Council, these were the ones who won a nomination time and again. Althea went back to the transcript and adjusted the record, noting that a 280 was representing the Ingas this week. If Althea wanted to be respected as a record keeper and future historian, she couldn't afford silly mistakes.

"That's not good enough," Carson-292 said. "We need security in the labs." He leaned back in his chair. "Those timers were stolen. This is sabotage."

The other Council members slumped in their chairs as if weary of an old argument.

"Don't be ridiculous, Carson," Inga said. "We'll post some Viktors there, but I'm sure they've just been misplaced by the new apprentices, that's all. They'll turn up soon."

Carson-292's lips tightened, but Althea noted in the record his assent to the proposal for new security.

Inga turned to her agenda. "Next item to discuss is the proposed modification of the de-extinction project. Samuel, since you've had the most involvement, would you like to address the Council?"

Althea's fingers paused on her machine. They were talking about the human, Jack. After that day in school, no one had seen him for a long time. Then suddenly he started appearing now and then, walking with his eyes focused on the ground in front of him, keeping to himself. Sometimes she'd see him carrying baskets of linen to and from the clinic. And then at the Declaration, he'd attacked Carson again. That was the first time she'd been reminded of the violence that shimmered just under the surface, the same violence that had ended with Carson-312 out of class for a week. Althea remembered the anxiety of the Carsons during their brother's absence. It'd made them jittery and short-tempered.

The brothers had been excused from class for the last few days Carson-312 was gone. They seemed about ready to fall apart, and the Council was concerned Carson-312 might fracture and there would have to be a Binding Ceremony. Althea had seen one once. A few years ago, a jaguar had come over the wall and attacked an older Hassan. He hadn't simply been injured, he'd been traumatized as well. He refused to walk any of the paths hidden in trees, and eventually he wouldn't even leave the Hassan dorm. His erratic behavior distanced him from his brothers, and when there was nothing more to be done, Althea had watched with the rest of the community as the remaining Hassan brothers said their ritualistic goodbyes before slipping a needle into the arm of the fractured Hassan. He'd drifted off, closing his glassy eyes, and then the community drank cups of punch and chatted solemnly about having uneven numbers at the Gen's next Pairing Ceremony.

Fracturing was rare, but it was painful for everyone. In the end, Carson-312 hadn't fractured. Everyone was relieved they hadn't needed the Binding Ceremony, and they subsequently remained silent about that terrible day. Althea avoided thinking about it all as much as possible. She couldn't help watching Samuel-299, however, wondering what he was going to say about Jack and the project that seemed to have caused so much trouble.

"First," Samuel-299 said, "I'd like to point out that the decision to exclude the subject—Jack—from the ceremonies and rites of passage for the Gen-310s, a decision I never thought was the best course of action, has not improved the situation. I'd like to ask the Council to allow him to apprentice with me. We agreed to it before, and nothing's changed."

"No one is denying you've done well with the subject, Samuel," Nyla-298 said smoothly. Althea enjoyed hearing an older version of her friend Nyla-313's voice, gentle but direct, and always poised. "But he's caused too many problems. I'm worried about the effect he'll have on the 310 generation. We know what happened to Inga-296. That was a direct result of her work with him."

"That was ten years ago," Samuel said.

A Viktor leaned forward. "Samuel, even you have to admit he's emotionally unstable. After what happened in Copan last year, I seriously think we should revisit termination. We need to move forward with another subject. Better yet, why not terminate the project altogether? I don't think it's even necessary."

The Nyla spoke again. "The project has provided us with valuable DNA. And this thing he does, the music, perhaps that's something we can use. Our spectral analysis shows there are number properties in the sounds he makes. The Kates, as mathematicians, may benefit if we isolate that particular gene and integrate it into the next Gen."

"Please." Carson puffed out his cheeks. "I for one am not comfortable integrating the defective genes of an asthmatic human with violent tendencies. It's time to end it, as we should have ten years ago."

"And to be fair," the Viktor said, "his intelligence hasn't made anything easier."

"Intelligence," Carson-292 scoffed. "I'd hardly call what we've seen *intelligence*. He has no impulse control. He's violent."

"That's not true, Carson," Samuel said. "Listen, this project represents decades of work. We can still learn from it."

Carson-292 leaned forward, punctuating his words with a finger thumping the table. "We have other avenues—"

"Avenues that have already failed us," Samuel said, looking around at the rest of the table. "All of us, we started this project for a reason. We simply cannot continue copying the exact same genetic material over and over again. The samples are degrading. I know you don't all see it, but we're losing something. Something Jack might help us get back."

"*Something?*" Carson said. "You can't even articulate what that *something* might be. Show me a DNA sequence, a genetic marker, anything! I'm done talking about *something.*"

"He's talking about that music nonsense Nyla brought up," Inga said. "It offers us nothing. Even you, Samuel, can't explain what that's supposed to be."

"It's more than that," Samuel said. "Carson, you're so quick to dismiss our human ancestry, but part of who we are is undeniably human. I'm worried we don't understand how important that part is, and as a result, it will disappear before we've even realized it's gone. I know how some of you feel about Jack, but let's not let a personal issue color our thinking on the matter."

"Personal issue?" Carson-292 exploded. "That boy is unstable! Carson-312 has a *scar,* on his *face.* Do you realize the damage it's caused, having a deformity that makes him so distinct from his brothers?"

An image entered Althea's mind. She pictured the boy on top of Carson, tears streaming down his face and his body bunched into an angry coil, more primitive than anything she'd ever seen.

"Oh, please," Samuel said. "It's barely noticeable, a scratch above his eye." He gestured around the table. "Hassan-295's nose is different since he fell from a tree when we were nine, and Mei-298's got the scar on her chin from tripping on the dorm steps. This is nothing."

"It's the *way* he got it," Carson said. "He was attacked, in his own school, by a human who has no more self-control than a chimp."

"Did you ever consider it was the isolation itself that caused his violent behavior? That his hostility toward us is a result of the segregation *we* imposed on him, are still imposing on him?

Let him truly be a part of the community. There's a Pairing Ceremony tonight, if he can't have an apprenticeship, let him participate in that at least."

Althea's hands froze in their note taking. Let him participate in the Pairing? Would the Council actually consider such a thing?

"Samuel," Inga said firmly, "the Pairings are for the nine models, with ten siblings each. How would that even work?"

Samuel made an obvious effort to soften his tone. "Well, why couldn't it? We continue the ceremony when a model loses a sibling, don't we? Inga-296 wanted to give him a human environment, but what he needs is for us to allow him to be one of us. He has no brothers, and the Gen-310s have never really accepted him. We haven't been fair to him. Even the animals in the jungle have families."

Carson-292 laughed. "Then let him live in the jungle. The thought of him taking part in the Pairing turns my stomach."

"Samuel," Nyla said kindly, "I think you're too close to the subject to be objective. The next time we discuss this, we'll have one of your brothers stand in for the Samuels."

"You think I can't represent the Samuels?" Samuel said, struck.

"Not in this instance, no." She looked around the table. The Council members all joined hands, and Althea felt the threads of intricate thought weave through them as they eased the tensions and communed on their decision.

"Good," the Nyla said as their linked hands dropped. She closed the agenda. "There's too much resistance to him participating in the Pairing, but he may have an apprenticeship. It must be in the clinic, and only with you, Samuel. The others don't want to work with him."

Althea had never witnessed such a conflict among the older generations. She'd always thought by the time a cohort was thirty or forty, they'd gotten over their squabbling and differences. And to see such argument at a Council meeting, where they were supposed to be acting in everyone's best interest, being mature and rational . . . *Why, they're no better than the rest of us,* she thought. Her sisters, with their disagreements about which pattern of new dress to sew, the bickering with the Kates, a Carson trying to push others around, a Hassan getting petulant about the inflexible Ingas. Althea unexpectedly felt the decades of her life stretch before her, taking part in the same arguments and conflicts over and over again. Except with each decade, the stakes would be raised. It wouldn't be about dresses and ceremonies anymore; it'd be about important scientific experiments, food resources, and the embryo tanks. She'd been so pleased to choose her recorder apprenticeship. It was a privilege to sit in on Council meetings and hear important decisions being made. But this fighting hadn't been what she expected.

That was exactly why the Pairing tonight was so important, she realized. If they couldn't get along at a Pairing Ceremony, how were they going to learn to work together when decisions were more critical? Althea resolved to have a better attitude than she'd had for the past few days. She would Pair with a Carson, just like her sisters, and everything would be smoothed over, paving the way for the future ahead.

Althea caught her breath that night when she saw the Commons fully decorated for the Pairing Ceremony. Last month had been the Altheas' turn to host, and Althea had to admit that the Meis were better at it. They'd obviously put such care into everything.

Lights hung like fireflies from the flowering trees in twinkling paper baskets, and the colored rocks glowed around the perimeter of the kapok. Fig and cherry trees dipped pendulously over tables overflowing with food.

There was the usual colorful rice cooked in banana leaves, each different hue representing the nine models. There were carved pineapple cups filled with jewels of corn in red, blue, and purple, and peppers modified to sparkle like gems in the lamplight. Avocadoes, molded to look like large-eyed spider monkeys, filled mango-wood basins. Under the direction of the Meis, the Hassans had put together a table of desserts; oil cakes covered in sugared violets, glitter-dusted breads that the little seven-year-old Gen-320s grabbed as they ran past, and jelly candies with almonds suspended inside. They'd even made flavored red ices in glass bowls, an obvious appeal to the Ingas in their red robes, whom the Hassans seemed to be hoping for tonight. It wasn't too likely, though, from the way the Ingas laughed and rolled their eyes at one another. They'd already decided on the Viktors, Althea had heard, now that they knew the Altheas were choosing Carsons.

Althea took a crystal cup from the table and tasted the drink made from melons and ginger. It was sweet, and as she held it, the drink changed color like a chameleon to match her yellow robe. All the sisters' Pairing robes were in their traditional colors. Tonight the Altheas' were seeded with pearls and sewn with gold thread, and their hair, in trembling curls across their shoulders, shone with tiny gold charms. When her sisters separated, they spread like glimmering sunlight into the throng of girls that had converged on the Commons.

The boys wore their cotton robes in their designated colors, crisscrossed with matching leather belts that wound from their waists to their shoulders. The Viktors were in teal, the Carsons in purple, the Hassans in orange, and the Samuels in a deep navy blue. The Meis had wrapped their braids in scarves flecked with copper; the Kates, in green, wore jade earrings; and the Altheas draped knit yellow shawls over their shoulders.

While Althea sipped her drink and admired the transformed lawn of the Commons, Nyla-313 skipped over to her. The Nylas' color was silver, and Nyla-313 wore a gray robe with silver trim that skimmed the top of her silver sandals, and bracelets on her arms that jingled as she held out a bowl of turquoise-tinted strawberries.

"They're beautiful!" Althea said.

"Try one." Nyla tilted the bowl toward her.

Althea eyed her friend. "It's not going to start squirming, is it?"

"That happened once," Nyla said, tipping her mouth down. "And it still tasted good."

Althea bit into the strawberry. The juice dripped onto her lips. "It tastes like sugar and . . . What is that?"

"Chocolate." Nyla beamed. "I spliced them with cocoa beans."

"How has no one thought of that before?"

"They did, actually. It's just been years since anyone's done it. I found the sequence in the botany logs. I added the color myself. It's from the flowers on the fiddlewood trees by the river."

"Well, it's brilliant. It might be my favorite thing you ever made."

All ten generations crowded the Commons, from the children weaving in and out of the crowd, unconcerned with the history and solemnity of the ceremony, to the Gen-230s seated in carved chairs, their Pairing days behind them. The other Gens each had their own monthly Pairings, but tonight was the Gen-310s', and after everyone had eaten and chatted, the Meis lined up the 310 boys in the circle of stones and shooed the other generations into a larger circle around them to watch.

At first, ushered by the Meis, the girls entered the center of the Commons single-file. Each of the four sets of sisters linked hands in a circle, as did the four sets of boys outside the border of lighted rocks. Althea took a breath. She looked into the sky, up at the numberless stars, and then closed her eyes. A warm breeze lifted her hair from her forehead, and the air smelled of hyacinths and lemons. She reached out in her mind, feeling the presence of her sisters as an immense current drawing her into a deep, warm liquid. It picked her up, and she gave herself to it so it spun farther, not just to her sisters anymore but to all of Vispera, gathered now in one place. In a quick, exhilarating wave, her thoughts and feelings seemed to amplify and then whirl out again like eddies in the bubbling Blue River.

With the clear ring of a bell struck by a Mei, the models dropped hands. The connection receded, and Althea exhaled softly, feeling the swift race of her blood and the sheen of sweat on her brow. This feeling, she thought, of connection with the community—with her sisters, her Gen, and all of Vispera—was why they held any of their ceremonies. Everyone talked so much about the traditions and history of the Pairing Ceremony, the Binding Ceremony, and then the final Yielding Ceremony, the one that gave a peaceful end to the oldest, hundred-year-old generation, allowing the community to celebrate the birth of the new generation from the tanks. But really, all the ceremonies centered on that one moment when they joined hands and everyone felt a surge of emotion swelling within them. Any disagreement, any confusion, it all fell away. They understood each other, and in their understanding, they became one. How could the Council even think of including the human in this sacred tradition? He couldn't commune. At best he'd be a nuisance, a distraction to their ritual; at worst he'd be a wall separating them. There was no question, it'd be a disaster.

As the girls fanned out and the Meis separated from the larger group, the sisters' colors mingled and they began the dance that preceded the Pairing. The Commons was silent except for the shuffling sound of the girls' feet and the hum of insects in the trees.

The Altheas' dancing was practiced and steady. Althea held the eyes of her sisters and the encircled boys while she concentrated, silently counting steps, remembering when to turn, when to spin, when to sweep her foot in a slow kick, trying to time it just right with her sisters. The evening glowed with candlelight, and Althea could hear the ripples of Blue River through the trees.

The wooden bowl in the center of the dance overflowed with silken ribbons. The Meis plucked ribbons from the bowl and handed them to the girl whose color had been chosen, determining the order of the Pairing and which sisters got first pick.

Althea continued the dance while girls were handed their ribbons. The first girls picked didn't take the Carsons, since by now everyone knew the politics of the Altheas' choice. Then Althea-313's ribbon was drawn, and she danced gracefully over to Carson-319 and took his hand. She wrapped her yellow ribbon around his wrist and through his fingers until she came to the end, where it dangled from his thumb. He smiled when she took his hand and led him to a spot outside the circle, which was dwindling now, as were the ribbons in the bowl. And it was done. The Altheas had chosen the Carsons.

Althea watched each sister as, one by one, her yellow ribbon was selected and she walked away with a Carson. All the Ingas sat outside the circle with the Viktors, the Nylas chose the Hassans, while the Kates were with the Samuels.

A hand touched Althea's in the midst of the dance. It was a Mei presenting Althea with her ribbon. The girl looped the satin over Althea's wrist, and she felt the silky slip of it tickle her skin.

The older Altheas all nodded their approval. The oldest Altheas, the Gen-230s, tapped their feet while watching the dance. Their faces were barely wrinkled. Any one of them could have been mistaken for an Althea thirty years younger, even though in three years their generation would have their Yielding Ceremony and they'd be gone forever. In eighty years, Althea and her sisters would be like them, finishing their lives and guiding the next generations. It seemed impossibly far away to Althea, and she couldn't wrap her mind around it. Though she already knew when looking into the face of the ninety-seven-year-old Altheas, quietly watching the ceremony, exactly what she herself would look like when she was old. During the Pairing, she could look around the Commons and see the rows of Althea generations, see her own face age decade by decade. But that didn't make it any more real. What was it like for the older generations, to see their own faces and bodies, forever young, dancing before them?

Beginning the next phase of the dance, Althea slowly unwound the ribbon from her wrist. The Mei walked away from her, back to the bowl to pull another ribbon. All her sisters sat with a Carson under the kapok tree. Still dancing in the silence, Althea turned to the last Carson. It was Carson-312. He stood with two Hassans to his left, though a Nyla was already dancing toward one of them.

Althea approached Carson-312. She could see the beginnings of a good-natured smile on his face, expectant and pleasant. She could tell he understood what the Altheas were doing, and he appreciated the gesture. They were willing to let bygones be bygones, and why shouldn't they be? After all, overlooking the Carsons at Pairing had all been a misunderstanding. There had been some ugliness recently, but that was the human's fault, not Carson's. Previous Althea generations had never had a problem with Carsons. Why should hers be any different?

While she danced, Althea's eyes wandered to the scar that puckered Carson-312's left eyebrow. It didn't hurt his features, really. The Carsons had fine, straight noses, and their hair curled nicely around their ears. Carson-312's expression remained unchanged, still mild and friendly, but Althea felt a sudden, sweeping vertigo. She faltered in the steps of her dance as his smile distorted into a cold, menacing smirk. She knew it was all in her mind, but what she saw in that very moment was one young boy standing over another, flicking pebbles.

Mere steps away from Carson-312, Althea spun right, swaying to regain her balance at the abrupt shift. With barely enough thought to make a decision, she stopped and her feet flattened to the ground in front of Hassan-318. When she took his hand, voices murmured around her, and panic rushed through her chest. She refused to look around, however, especially at Carson-312, and instead she held Hassan-318's eyes as she wrapped

her ribbon around his hand and through his fingers until the end
dangled from his thumb.

That evening, Althea couldn't concentrate. The newly formed
pairs had all dispersed to the rows of glowing tents erected on
the outskirts of town. The Meis had chosen an elaborate décor
of gold-fringed rugs, piles of pillows embroidered with roses,
jasmine-scented candles in glass cups, and brilliant flowers in
orange and red. The walls of the tents were crimson trimmed in
gold, and fashioned with a netted skylight, letting cool air flow
into the small space. Despite all the distractions and amusements
that were supposed to accompany a Pairing night, Althea felt
sick. She'd ruined the Pairing, taking a Hassan from the Nylas,
and leaving a Carson to Pair with someone other than an Althea.
The sisters and brothers wouldn't share the same experience of
the Pairing now, and it would cause all kinds of disruptions. The
older Altheas would be upset, and the Carsons would be angry.
Althea and her sisters would have to come up with some new
way to make it up to them.

Althea felt herself going through the motions of the Pairing.
Hassan-318 kissed her, and his fingers slid up her arm. His kisses
were warm and hesitant. She tried to focus, to keep her thoughts
pleasant. He did have warm, tan skin, and lovely dark eyes with
lashes so black they looked painted on.

Althea couldn't remember if she'd Paired with Hassan-318
before, but she remembered what Hassans liked. She pressed
against him. One of her sisters had clearly taken the time to
teach Hassan-318 a few things. He touched her the way Altheas
liked to be touched, and he knew enough to be slow. He slipped

from his robe and she untied hers, letting it fall to the pillows at their feet. She kissed him and then slowly pulled back. His hands roamed down her sides, and she let her own linger on his shoulders. They fell back on the pillows and nestled there, facing each other. Then he braced himself on an elbow and looked at her.

"Should I do something different?" he said.

"What do you mean?"

"Your mind is somewhere else. It's pretty obvious."

"Oh." Althea lay back and gazed at the stars through the tent's skylight. "Sorry."

"What happened with the Carsons tonight, anyway?"

"I don't know," she sighed. "But listen, it doesn't have to ruin our whole night. We can still Pair if you want. No sense in everyone being miserable."

He tilted his head at her. "Nah, it's okay. Sometimes I don't mind an early night."

Althea sighed and nestled closer to Hassan. It would have been nice to let the Pairing take her mind off everything, but it would only work for a few moments, and it wasn't fair to Hassan that she was so distracted. She didn't even know why she hadn't picked the Carson like she was supposed to. Part of her blamed the Council meeting for putting all those thoughts in her head about things that happened ages ago.

Althea and Hassan lay together while he talked about his apprenticeship in the greenhouses and the new hybrid seedlings. She didn't mind letting him chatter while her head rested on his shoulder. After a long while, they dressed and Hassan lifted the flap of the tent. The insects outside had grown louder. Althea breathed in, relieved to be out of the heavy, scented air of the Pairing tent.

"Althea, Hassan!" Nyla-313 emerged from her own tent nearby and pranced toward them, her half-tied gray robe falling from one shoulder. She grabbed Althea's hand. "I'm glad I caught you. Come with us, we're exploring!"

Now that the Pairing Ceremony was done, small groups were forming and heading to the dorms or back to the Commons to spend the rest of the evening enjoying the celebrations. Althea was tired, though, and didn't want to have to explain herself to her sisters tonight.

"I'd rather go home," she said. She turned to Hassan-318. "You can go with them if you like."

"Oh, come on," Nyla said. "Come with us. You can't go sulk in the dorms for the rest of the night." Nyla pulled Althea aside. "If this is because of that Carson business, I tried to soften that a bit for you." Althea wasn't sure what Nyla meant until Carson-312 emerged from the same tent as Nyla, fastening the leather belts around his robe. Althea hadn't seen what happened at the rest of the Pairing because she'd rushed off with Hassan, hoping to avoid the glares of the Carsons and her sisters. Now Althea understood. Nyla, trying to ease the sting of Carson-312's rejection, had paired with him, while her sisters had all Paired with the other Hassans. Althea suddenly felt even worse. Why couldn't she have just dealt with it and paired with Carson-312? It was all so stupid.

"Come hang out with us," Nyla said. "It might make things better. Carson-312 says Copan sent a shipment of Somnium last week and he knows where to find it." She leaned in to whisper. "He specifically said he wanted you to come. You can't very well reject him twice in the same night."

Althea wasn't interested in Somnium. She never liked the way it made her feel, the strange thoughts it put in her head that felt like they'd come from somewhere else. She saw her sisters heading back to the dorms. They were alone. After what Althea had done, their own Pairings might have been as beside the point as hers. It'd be better if she faced them tonight, but if she went with Nyla, maybe later she could tell them how she'd made a special effort to be nice to Carson-312, soothing his ego and any lingering resentment.

Althea nodded to Nyla-313, her decision made. "Okay," she said. "Let's go."

*Chapter Four*

# JACK

Jack hated the nights of Pairing Ceremonies. He could always feel the silence descending on the town, even from inside the labs, and he knew everyone around him was celebrating.

At these times, when the clones working in the labs had left, all he had were his books. Tonight he was reading *The Call of the Wild* again. His mother had first given it to him because the author had his name, and he'd loved reading about the dog racing through a strange, frozen terrain, so different from the lush jungle Jack had always known. The story stirred something in him. It was violent, and Buck suffered awfully from cold and hunger and the brutality of the other dogs, but he was also wild, powerful, and free. Jack wished he could be more like that instead of stuck inside a sterile, polished lab. He imagined racing headlong through the trees, quick and alive, the walls of Vispera far behind him.

When he'd lived in the cottage, he and his mother would go for long walks in the jungle, a canopy of broad leaves above them and paths made by animals much bigger than either of them. Once, halting in the middle of dense vine tangles, she'd pulled down the branch of a thin tree with a crown on top shaped like a candelabra.

"Look," she said, pointing to a train of ants. "They're called Azteca ants. They live in the trees, and their whole lifetimes they never touch the ground."

"The clones made them that way?" Jack asked.

"No. We've been around only a few centuries. These ants have existed for a thousand thousand years. They evolved." She let the branch go, and it snapped back into place. "Everything evolves."

"Vispera doesn't," he said. "The clones don't."

His mother laughed. "We like to think we're perfect, don't we? But everything changes, Jack. Everything."

She taught him to watch where he stepped, to be wary of trees with needle-sharp barbs spiking from the bark and snakes coiled near rocks. She taught him to always be aware, that the jungle could easily kill you, and without the walls, there was no protection. But Jack had always felt safer out there with her than he did inside the walls of a town that, for him at least, seemed more menacing than the jaguars roaming the rainforest. Someday he would go back to live in the cottage. The clones almost never left the confines of Vispera except to travel by boat to one of their other walled-in towns. One day Sam would come to visit and find him gone, and he'd be free.

Flipping the pages of *The Call of the Wild,* Jack froze as noises came from the hallway. There were whispers and shuffling outside the lab door. Lab workers didn't come by this late.

"I don't know about this," someone said in a hush as the door to the lab opened. It was a girl's voice. "Where did Nyla and Hassan go?"

"I told them to search South Lab. We'll catch up with them later," a male voice answered. "Come on, quit acting like such a Gen-320 kid."

The door to Jack's room opened onto the lab. At night, he often didn't close it, and he never locked it. Why should he? Nobody came by except Sam. After more shuffling, the owners of the two voices peered into his room. He heard a gasp from the girl as she saw him. He refused to react or even sit up from the bed. If kids were going to sneak into the lab to gape at him like he was some kind of specimen, he wouldn't give them the satisfaction of acting like he cared.

The girl was an Althea. The guy was a Carson. Of course it was a Carson.

The two approached him, the Carson with his thumbs hooked in his belt, the Althea standing slightly behind, wide-eyed. Resting his arm casually on his knee, Jack gazed back at them.

"What d'you know?" Carson said. "It's monkey-boy." Carson rocked back on his heels, pleased with himself.

The Althea glanced from Jack to Carson and back again, a frown suddenly on her face. "You knew he was here. You've got Nyla and Hassan off looking for Somnium, when you just wanted to come here."

"What?" Carson shrugged. "He's just sitting by himself. Maybe he'd like to have some fun with us." He winked at Jack. "What do you say?"

Whatever the Carson had planned, *fun* wouldn't have much to do with it.

Jack glanced at the Althea's wrist, but her knit shawl covered it. He couldn't tell which Althea she was. Not that it mattered, he told himself. They were all the same. There was no sense reading much into a smile two years ago.

Carson strode up to Jack and grabbed the book out of his hand.

"Hey!" Jack said.

"I just want to see what's so fascinating," Carson said, flipping through the pages.

Up close, Jack saw the jagged scar above the Carson's left eye bisecting his eyebrow, which confirmed what Jack already knew. It was Carson-312. It was always Carson-312.

"Carson, stop it," the Althea said. "You're being a jerk."

Carson turned to Althea. "You're very concerned about the monkey-boy. Isn't that interesting?"

"What are you talking about?"

Carson made a show of licking his lips. "Nothing. Just wondering why you care."

"This is stupid. I'm going back to the dorms. I don't like the way you're acting."

She headed toward the door of the lab, but Carson tossed the book to the floor and cut her off. He braced his arm against the wall by her head, blocking her way out. "You're going home, just like that? Come on, have a little fun. You Altheas, you think you're too good for us." He lifted a strand of her dark hair and twirled it around his finger. "What makes you think you're too good for us?"

She pulled her hair from his fingers and tried shoving him away. "It was just one Pairing, Carson. Don't make a big deal out of it."

Carson pressed harder against her, not letting her get to the door. "I'm glad to hear it wasn't a big deal. It's still a Pairing night, you know. Maybe you'd like to make it up to me now?"

"Stop it." Althea glanced nervously toward Jack.

Jack had no idea what they were arguing about or why he'd ended up the audience for their little drama, but he didn't like the way Carson nuzzled his face into the Althea's neck.

Jack, unable to stop himself, said, "Let her go."

Carson didn't let her go. Instead he tilted his head in Jack's direction. "Ah, there he is. I knew I could get you to play. So, monkey-boy, I should let her go? What are you going to do about it?"

"Nice scar on your face—maybe I'll give you a matching set."

Carson's eyes narrowed. He didn't respond to Jack, but put his mouth to Althea's ear and whispered something.

"Carson!" Althea pushed him away with both hands. "The Pairing's over. I'm going home."

"Yeah, that's what I thought you'd say," Carson said. He seized Althea's arm and led her to the bed where Jack still sat.

Carson was trying to play off his actions like he was joking, but there was something sharp and mean in his eyes. Jack was used to seeing those eyes narrowed on him. Seeing a Carson target an Althea, that was new.

Carson turned Althea so she was forced to face Jack, her back against Carson's chest and his arm clutching her shoulders. "Maybe you and the monkey could have a good time together," he said, his lips brushing her ear. "I can tell you feel sorry for him. I *feel* it when I touch you, so much it makes me sick. You clearly don't like Carsons very much, and it's so obvious you didn't Pair with Hassan tonight. Maybe this thing is more what you're into."

Jack hated the Carsons, but this girl feeling sorry for him was somehow worse than the contempt and disgust he got from the others.

The Althea squirmed in Carson's grasp. Before Jack knew what was happening, Carson shoved her. She screamed as she crashed into Jack. He caught her around the waist to stop her falling from the bed while Carson slipped out the door of the room and locked the latch behind him, trapping Jack inside with the Althea.

She looked up at Jack from his arms and then pushed away, falling against the wall. One hand pressed the bed frame while the other stretched before her as if warding off an attack. The shawl fell from her arm, uncovering the thin white scar circling her wrist. Jack's eyes jumped to her face.

It was Althea-310. The only girl who had ever looked at him and smiled.

Now her face twisted with fear.

"Carson!" she yelled. "Get back here!"

Carson stood in the hall, his face in the window of the door. He rubbed the uneven scar on his eyebrow, a sly grin barely showing his teeth.

*Chapter Five*

# ALTHEA

Althea was practically in Jack's lap. She found herself looking into gray eyes that registered as much surprise as she felt, but she didn't see any of her fear reflected back.

She scrambled away from Jack and yelled at Carson to let her out. What the hell did he think he was doing?

"This isn't funny, Carson. Unlock the door!"

Carson sneered at her through the window. "If you'd rather Pair with *him* than me or Hassan, here's your chance."

Althea glanced at Jack, who'd backed away from her. Carson was right, she had felt sorry for him, but she'd also seen him dragged away from attacking someone, twice now. He was violent. As if to prove the point, he was suddenly at the door of the lab, pounding it as if he could break it down. When he gave up, he looked out at Carson. "Open the door."

Carson laughed, and Jack's face darkened. *If he gets out of this room, he'll kill Carson,* she thought. It was in his eyes, like he was holding something in that might explode.

"Just let me out," Althea said. "I swear, I won't tell anyone."

"Have fun, you two," Carson said, rapping the window as if offering a friendly goodbye.

"Carson!" Althea yelled. "Don't you dare leave me here!"

But it was too late. They could hear Carson laughing as he walked away down the hall.

Althea put as much distance between herself and Jack as possible in the small room. She crouched warily against the wall and watched him pacing the small space. It was no longer just that he didn't commune that made him different, or even his strange-colored eyes. When the boys were all fifteen, they and Jack had been basically the same size. Now, only two years later, he was bigger than any of them. He was several inches taller than the Carsons, and at least a head taller than the Hassans.

One time, some little Gen-320s had chased an injured monkey into a tree. It had been hurt badly enough that it wasn't able to climb down, and they threw sticks at it and jeered. Jack scared them away, practically growled at them until they scattered, and then climbed the tree to get the monkey. The others had laughed, gone back to calling Jack "monkey-boy" anytime they saw him. But that was when Althea had first noticed that Jack was less . . . willowy than the other males. Not quite as delicate as the Viktors, Samuels, Hassans, or Carsons. She hadn't felt sorry for him then, even as the others taunted him mercilessly while he climbed. She hadn't been able to stop staring at the way his hands grasped the thick branches, and his arms flexed as he pulled the weight of his body up limb by limb.

Jack stared mutely at the locked door and then turned away.

The humans were so strange. How did they convey feelings to one another if they couldn't commune? They must have gone through their lives in an unbearable state of uncertainty, trying to guess at people's feelings all the time, misreading the emotions of even those closest to them. Perhaps that was what made Jack seem so angry all the time. He was isolated, and no one in Vispera could feel what he did. Though, watching him kick the door in frustration, Althea realized it wasn't all that difficult to discern his emotions, even without communing.

Althea couldn't remember if the Council had said what year Jack's sample was from. If it was a few decades before the Slow Plague, that would put his original's birth around A.D. 2000. She studied his belongings, trying to remember what she knew of humans. Human history was impossible to keep straight. It had, after all, lasted thousands of years. So many of the records had been lost, whether because of the Slow Plague or the carelessness of her own people in the three hundred years since they'd been created.

Jack's room was littered with stacks of human books, a few games. Jack picked up his book from the floor and sat back on the bed. Instead of reading it, however, he dropped his head in his hands. Althea found herself wanting to touch his arm, to comfort him the way the brothers and sisters would do with each other.

He had hair, she noticed suddenly, on his arms and chest. She could see it peeking from the V of his shirt, soft and pale like a fine down. There was even a shadow of hair on his face. The male bodies in Vispera were bare except for the hair on their heads. As he sat under the fluorescent bulbs, the hair on his arm caught the light like glints of gold.

"Damn it!" Jack said, hurling his book away. Althea jumped

to her feet, all thoughts of going anywhere near him flying from her mind. He looked at her for the first time since Carson had left and then shook his head.

Althea sat on the floor again, keeping a cautious eye on Jack. "You shouldn't have mentioned his scar," she said.

His lip curled. "Yeah? Well, what'd you ever do to him? I wasn't the only target here."

Althea pressed her lips together. She had no desire to talk with this boy about the Pairing. "He's always had it in for you. You shouldn't have attacked him that time in school."

Jack laughed, his eyes cold. "I'll be sure to make better choices next time someone's trying to kill me."

"Don't be an idiot—he wouldn't have killed you."

"Why don't you tell me how you react next time it's thirty kids against you?"

"The Altheas weren't part of what happened. We didn't do anything."

Jack leveled his gaze at her, his eyes clear and accusatory. "Exactly."

Althea realized what he was saying and felt her face flush. "There was nothing we could do."

"Listen, don't talk to me. I don't need you feeling sorry for me. Someone will figure out you're gone soon enough. Just wait till they show up."

She did feel bad for Jack, though why that should upset him was a mystery. She hadn't been aware her feelings surrounding him were palpable to the others, but they must be if Carson had picked up on them so easily.

Althea had no idea how long it would take for someone to find her. The situation, it seemed, was perfect for her to be stuck all night. She'd felt her sisters' irritation and anxiety earlier. They would probably conclude she was avoiding them after the disaster of the Pairing Ceremony. In any case, they'd be asleep by now. They wouldn't be looking for her tonight.

Althea felt jumpy. Jack must have noticed how wary she was, because he rolled his eyes.

"Settle down, would you?" He collected his book from where he'd tossed it and then sat on the floor, leaving her the bed. "I'm going to read, which is what I was doing before your friend ruined my night."

"He's not my friend. And what am I supposed to do?"

"Take the bed. Sleep or something—I don't care."

"Don't you sleep?"

"Of course I sleep. Do you think I don't sleep? You people —you clones—why do you think I'm so different from you?"

Althea didn't like the way he said *clones,* as if it was something bad.

"But you are different. Aren't you?"

"No," he said, though Althea suspected he had his own doubt on the issue. He settled into his book, disregarding her.

There was no way she was going to fall asleep while locked in a room with the human. She took a book from the bookshelf. *Silas Marner,* the cover read. It had a picture of a human man holding a yellow-haired child.

Jack gave an exasperated sigh.

"Not that one," he said, snatching *Silas Marner* from her hand.

He handed her the book he'd been reading, *The Call of the Wild.* He went back to his spot after selecting a new book for himself, seemingly at random. He didn't look at her again. Althea took the book and gingerly sat on the edge of the cot.

Jack spent the next long hours apparently content to turn pages, barely shifting position. Althea had a harder time. She started the book, but none of it made sense. It took ages before she realized that the story wasn't even about a human. It was about a *dog*. But that was such nonsense. She wasn't a complete idiot about human history; she knew back then they didn't have dogs with human thoughts and feelings. The further she read, the worse it became, with page after page about clubs, fangs, blood, and wild animals in ice-frozen forests.

Of course the human read such things.

*He was mastered,* she read, *by the sheer surging of life, the tidal wave of being, the perfect joy of each separate muscle, joint, and sinew in that it was everything that was not death, that it was aglow and rampant, expressing itself in movement, flying exultantly under the stars —*

Flying? The dog was supposed to be *flying?*

"Oh!" she exclaimed, flinging the book to where it landed, for a third time, on the floor.

She was secretly pleased when this time Jack jumped at her outburst. He scowled at her, then fished the book from under the desk. It had landed face-down with the spine bent. He carefully flattened the pages and closed the book, then took up his own again.

She had no idea what time it was, but surely this interminable night was almost over. She couldn't tolerate being stuck here anymore. If he liked reading that jumble of nonsense, he really was a strange creature.

"How can you read those things?" she said, gesturing to his books, horrified by the sheer number he'd collected. None of it made any sense. "Anyway, these books should be in the Tunnels. I don't think you're even supposed to have them."

He shrugged, unconcerned.

"And you read them?"

"Of course. You read, don't you?"

"All the Altheas do. But we read textbooks and essays. That thing." She indicated the book he still held in his hand, pointing to it like she would to a spider. He held it like it was something precious. "It's . . . awful."

"Then don't read it."

"The Council said you were intelligent. You don't actually believe a *dog* can tell a story, do you?"

She hated the way he shook his head, like she was the one being dimwitted.

"It's not real, obviously. It's made up."

"It *is* made up. It's lies. You're reading about things that never actually happened." Althea crossed her arms. "Seems like a waste of time to me."

"Never mind," he said, turning his back to her. "Stare at the wall the rest of the night for all I care."

"It's a better way to spend the night than reading about flying dogs."

"They're not—" he said, then shook his head in frustration and went back to his book. "Forget it."


Althea must have fallen asleep, because the next thing she knew, the lights flickered on in the lab and shocked exclamations came from outside the door. When she opened her eyes, the lab workers—mostly Nylas and Kates—were in the room and staring at her and Jack, aghast. She stood to find Samuel-299, the one on the Council, looking sternly at them both, as if she'd had something to do with this mess.

"Finally," Jack muttered. He winced as he stood, sore from having sat on the hard floor all night. Without a glance at her or Samuel-299, he lay where she'd been on the cot, his back to the rest of the room. He was going to fall asleep, just like that. If he could dismiss her so easily after she'd been stuck there all night, she was capable of the same.

"Jack," Samuel-299 said, glancing from Althea to him, "what's going on? What's an Althea doing here?"

Jack pretended he'd heard nothing, his eyes already closed.

Althea smoothed the wrinkles from her Pairing robe, inexplicably embarrassed to still be wearing them the morning after the ceremony.

"Althea," Samuel-299 said. His eyes wandered to her wrist, which she moved to cover with her shawl. "Althea-310, is it? What happened? How'd you get in here?"

Carson-312 had been a jerk, but there was no point in telling on him to the Samuel. They weren't children. She could handle the Carsons. "It was a dumb prank," she said.

"Okay," he said, drawing the word out. "Are you all right? It was a Pairing night. Did anything . . . happen?"

A muffled sound came from the cot, and Althea narrowed her eyes at Jack's back. Did the Samuel actually think . . . and did the human just *scoff*? She turned to Samuel-299. "I'm going to pretend you didn't just ask that."

Althea knew she shouldn't talk this way to a Gen-290, but she was tired and achy. The Pairing, Hassan, Carson-312, the endless night—it was all too much. She was mad at the Carsons for being jerks and annoyed at Samuel-299 for his implication. She was mad at herself for the situation she was in. And everything about Jack was incredibly irritating.

"So you didn't . . ." Samuel-299 said, his voice trailing off.

She looked at the Samuel pointedly and smoothed her robe once more. "I'm tired, I just want to go home." She nodded toward the bed. "If he wants to be alone so badly, let him."

Samuel-299 rubbed his hand across his face and Althea noticed for the first time how haggard he looked. It set him apart from the other Gen-290s, who didn't have those circles under their eyes.

"You didn't get along, then?"

Jack's back was turned. He hadn't even pulled a blanket over himself. His knees were bent, and his arms folded across his chest. She knew his sleep was feigned and that he was listening to hear what she said. *Well then, fine.*

"The subject is not what I'd call *well-socialized*," she said, immediately pleased with her turn of phrase. She usually wasn't mean-spirited, but all night he hadn't been the least bit friendly, or made any effort to put her at ease. He acted like she and the rest of Vispera—*you people,* he'd said—were beneath him. Beneath a *human.*

Jack hugged his arms a bit tighter across his chest, and something in that slight motion gave her a stab of guilt. After all, she'd probably made things harder for him, too.

Before she could say anything else, Samuel-299 stepped away from the door to let her through. He was too distracted to chastise her for talking to him so dismissively. It was just as well, given her mood, which was worsening by the second.

Turning back just before she left, she caught sight of Samuel-299 standing before the bed, his hands in the pockets of his lab coat, gazing at Jack's still form. Samuel-299's feelings were difficult to read, a map of conflicting emotions. He was angry, that was clear, probably with the Gen-310s for playing pranks that disrupted his lab and his project. He had the usual distraction of a Samuel working through a problem, methodical and rational. But he was also concerned, exasperated, and . . . What was it? Sad, she decided. He was so deeply sad. It took her breath away once she felt it, and then it was all she could feel. It consumed him, and in that moment, he was as foreign to her as Jack. He wasn't one of the Samuels at all; she didn't know who he was.

She shook her head. That was ridiculous. Of course he was a Samuel. She just needed sleep, and she'd messed up her brain trying to read that book about the dog. All she wanted was to curl up in bed back at the dorms, with her sisters' beds lined up next to hers in a neat, orderly row.

She knew however, as the door closed behind her, that the Council had been right—the Samuel was too close to the project. Regardless of what the Council decided about their experiment, it was tearing the Samuel apart.

As she headed back to the dorms in the early mist of dawn, she stopped in front of Remembrance Hall and looked up at its white steeple. She didn't know what would happen to Jack, and after that long night in the cell, she wasn't sure she even cared. He didn't seem to want anything to do with her or Vispera.

The morning light shone against the stained glass of the building, casting a brilliant red into the sky. Althea's usual composure trickled back with the warmth of the light.

Samuel-299 could take care of himself, she told herself, and what happened to Jack was none of her concern.

*Chapter Six*

# JACK

I t'd been a month since the Pairing Ceremony that brought Carson-312 and Althea-310 to Jack's room. He'd been spending his days in apprenticeship with Sam at the clinic. Once or twice he'd been allowed to assist Sam with a clone injury—a Viktor's broken finger, a Kate who'd burned her arm. But the clones didn't like him treating them, even if he was just assisting Sam, so mostly he did what the Gen-310 Samuels didn't want to bother with, like rolling bandages, cataloguing pills, or organizing closets. In the evenings, he spent hours at the cottage reading through the books and papers left behind in his mother's office, hoping to find some clue to why she'd raised him so he'd never be accepted by the other kids his age. He loved her, and he missed her, but what had she been thinking?

*Where you came from is important, Jack,* she'd said, bustling into the cottage with armloads of books and art she'd snuck out of the Tunnels. *Nobody here understands how important it is. The Council doesn't know; they don't understand that we* need *you. Don't give up. This is your past, your* human *past. These things are for you. They belong to you.*

But she was the one who hadn't understood. The human world wasn't his past. He'd grown up in Vispera, in the same time as the clones. Anything in him that was human only made him more alone. His mother had told him not to give up, but she'd never told him why any of it mattered.

Then, two nights ago when the Gen-310s held their next Pairing, Jack found himself spending the whole night in his room, anxious and fidgeting. He kept watching his open door, waiting to see if anyone would come in through the lab to ogle the human.

He told himself he was relieved when nobody showed. If anyone did come, it would probably be another Carson anyway.

*Not well-socialized,* she'd said, sounding as arrogant as the Carsons. How exactly had she expected him to be? She'd acted like he was about to attack her. She was apparently too blind to realize that Carson-312 was the dangerous one that night. He'd seen Carson's face. She was lucky Carson hadn't done worse than lock her in the room for a night. Jack shook himself, blocking the images from his mind of what could have happened.

If she wasn't smart enough to be afraid of Carson rather than Jack, why should he try to be sociable with her?

He pulled off his shirt and grasped the edge of the bathroom door frame. Hoisting himself up, he felt the release of built-up energy that came when he focused too much on things he couldn't control. After a while, he stopped counting and simply took pleasure in the strain on his muscles and sweat in his eyes, the ache that let him know he would be too exhausted to let thoughts run unbidden through his head.

Caught up in his workout, he wasn't aware of someone else in the room until he heard soft breathing behind him. He dropped to the floor, shaking out his hands.

Maybe it was the Althea, he thought, before dismissing the idea. She hated him. Why would she come back? But he didn't dismiss the thought quickly enough to avoid the sting of disappointment when he turned to face one of the young Nylas standing in the doorway.

She gazed down the length of him, her eyes somehow both tranquil and intent. He knew what he must look like. He was sweating and breathing hard, his hair was plastered to his forehead, and he towered over her, his muscles and broad shoulders unnatural compared to the delicate Samuels and Hassans. The hair on his arms bristled when her gaze followed a path from his chest and down his stomach. His lip curled. Just another zoo animal. He drew a shirt on and stared back at her.

"You want something?" he said. "Or did you just come to stare?" He pressed his lips together, hating the resentment in his voice. *Not well-socialized,* he heard in his head.

"I . . ." She seemed at a loss for words. "I was talking to . . . my friend, Althea-310. She told me about you."

"Yeah? I bet she had a lot of great things to say. Did she tell you how dangerous I am?"

"You are?" The Nyla's eyes widened.

Jack shook his head, beyond exhausted by the way they all stared.

So the Althea had talked about him. What could she have possibly said? That he was an unfriendly brute who wasted his time on books that made her scream in revulsion?

Feeling like an idiot, he asked, "What'd she say?"

"She told me you were lonely."

Cursing himself for asking the question, he shrugged his shoulders and made to turn away. He didn't want their pity.

"I was also told you were smart, and could be funny and nice, and that you're so angry all the time because you're lonely. Is that true?"

Now she was making fun of him. He was supposed to believe Althea said all that?

"Did a Carson put you up to this?"

Her brow creased. "I haven't talked to the Carsons."

In a way, the Gen-310s were worse than the 290s and 280s. He never really knew why the older Gens did what they did with him, but he knew their day-to-day motives. They gave him tests to take—personality tests, intelligence tests, blood tests, and sometimes injections of medicines and drugs the nature of which they never explained. But the clones his age, they always seemed to be playing some game, and he was sick of not knowing the rules.

"So what, you thought you'd come over for tea?"

"No," she said, her dark eyes blinking at him. "Not tea." She closed the door behind her.

He backed away. "Okay."

She approached him, smoothly confident. She circled his small space, her fingertips lightly tracing over his desk, his books, as she casually looked over the few things he owned.

"You don't have very much," she said.

"Listen, you shouldn't be here."

She peered at him over her shoulder, and her mouth softened into a smile. "So—are you?"

"Am I what?"

"Lonely." She approached him with her hand raised, delicate and graceful, as if she was about to touch his face with the back of her fingers. A cup of pencils rattled on a shelf as he bumped against it.

"I don't understand." And then her fingers brushed his cheek. He swallowed as her touch slid down to the center of his chest. "What are you doing?"

She touched his lips with a fingertip, and her mouth formed into a *shhh*. With one hand, she picked up his, and with the other, she reached into the pocket of her robe. She withdrew a silver ribbon and draped it around his wrist and then over his palm and through his fingers, until it wrapped finally around the end of his thumb.

Jack knew what went on at the Pairing Ceremonies. He'd read about the customs in the Vispera histories and textbooks. And he'd read Sam's books on physiology and psychology. He'd also read his own books, his human books, and those stories often dealt with things like romance, love, and sex. It was his books, not those of the clones, that told him what people did when they loved one another. Whatever he knew, his mind couldn't form a coherent thought when she slipped the silver-gray robe from her shoulders and let it pool at her feet. She wrapped her arms around his neck and pressed herself against him. He gave way until they lay back on the narrow bed.

As much as his books had tried, they'd failed utterly to prepare him for what this was. Her touch burned. Her lips inflamed every part of his body as they caressed his own. He felt like an electric current was running through his skin. Her softness and warmth was like sinking into a bottomless pool that made him want to sink farther, and when her warmth enveloped him completely, he finally understood what loneliness truly was and that he'd been drowning in it his whole life.

After, they lay side by side on the bed, and Jack ran his fingers along her brow. She touched his necklace, holding the bead so it faced the candle he'd lit. She ran her finger along the curve of the heart design.

"Why do you wear this?" she said, contemplating the bead. "I've never seen a boy wear a necklace."

"Inga-296 made it."

He'd seen the older Nylas in the lab every day for the past year, but he'd never noticed before how their black lashes sloped up at the corners of their eyes or how their petal-soft skin smelled of violets.

"They had a Binding Ceremony for her, didn't they?"

"Yes. The bead is made from a cohune nut we found in the jungle after she ran away from Vispera. She carved it one of the nights we were gone. I've worn it ever since."

Nyla's nose wrinkled. "Why?"

Jack had never known a clone to be sad in the face of death. It would be hard for Nyla to understand why he wore the bead. The clones simply moved on as if each life were replaceable. But his mother wasn't replaceable, and he wanted Nyla to understand.

"I don't want to forget her, and the bead reminds me of her."

Nyla thought about that for a moment. "Why would she run away from Vispera?"

"She'd fractured," Jack said simply.

"Well, it's good they held the Binding."

Jack was silent, not wanting Nyla to hear the tightness in his throat. He'd never talked to anyone about his mother except Sam. He wished he knew more about her. He remembered her making him bowls of amaranth stirred with honey and then watching him run through the yard of the cottage. Sometimes he'd get so mad at her for turning him into such an outsider. He forgot how, back then, he always felt like he belonged. He felt loved.

The night she ran away, he was seven. He remembered her panic. She was talking about the Council, and her sisters, and how the asthma that Sam had recently diagnosed meant he wasn't safe anymore. She rushed haphazardly through the cottage, hurriedly packing mismatched shoes and random food. That first night in the jungle, she laughed with a tinge of hysteria at finding among their supplies a useless bag of cornstarch. She made a circle with it around their fire, telling him the white powder would magically keep out the snakes and bugs. She wrapped him in a blanket and then stayed up the whole night keeping watch.

By the third night, Jack wanted to go home. He missed his bed; he was hungry. The nights were cold. She told him they had to keep walking, that they'd be safe once they crossed the mountains. They never reached the mountains, though. The Viktors caught up with them and forced them to go back to Vispera. They told Jack she was sick, and her sisters were suffering because of it. She fought them every step of the way, and once in Vispera, they rushed through the ceremony. Jack didn't understand what was happening, and then they were holding her down, the needle that would kill her poised above her arm. She grabbed Sam, her fingers white as they pressed into the flesh of his neck. *Protect him!* she said. *Promise me!* Sam stumbled backward, repulsed by her vehemence and how unhinged she'd become.

She died never hearing an answer from Sam, but he'd brought Jack to live in the little room in the lab, telling him the Inga had fractured, and there was nothing anyone could have done. Jack didn't know what Sam ended up saying to the Council, but he was an experiment they let continue, asthma and all.

Nyla continued to fondle the bead, making it wink in the flickering light of the candle. "If you like the Ingas so much, you could always Pair with them, too."

Jack's hand covered hers, stilling the fingers that idly twirled the bead on its string. "I didn't like her in that way. And I don't like the other Ingas at all. I like you." He turned to face her. "Nyla, why'd you come here?"

"I wanted to. Are you sorry I did?"

He held her close. "Of course not."

She tilted her head. "I was curious what it would be like with you."

"And?" he asked, suddenly self-conscious.

"You're different than the others during the Pairing." Jack felt a twinge when she mentioned others she'd been with. He pushed the thought away. "With you," she said, "it's like you think the whole world might end if we stop."

"Maybe it would." He smiled.

She shoved him playfully. "I was going to teach you the rituals and what the Nylas like. That's usually how it is with the first year of Pairing. I mean, if someone hasn't been with a Nyla before. You show him what to do to pleasure us, and he'll show you what pleasures the model he belongs to."

Jack's discomfort intensified the more she talked about it, but he didn't want her to stop. He wanted to hear everything, know everything about her. "Show me," he said. "Show me what you like."

"Well, that's the thing. You make it seem like none of the rituals matter. Does that make sense?"

Jack leaned over her. "Show me anyway. I want to know."

She smiled, slipping out from under him. "I have to go."

He drew her back into his arms, where she settled for a minute before she sat up again and collected her robes. Jack leaned on his elbows, watching her dress. "Do you have to leave?"

She looked at him strangely. "Don't be silly. My sisters are expecting me."

He grasped her wrist, pulling her down to sit on the edge of the bed, and ran his fingers along her arm. "Can I see you again tomorrow?"

She laughed. "I can't tomorrow."

"When?"

"You will," she said. She stood up and then leaned down to kiss his cheek. "But listen, don't talk about this, okay? Let it be our secret."

"Okay," Jack said. "But wait, I don't even know . . . which Nyla are you? I don't even know."

"Nyla-314," she said, laughing again.

After she left, Jack lay in bed with his hand resting on his chest, feeling the beat of his heart pulsing into every corner of his body. He fought to keep his eyes open for fear he'd fall asleep and miss a moment of the peace that had come over him, a peace he'd never known was possible.

*Chapter Seven*

# ALTHEA

The Council was talking about the cornfields, and Althea was finding it difficult to pay attention. She hadn't seen Jack since spending that awful night locked in his room, but for reasons she didn't understand, she couldn't get him out of her mind.

Althea had always been so proud that she was an Althea, the model that was supposed to be full of compassion and understanding. She hadn't been very understanding that night. She and Carson were the ones who barged in on Jack, and Carson-312 —all the Carsons in fact—had made a game out of tormenting Jack anytime they saw him. Jack took it all silently, with only the tense muscles of his jaw betraying emotion.

For some reason, the image of Jack climbing that tree to rescue the injured monkey kept coming back to Althea. The monkey had died in the end. The Ingas mocked Jack when he took the body outside and buried it in the ground, a strange, human ritual. The Ingas were as bad as the Carsons sometimes, blaming Jack for Inga-296 fracturing years ago. The more Althea thought about Jack, the more she realized how terrible everyone had been to him. True, no one ever attacked him the way he had Carson, but Althea was beginning to understand that there were other ways to hurt someone. And she'd thought it didn't have anything to do with her, but it did, didn't it? She could have at least tried harder to be nice.

She thought perhaps she should go to him and apologize.

"It's sabotage!" Carson-292 yelled suddenly, startling Althea back to the meeting.

They were still talking about the cornfields. A whole section of field had failed, and when they tested the soil, they found the ground had been doused with vinegar. No one knew how it happened. The Hassan at the table in charge of food production was alarmed.

"If it was the same vinegar we use to treat weeds," Inga said, "it must have been an accident. The machines in that particular field simply malfunctioned."

"The machines can't hold enough vinegar to drown a whole field," Carson-292 said. "This was no accident. This was purposeful."

"Who would sabotage the field, Carson? That's our *food*," Samuel-299 said. "If the crops fail, we all suffer. No one in Vispera would do such a thing."

The Samuel was right. The community always worked together. The idea of any brothers or sisters sabotaging Vispera was inconceivable. They'd only be hurting themselves. It simply made no sense.

Carson-292 raised his eyebrows. "No one?" he said.

Samuel-299 glared. "It wasn't Jack."

"And I suppose it wasn't him who stole the timers for the amniotic tanks? We can't have him wandering around, free to do whatever he wants."

"We should lock him in the labs again," Hassan said. "This wasn't some prank. We'll have grain shortages in the fall now, and nothing to send to Copan."

After several more moments of discussion, the Council adjourned the meeting, and Althea caught Samuel-299 as he headed for the door.

"Samuel?" she said.

His eyes grazed over her face. He was distracted by the debate inside, the way they'd all accused Jack.

"Can I help you, Althea?" he said.

"I wanted to say that I was sorry." Samuel clearly had no idea what she was talking about. She continued, "About Jack, I mean. I feel like that night I could have been nicer about everything. I was mad, and I took it out on him. Not that he was really nice about anything, but anyway—" She shook her head. "That's not the point." She stopped and thought out what she really wanted to say. "You remember that day when you taught our class, the day you brought Jack to school?"

Samuel-299's mouth turned down. "Of course."

"That day, you told us to behave. You told us, actually, to be kind. We weren't very kind. And no one has been very kind since."

"The Carsons tend to—"

"No, I don't just mean the Carsons," Althea said. The Samuel might not know how badly her Gen had treated Jack whenever they'd seen him around town. How they mocked him, called him names, tried to get him to lose the control he always seemed to be clinging to. "The Carsons behave badly sometimes, but that's nothing new. It's the others, too. And those of us who don't do anything about it, we're just as bad, aren't we?"

Althea couldn't see Samuel-299's face. He seemed to be studying the palm of his hand, rubbing it with his thumb. Maybe he was thinking of himself that day. While the Carsons threw pebbles at Jack, he'd been standing behind a window with a notepad.

"Can I ask you something? Do you really think he'd try to hurt us? That he's the one doing those things to the fields and the tanks?"

"I think he's given them reason to suspect him, and they've given him reason to do those things. But he didn't, and so far, the Council has decided to tolerate him."

"But you think they'll change their minds."

"Yes, I do. But don't worry. You'll know when that happens."

Samuel turned to walk away, his shoulders tense.

"Wait, what do you mean?" she called after him. "What happens when they change their minds?"

Without slowing down or turning back to face her, he replied, "He'll be dead, Althea."

*Chapter Eight*

# JACK

It was the sixth week Nyla-314 had come to him, and each time was wonderful and different, and they learned more about each other. He felt he knew her inside and out, the feel of her skin on his, her breath in his ear, their legs entangled, her soft whispering. And when she left, he'd lie on his bed and replay everything in his head, eyes closed, dazzled by the way she'd changed everything. How long, he always wondered, before she'd return?

Jack spent the whole week waiting for the night she'd arrive, waiting to spend those few hours with her. He'd think of her, of her depthless dark eyes, the way it felt when she touched him. And as much as he loved what they did together, he cherished more the moments after, when they'd lie together and his hand would drift over her body and he'd listen to her talk about the parties she'd be going to, or the experiments she was working on in one of the labs. In the daytime, he would seek the Nylas out in town and watch them from a distance. He could always pick her out from the way secret smiles seemed to pass between them. He wanted to be with her the way her friends were, but he couldn't ask for too much, not so soon. He didn't want to do anything that could jeopardize these few nights they were able to share.

For the first time, he felt like he had someone to talk to. He told her about the books he liked, and she would murmur in understanding, all while running her fingers through the hair on his chest, which was a never-ending fascination to her, but he didn't mind. He told her about growing up in his cottage on the hill with Sam and his mother. He talked about his music, though her eyes drifted away on that topic, so he'd bring their conversation back to something that made her face light up again, like one of her parties or a clever experiment with food flavors. She told him about the pigs they were breeding. She and her sisters had manipulated their genes so that, when roasted, the meat would be infused with the taste of pineapple. Jack couldn't imagine such a thing.

"You're the prettiest Nyla," he said.

They were in his bed with the door to his room locked, and the drifting calm had come over him. He felt like he could sleep with his arms around her forever, but he didn't want to miss one second of being with her.

Her forehead wrinkled, and the laughter faded from her eyes. "That's a funny thing to say. We all look alike."

"You're more beautiful than them."

"Don't say such strange things. You're already strange enough."

Jack quirked his mouth at her. "Okay, then. The Nylas are more beautiful than any of the other clones."

He was pleased to see her mood lighten. "Stop it," she said, poking him in the ribs. "And don't say *clones*." She turned solemn again. "Anyway, everyone looks the way they look, that's all. Why would you bother comparing?"

"As long as we're comparing, I must be the handsomest human you've ever met."

"You're also the only human I've met," Nyla said, gently punching him again, but no longer irritated. She got up from the bed.

As he always did, Jack pulled her back. "No, stay longer."

"You always say that."

"You always stay longer when I do."

She settled back down with her back to his chest, and he ran his fingers along her arm. They'd just Paired, and already he was aching to feel close to her again. Every time she left, it became more difficult.

"Nyla," he said, trying not to hesitate in what he planned to say, but sometimes he couldn't predict how she'd react. "Do you like being with me?"

"Yes," she said, picking up his necklace from the bedside table. He always took it off now when she visited. He knew she thought it was strange for him to wear it, and he didn't want her to think he was strange. "It's fun, Pairing with you. You're different from the others." She rolled the bead in her fingers.

Jack cleared his throat, pushing away the images that came when she mentioned the others. A Gen-310 Pairing Ceremony was coming up. He knew the Nylas had hosted the last one, so she'd definitely participate in the next one. If he had his way, she'd never Pair with anyone but him. Jack wondered if that meant he loved her. Was this the feeling so many of his books dwelled on?

"I was thinking," he said, letting his touch roam to her shoulder, feeling a slight scar at the base of her neck, shaped almost like a heart. "Maybe you don't have to participate in the Pairing."

Jack envisioned them spending the Pairing nights together. It would almost be like he was finally allowed to take part in the Pairing. Except now, after all these years of not being able to, he didn't even want to. He only wanted to be with her.

"Don't be silly," Nyla said. "I can't miss the Pairing."

"But don't you want more than this?" Jack sat up. "Why do we need to be a secret?"

He stood while she gathered her robes. She wasn't really paying attention to him.

"Why do you wear this?" she said, dangling the bead she still held by the string. "I've never seen a boy wear a necklace." She dropped it back on the table, not noticing as it rolled to the edge.

Jack's chest tightened.

"Why would you . . ." he said, but his voice died in his throat. He bent close to her, hearing a *tap tap tap* as the bead fell off the string and rolled over the edge of the table. His heart went silent as it missed one beat and then tripped to a start again. He tilted her chin to the side and brushed his thumb over the heart-shaped crease of skin. "Has this always . . ." His touch wandered to her chin, her forehead, her hair. He squinted, staring intently, like he was trying to see into her mind, her heart. A feeling overcame him, making him choke on the breath he'd just taken in. "Oh, God."

She brushed his hand away and continued fastening her robe. "What?"

He couldn't breathe. The panic of losing his breath swelled his lungs further, and he desperately wanted his inhaler from the bedside table, but he kept his hands clutched at his sides. He refused to let her see him like that. As if it were happening to someone else, he saw his hand reach out to recover the polished bead from the floor, and he stumbled to the wall. He let his forehead rest against the cool tile. Slow and deliberate, he said, "Who are you?"

"Jack, I'm Nyla. What are you talking about?"

He squeezed his eyes shut. Breathe. Just breathe. But his lungs were filling with cotton, and he couldn't get the breaths out.

"Nyla-314?"

"Nyla-313," she said, as if it were the most obvious thing in the world. As if his chest weren't squeezing down into a tiny suffocating pinpoint.

He turned on her, this Nyla. He took her arm, gripping it hard. He couldn't stop himself. "Why aren't you Nyla-314?" Nyla-313 stared at him as if he'd lost his mind. Jack tried again. "Where's Nyla-314?"

Nyla-313 shrugged. "She's home, in our dorm."

He squeezed harder and the Nyla winced. "Why didn't she come?"

"You're hurting me." She wrenched her arm from him and rubbed it where he'd held her. "What's wrong with you? You haven't Paired with Nyla-314 since that first night, weeks ago."

He felt sick. He was going to be sick.

Jack sat down heavily on the cot. He stared at the Nyla, feeling like he knew her intimately — her eyes, her lips, every length of her violet-smooth skin — but he didn't know her at all.

"Nyla-314, I thought — She was —" He ran a hand through his hair, struggling with his words. "We talked. I told her things, things nobody else —"

Nyla-313 watched him, bewildered. "There's nothing special about Nyla-314. We're all sisters. You know that."

Jack looked up at Nyla-313. She blurred in front of him. He blinked, trying to see her clearly. "You were a different one every time," he said, fighting not to believe it. Moments ago she'd been in bed with him. He'd spent only a few hours with her, only a few hours with any single Nyla, and he didn't even know which ones had been in his bed and which hadn't.

Nyla-313 smiled gently at Jack. "The Pairing has gotten better each time, hasn't it?" She knelt in front of him, placed her palms on his knees. "My sisters, we all learned what you like from each other."

"You *talked* about me? You took notes and then came here and made me think . . . ?" His voice sounded thin from lack of air. He pressed his hand to his mouth, feeling more ill by the second.

"It wasn't like that, Jack. We weren't out to make you think anything. We wanted you to enjoy the Pairing as much as possible. This wasn't some kind of trick. We're sisters; we share experiences. We share everything."

*We share everything.*

Jack suddenly felt very much like a thing.

Like a human.

Nyla-313 put on her shoes and went to the door. "I'm sorry, Jack. But you should see why it doesn't matter. I mean, we're all Nylas."

The familiar anger bubbled up again. *We're all Nylas.* Of course they were all the same; they were clones. It had certainly taken him long enough to figure it out. Althea-310 was right, he really was an idiot.

She stood halfway out the door. "Jack, don't be upset. Samuel-299 said—" She stopped herself.

"What about Sam?" Jack asked, and it came to him, what he should have figured out weeks ago. "He sent Nyla-314 that first time, didn't he? He sent you all here."

"Don't be mad at him. He wanted to help. He told us it would help you be . . ." She considered a moment, thinking back to the words Sam had used. Jack closed his eyes, already knowing what she was going to say. "Help you be more socialized."

In his mind's eye, Jack saw a succession of Nylas slipping in and out of his room, with Sam standing by, smiling at his experiment. He couldn't deal with it, not all in one night. He had to leave. He grabbed a bag and started gathering the things he would need from his room.

"What are you doing?" Nyla said.

"Leaving. Leaving Vispera."

"But . . . are you allowed to leave?"

"Nobody owns me. I can do what I want."

"Where are you going to go?"

"The jungle. They won't find me there."

"You'll die in the jungle. No one could survive out there, not by themselves."

"I can take care of myself."

Nyla's hand tightened on the door.

"You're going to tell them, aren't you?" When Nyla didn't answer, Jack shook his head. "I'm sorry, Nyla, but you're staying here." He moved toward her, and she edged farther into the hallway. "You can't leave. I don't want to hurt you, but you can't leave."

Nyla-313 stared at him, hugging her arms, and then backed away from the door.

"Someone will be by in the morning," he said. "You'll be fine."

She would be fine, too. He'd been locked inside this room more than once. He'd survived.

Jack passed her quickly, his bag in hand, and once outside the door, he turned the lock, trapping her inside. Without looking back, he left the lab building.

Outside, staring up at a half-moon barely visible in the tempestuous sky, he breathed in the humid air.

He wanted to run, to find the paths he knew at the edge of the jungle, past the wall and through the mango trees and ferns. He'd run until his legs gave out and he fell in the yielding dirt, blanketed by stars. Then he thought of the cottage far up on the hill, shielded by trees and outlined against the night sky. That was where he had to go. He would stop there for anything else he might need. If his mother thought she could do it, he could too.

He took a breath from his inhaler, waited for the cotton in his lungs to break apart, and then ran.

Halfway to the cottage, the sky broke. Rain poured down, thrummed against his skin. As if the rain gave him energy, he ran faster, slipping again and again on the muddy path up through the trees and over the wall. He tore open the door of the cottage. It'd been abandoned after his mother's death. No one else had use for it. Only Sam knew that Jack still came here; the others never left the confines of town.

The air inside swelled with the dampness outside. The windows, covered in thick drapes, trapped the dust in the dark house. The rooms smelled of animals nesting in the shadowed corners. Jack collapsed on his bed and pulled the quilted blanket over his shoulders. He willed his muscles to relax as he listened to the rain sweeping through the trees and to distant peals of thunder. He'd fallen asleep to this countless times, hearing those identical sounds in thunderstorms. This storm felt different. He wasn't the same person he'd been when he slept in this bed as a child.

The clones would come looking for him in the morning, after they found the Nyla. He had until then to gather what he'd need and escape to the jungle. How could he stay? What Sam had done, and the Nyla too, felt worse than any of the pranks or taunts he'd endured before. There was something wrong with them, with all of them. His mother must have thought so.

Jack wished she were still alive to tell him what to do.

He was tired, bone-tired, in mind and body. He lit a candle against the dark, then curled on his side. He felt betrayed, but he would still miss Sam. Sam was the one person who at least tried to care for him, who halfway understood him. Sam hadn't been much of a father, but it wasn't his fault. For all Jack knew, human fathers had also failed their sons at times. And as much as Jack resented Sam sending the Nylas to his room—and his face burned with anger when he thought about the conversations they must have had about him—he knew Sam well enough to know what he'd been thinking. In his own way, Sam was trying to make Jack part of the community—to *socialize* him.

Even the Nylas hadn't done anything wrong, not really. What she'd done with him—what *they* had done with him—that was how the clones Paired. It'd been his own fault for thinking she was different.

The rain would stop soon enough, and when it did he would leave. Jack closed his eyes, wanting sleep to claim him, just for a few minutes.

He'd only just drifted off when he heard the front door creak open. They'd tracked him down quickly. But it wouldn't have been hard. He'd figured he had until morning, but of course Sam would have told them to look in the cottage.

Then he heard a quiet, familiar voice calling, "Hello?"

*Chapter Nine*

# ALTHEA

Althea had seen Jack run from the labs. She'd been heading there to apologize when he burst through the doors. He'd pulled a hand through his hair, his head bent low as if distraught, then in a single, unexpected movement, he'd run full force, past the banana trees shaking in the night air, a bag slung over his shoulder. Something had dropped from the bag though, and when she went to pick it up, she found it was his inhaler. So she followed him. She'd barely kept up, watching through the leaves for glimpses of his hair, flashing silver-white in the moonlit clouds. By the time the rain started, she'd already followed him halfway up the hill, to the wall of the town that appeared through the sheets of rain on the steep side of the slope.

Hidden among vines was a makeshift ladder leaning against the wall, and she climbed it, only to find no such ladder on the other side. She had to jump from the top to the ground, which Jack probably found simple enough, but her dress tore, and she rolled her ankle and skinned her knee while awkwardly trying to lower herself down the stone barrier. It would have been easier to go through the gated bridge by the river, but by then she would have lost him, and at some point in all the difficulty, she became determined to deliver the inhaler. Once over the wall, she discovered the ramshackle house with loose shutters, its front door hanging open. Althea stood for a moment, breathing hard. She felt exposed outside the safety of Vispera. She stood in the shelter of the porch for a few moments, then went inside.

"Hello?" she said, following the muddy footsteps that headed upstairs. She'd never seen a place like it before. Dusty and damp, it was so unlike the clean, well-ordered dorms she grew up in.

The door to the room upstairs was closed. She raised her arm to knock, paused, then simply opened it.

Jack was sitting on the bed. He must have heard her come in, because he didn't act surprised to see her.

"Jack?" she said, feeling strange about being there. She suddenly felt like a trespasser.

He absently twirled a white ball sewn with fraying red thread in his hands. His hair, dark with rain, fell across his eyes, but he seemed not to notice or care. When he looked up, his eyes weren't as gray as she remembered. They seemed almost blue, even in the dim room. A candle glowed in a narrow circle of light on the desk. The reflection of water from the windows cast broken paths on the striped wallpaper, drops of rain spilling down.

Jack tossed the ball next to him on the bed. "You followed me," he said, his voice flat. It wasn't a question.

The room was sparsely furnished. There was a chair by the desk, but she didn't feel like sitting down. He didn't seem to want her there, just like when she'd showed up in the labs with

Carson. He scanned her briefly, taking in her wet clothes, her skinned knees, the hair sticking to her neck in damp strings. Her hands folded and unfolded.

"Listen, I don't know what you're doing here. Go home."

Althea blinked at him, momentarily forgetting herself why she'd followed him. "You dropped this," she said, holding out the inhaler.

He snatched it from her hand as if embarrassed that she should have seen it.

"Okay. You can leave now."

He was being rude. She ignored him. What reason had anyone in Vispera ever given him to be nice?

"Did Samuel find you another guitar?" she said, spying the instrument propped in the corner.

"You mean after Carson smashed the first one? Yeah. You want to tell him about it, in case he's itching to destroy another?"

"Show me how it works."

He eyed her suspiciously.

"I'd like to see." She picked it up, surprised by how heavy it was, and plucked one of the strings. "Please?"

At first his eyes narrowed, as if he was trying to figure out whether she was making fun of him, but then he took the guitar and his fingers fell naturally against the strings, finding placement without him even thinking about it.

"You're not going to like it," he said.

She shrugged.

He fiddled with the keys on the end, plucking the strings here and there, and then let out a slow breath. With a brisk movement of his fingers and hands, the guitar vibrated.

The sound made her gasp. It seemed to shake everything in the room, filling each inch of empty space the way the rain filled the air in the jungle outside. It was in her body, her lungs, that thrum and movement, a noise that clattered through her brain like the itch of a memory just out of reach. Right when she thought she couldn't stand it anymore, he stopped, pausing to let the last tremor of the strings still to silence.

"That's it?" she asked, more than a little confused.

"That's it," he said, like he didn't feel the need or desire to explain it. Which was fine. At least he seemed calmer now. His anger when she'd first showed up had softened.

He held the guitar, his hand distractedly caressing its curves. As she watched his fingers ripple with the contours of the instrument, her skin, cold and damp from the rain, began to warm with a heat stirring in the pit of her stomach. He looked up to see her staring at him, and the warmth seemed to stir the air between them, a kind of communing unlike anything she'd known before. It was similar to the Pairing, actually, but at the same time so different that, without any warning, it scared her.

She suddenly wanted to see his smile. Maybe if she saw it, these feelings would go away and she could go back to her sisters without thoughts of him intruding on her, which seemed to keep happening. She only wanted his lips to part and reveal the slightly crooked bottom teeth, something she'd seen once and thought an imperfection, but somehow it no longer was. Unable to stop herself, she reached her hand up to trace the lines of his mouth.

His eyes shuttered as he turned his head away, leaving her more confused than before. He must have felt what happened between them, but he went back to his guitar as if it'd been nothing. After a minute, he was lost in his thoughts, but she didn't want to leave.

Her room with her sisters was a simple, white-painted dorm, a row of beds on one wall with matching yellow coverlets, a row of desks on the opposite wall. It was exactly like all the other rooms in the Althea dorm. Jack's room was crowded and chaotic. His bed was draped with a quilt of trim blue squares and white thread sinking into soft cotton. The walls were covered in pictures and paintings. There was a large poster of a human man, tall and dark, leaping into the air, a bright orange ball cupped in his palm.

"Football," she murmured, recalling what little she knew of human history.

Jack finally acknowledged she was still there. "What?"

She pointed to the poster. "That's what he's doing. It's a sport. Humans played it."

Jack didn't look at the picture. "Basketball," he said. "You were close."

"Samuel-299 gave you all this stuff?"

"My mother. She liked to find human things stored in the Tunnels and bring them to me. Like that," he said, tipping his chin to the poster.

Jack had books stacked haphazardly on a shelf. They spanned at least five hundred years of human history, maybe more. If Inga-296 was trying to recreate a human's room, Althea couldn't pinpoint what century she'd meant to be represented. There were countless human artifacts in the Tunnels. They contained everything the humans and the Original Nine had wanted kept safe. It was deep underground, climate-controlled, and safe from contamination. Except for the Sample Room, the items in the Tunnels were merely of historical interest. Althea was intrigued by them, but only because she'd always liked history. Otherwise, the things kept there were mostly what the humans had valued but that Vispera had little use for. Things like the poster on Jack's wall.

Althea straightened. Jack was still softly plucking the strings of the guitar.

"Well," she said awkwardly. "I just thought you might need the inhaler."

He glanced up. "Wait." He put down the guitar and stood in front of her with his hands shoved in his pockets. He struggled for what to say. "It was nice of you. Thank you."

"It's okay," she said. She'd only gone to the labs to talk to him, to apologize. She hadn't really meant to be here, in this cottage with him. "I'm sorry for what Carson-312 did to your other guitar. I'm sorry I didn't do more to stop him." Althea didn't just mean the Declaration, and she thought Jack could tell. "Also, I didn't . . ." Althea meant to apologize for calling him unsocialized, but she couldn't bring herself to say it again. "I'm sorry I didn't like your book," she finished lamely, tucking wet hair behind her ear. "Those dogs that fly . . ." She trailed off.

He smiled. It was what Althea had wanted, to see his smile, and it was supposed to make these strange feelings go away, but they didn't. She was only left frustrated and wanting more.

"You didn't have to like the book," he said. "And the Tunnels have lots of guitars." They stood for several moments, at a loss for what to say or do next, until Jack startled Althea by abruptly turning around. "Hold on," he said.

He rifled through his bookshelf, scanning several before he found the one he wanted. He didn't hand her the book, however, but instead a piece of paper tucked inside. It was a page of words written in a precise script.

"It's not a story," he said. "It's a poem. You might like it better."

She held the paper, then twisted her mouth skeptically. "Did a human write it?"

"Sure," he said. "A woman wrote it. I know you didn't like the story because it was made up. This is different."

Althea felt Jack watching her as she read the words of the thing he called a *poem*. It was about losing things, how it was easy to lose things—keys and watches and such. It said that losing things was an art, which made Althea more puzzled than ever about what the humans thought *art* meant. *The art of losing isn't hard to master,* it said, over and over, as if the human writing it was trying to convince herself more than anyone else. Why didn't she simply say what she meant straight out?

She talked about losing names and places, although how could you lose a place? Althea's irritation almost made her put it down, just as she had with the book about the dog. She didn't, because Jack was watching her, and perhaps, she thought after a moment, the loss of a place could mean losing a memory, like forgetting. Though it was such a peculiar way to say it, and anyway, Althea had a very good memory and certainly couldn't relate to the idea. She kept on:

*I lost my mother's watch. And look! my last, or*
*next-to-last, of three loved houses went.*
*The art of losing isn't hard to master.*

*I lost two cities, lovely ones. And, vaster,*
*some realms I owned, two rivers, a continent.*
*I miss them, but it wasn't a disaster.*

*—Even losing you (the joking voice, a gesture*
*I love) I shan't have lied. It's evident*
*the art of losing's not too hard to master*
*though it may look like (Write it!) like disaster.*

She read it all the way through twice, and then turned to Jack. "You called it a *poem?*"

Jack nodded. "My mother—Inga-296—she loved it. She found it in the Tunnels and wrote it down so she could keep it with her." He waited patiently for her to say something. This was a gift he was giving her, a sort of thank-you. He wanted her to like it, to understand it, but she didn't.

"In the words, there's a pattern," she said, struggling for something to say.

"It rhymes."

"I guess so." She studied it further. Althea saw a mathematical rhythm to the words beyond the rhyming Jack meant. "There's a pattern, like math." She wasn't explaining it well, but it was the best she could do.

Jack seemed to grasp what she was saying, however. "Sam could never see the patterns," he said. "So you don't want to throw it across the room?" He was teasing her now, but she didn't mind because the smile was back again.

"Is it real?" she asked.

"It was real for the woman who wrote it. And real for my mother. It's more than real. It's true."

Althea had no idea what he meant when he talked about something being more than real. If something was real, of course it was true. The idea of what was true seemed important to him, though. Was that why he'd given her this poem? Was it true for him?

Althea's gaze followed the walls of the room. It was small, made smaller for being cluttered with the remnants of a world that no longer existed. Jack had spent his childhood here, with no brothers, no Gen. For the first time, Althea considered that the Council had made a mistake when they created Jack. A poster on the wall and a stack of books wasn't enough. In the end, it must be wrong to bring someone into being who had nothing to connect him to the world he was thrust into.

The poem was about loss, and it occurred to her that he had lost so much. The people he came from had lost everything— like the poem said, realms and continents, a whole civilization. And he had lost them, too. Not in the sense that he'd had them to lose, but that he'd never been given the chance to know them, to know others like him and the world they'd built. It must have made him sad. He would always be alone, the only one of his kind. That was why Inga-296 had tried to give him a human existence, so he would have something that was his, something to connect to. Even tonight, a sense of loss lingered over him like the night circling the glow of the candle.

Looking back at the last few words of the poem, she wondered also if something in it had spoken to the Inga because she'd already started to fracture. With fracturing, you would lose everything.

Althea stood and pulled the window curtain aside. Jack didn't notice her shivering in wet clothes.

Like Sam had said, Jack was here, living with them now. He might not be one of them, but they'd made him, and whether they wanted it or not, he was their responsibility. The Council would have to see that.

"Will you go back down, then?" she asked, watching the rivulets of water run down the hill where they would pour into Blue River. The rain would cause the river to swell, changing the character of the channel like a living thing.

"I don't know," he said.

She regretted asking the question when his eyes darkened. He was remembering whatever had made him run up to the cottage to begin with. He leaned back against the wall, staring at the ceiling and closing himself off from her again.

"Neither of us can go anywhere if the rain keeps up," he said. "Sleep downstairs if you want. I'd rather be alone."

He lay on the bed, turning away from her with his hands tucked under his arms.

Jack's face was still strange to her, and his mannerisms unfamiliar, but that night, even if he was trying to hide his feelings from her, he was failing. He said he wanted to be alone, but everything in his eyes, his whole being, made it a painfully obvious lie.

Althea sat next to Jack on the edge of the bed. Without being able to commune with him, she didn't know what would comfort him, so she touched his hair. It was what her sisters did when one of them was upset. They touched each other, seeking that calm they felt when they were all together, the soothing brush of fingers in their curls.

He didn't pull away from her this time, but his back stiffened. "I don't want to do anything," he said. "I don't want to Pair."

"Okay." She didn't lift her hand, but her face reddened thinking about how badly she'd wanted to touch him only moments ago. "I wasn't offering," she added with a slight scowl.

The room was quiet except for the rain and their breath, and she watched his chest rise and fall as the lines in his forehead faded with sleep. She stayed, brushing the hair from his closed eyes until it had dried, smooth and pale as corn silk, under her hand.

*Chapter Ten*

# JACK

Jack awoke to a low resonant crack followed by what seemed to be a rumble of thunder. He lay quietly for a few moments, remembering he was no longer in his bed in the labs; remembering that he'd planned to leave last night but had fallen asleep instead. The blanket at the foot of the bed was spread over him, and his muddy shoes had been removed. It must have been Althea, though he didn't remember her doing it. He remembered her weight on the bed next to him and her hand in his hair. Then the memory of what had happened with Nyla flooded over him, and he groaned softly.

Althea, standing by the window, glanced in his direction. He covered his face with his arm.

He wondered if they were all laughing at him. Sam, the Council, the Gen-310s, who'd probably heard all about it by now. Laughing at his ridiculous human response to their everyday rituals. To them it was nothing; it was just what they did. But maybe they weren't laughing at all, maybe they were disgusted by his behavior the same as they were by his music.

"Jack," Althea said, staring out the window toward town.

He sat up. The rain had stopped, and it was still dark, but the first light of dawn outlined the window in a gray veil, silhouetting Althea against it. He wondered if she'd slept.

"Jack," Althea said. "There's something down there."

Jack got up and looked out. At first he didn't see anything, only the light through the trees, and then he saw it. A plume of smoke rising snakelike into the sky, and a thin finger of gold.

"Fire," Jack said.

"I think . . ." Althea said, trying to figure it out, "I think it's near the labs."

Jack's unease turned to alarm. The noise that woke him hadn't been thunder. It was an explosion. "Nyla," he said. He pulled his shoes on, jerking the laces closed.

"What about Nyla?"

"She's down there. She's locked in my room."

Jack raced down the stairs. Althea followed behind, calling his name, trying to figure out what he was talking about, but he couldn't wait for her.

He barreled down the path, outstripping the branches and vines catching his clothes, misting him with dampness from the rain. The sting of a thorn caught his face, and a sharp stick scraped his arm. At the wall, he grasped the top in one jump and hauled himself over, then tossed the ladder to the other side for Althea. He couldn't stop to help her.

The Commons was empty and still, the town unaware of the raging fire half a mile away, though someone must have heard the explosion. When Jack finally reached North Lab, flames had burst the windows on the far side and black smoke rose from within. The first door he tried was locked. The second was blocked by something. He backed up and smashed it in with a swift kick. Someone had barred the door with a wooden board from the inside, trying to keep people out.

He didn't know this side of the building well. He tried to avoid the labs unless he was in his own small part of the complex. He ran up a stairwell, down a hallway filled with smoke, and then at last reached the door to his room. He unlocked it, opened it wide, and found it filled with smoke, black and choking. Nyla lay unconscious on the floor at the far end. A chair was tipped over next to her, as if she'd tried to use it to break through the glass in the door.

He rushed to her, swearing and searching frantically for the alarm. It should have gone off, everyone in Vispera should have been there putting out the fire, but there was nothing, only snapping flames punctuating the silence. Then he saw the alarm, wires dangling from the bottom. Someone had disabled it. He cursed again.

He lifted her from the floor. The smoke was thicker now, and the crashing sound of a ceiling caving in reached him from the hallway. His chest constricted. He couldn't remember if he'd grabbed his inhaler before he left the cottage. It was too late to check his pockets.

Nyla stirred in his arms. At least she was still alive.

"Hang on to me," he said, his voice choked. "Don't let go."

Dodging a row of doorways walled off by crackling flames, he finally reached one that hadn't been blocked. He shifted Nyla, hauling her over his shoulder. With his free arm, he rammed his other shoulder into the door until it fell open. Outside, Jack laid Nyla on the ground, and Althea cried out the girl's name, Nyla-313. He'd forgotten which one she was—he knew only that she wasn't Nyla-314. Jack dropped to his knees, doubled over and coughing, unable to get the smoke out of his lungs. Even racked with coughs, he saw Althea's hand seek out Nyla's to hold. It was such a slight touch, both casual and needful, and Jack understood that they were friends.

His coughing grew worse. Althea glanced at him, her worry for Nyla clear on her face, though now it seemed focused on him too. He forced in a lungful of air, but then it felt trapped in his chest until every cough was like a dagger.

Althea bent over him. "Jack?"

He warded her off with his hand, feeling like everything near him was blocking the air, and also wishing she wasn't seeing him like this. The edge of his vision darkened.

The clones had started to arrive. They ran toward Nyla and Althea, and called to each other for water and buckets. They paid no attention to Jack, who second by second was more sure he'd pass out. The Samuels descended on the two girls, and then a hand appeared in front of Jack's face holding an inhaler. Jack grabbed at it, fumbled it to his mouth, and pressed, sucking in the acrid, chemical taste. He pressed again, and again, until finally the coughing eased and his lungs cleared. Jack sat back on his heels and looked up to see Sam standing over him.

"What happened?" Sam asked.

The Viktors shouted orders, sending people for hoses and buckets, telling them to go to the river.

"I don't know."

Jack watched sheets of flame leap from the building. It was fully engulfed, blazing orange. The North Lab was where the amniotic tanks were, where they grew the clones. It was all destroyed now. There hadn't been any fetuses in the tanks, not this year, but what would happen if they couldn't replace those tanks? They'd never be able to grow the next generation.

Jack realized that Sam wasn't watching the building. He was watching Jack, studying him. His eyes felt like sandpaper, he was scratched up from running in the jungle, and he'd slept all night in wet clothes. His breathing was still ragged, and blood ran down his arm from a gash he didn't remember getting.

"Are you okay?" Sam asked.

"I'm fine."

"What was Nyla doing in the labs?"

Jack paused, then said quietly, "You should know. You sent her."

Sam nodded, confirming what Jack already knew.

Nyla lay on the ground surrounded by Sam's brothers. They lifted her to a stretcher, and Althea covered her in a blanket. Nyla's sisters appeared, crowding themselves around the throng of Samuels. Jack thought a few of the Nylas were glaring at him, though some looked with simple curiosity, probably wondering what had happened. He supposed they knew Nyla had been with him last night. It had been only a short time ago, though it felt like longer.

He tried to pick Nyla-314 out of the crowd of Nylas and found he couldn't. In his mind, she'd looked so different from her sisters, sweeter somehow, more beautiful. Before, he thought they'd been sharing secret looks, but it'd all been in his mind. He shook his head, feeling deceived all over again.

Sam took in the scene. Althea and Nyla, the fire, Jack's scratched face. Jack watched Sam, calm and deliberate, trying to figure out what had taken place.

"Did you do this?" Sam finally asked.

Jack reeled as if he'd been struck. "How can you ask me that?"

"If you did this, you should run, Jack. Go to the jungle, don't come back."

Jack almost laughed. Sam didn't realize that was exactly what Jack had planned. "You said I'd die in the jungle."

"If you did this, destroyed the lab, hurt one of our own . . . they'll kill you, Jack."

Althea left Nyla and came to Jack.

"How did this happen?" she asked. "Why were you at that house while Nyla was locked in your room?"

Sam's head tipped toward Jack at this information. Jack swallowed, wishing he didn't have to explain any of it, and certainly not with Althea listening. No doubt she wouldn't care what Nyla was doing in his room. She was more familiar with the Pairing Ceremonies than he was, so she would think nothing of it. But he hated her hearing the details. Though perhaps the Nylas hadn't just talked with each other about him. Maybe Althea had already heard every intimate detail of what he and Nyla had done together. Maybe they'd reported and catalogued to one another all his physical responses, things he'd done on instinct, driven by desire and an imagined sense of closeness. Jack squeezed his eyes shut to block out the feeling of exposure.

The Samuels carried away an unconscious Nyla. He hadn't started a fire, but he had locked her in his room. He'd left her there. It shouldn't have mattered. She should have been safe. He spent every night sleeping in that room in the labs. So why did this happen now? It had clearly been done on purpose. Someone had aimed to destroy the labs, or maybe to harm him, and they'd instead hurt the Nyla. Could the Council have done it, trying finally to get rid of him? But they didn't need to sneak around to terminate their own project, and anyway, there were easier ways to get rid of him than destroying the whole lab. Maybe Carson-312—but then why would Carson start a fire in another part of the building rather than Jack's own rooms? In any case, Carson could be vicious, but Jack didn't think Carson would actually try to kill him.

Jack had no idea what it meant, but someone wanted to destroy the labs, and possibly kill him, and they'd very nearly succeeded.

"You should both head to the clinic, get yourselves looked at," Sam said.

"I told you I'm fine," Jack said, grateful Sam had distracted Althea from her questions.

Sam gave him a sideways glance, frowning. "You're bleeding."

"It's nothing." He was being stubborn, but it'd been a long night.

The fire still blazed. A hose had been hauled all the way from the river. Shouts came from those fighting the fire, and pockets of clones stood in clusters of the nine models. They touched each other's shoulders and backs in nervous, unconscious movements as they gazed unblinking at the destruction. When they weren't watching the fire, their eyes veered toward Jack, and they huddled closer to their sisters or brothers.

"You don't seem to understand, Jack," Sam said. "You'll take the blame for this. Go to the clinic. Take Althea-310 and go."

*Chapter Eleven*

# ALTHEA

The clinic was cold, and Althea pulled the blanket tighter around her shoulders and watched as the Samuels adjusted the machines Nyla-313 had been hooked up to. She hadn't woken yet, but the constant beeps from the monitors told Althea the Samuels had done all they could, and now they simply had to wait.

"Will she be okay?" Althea asked.

One of them nodded. "I think she'll wake up soon."

Nyla's sisters were outside the door, insisting that they had to get into the triage room. They needed to see Nyla, touch her, assure themselves she'd be okay. Althea knew how they must feel. It was like that with her sisters, too. They experienced the anxiety or pain of another sister like something lodged in their bones. But with Nyla still asleep, they wouldn't be able to comfort her in the way they were used to.

Althea wanted to ask Jack again how the disaster at the labs had happened. He slouched tiredly next to her in one of the clinic's stiff-backed chairs. He'd refused the blanket Samuel-299 had offered. His clothes, still damp and stained with ash, smelled bitterly of smoke, and a bandage wrapped his arm.

Nyla-313 had been locked in Jack's room, and it must have been Jack who locked her in. What was she doing there? Growing up, she and Nyla had told each other everything, or at least she thought they had, but something was going on that Althea knew nothing about. She folded her arms in frustration. Jack obviously didn't want to talk about it. She'd seen him last night. He'd been distraught. She was sure something had happened between him and Nyla.

She briefly considered whether he'd had something to do with Nyla being in danger, but she'd seen the way he raced away into the building. Jack had saved her, and he'd done it without thinking, ignoring the danger, almost dying himself. He couldn't have tried to harm Nyla.

Althea knew she should go back to the dorms and be with her sisters, but she wanted to make sure Nyla was okay. And Jack couldn't leave. He'd stood earlier as if he wanted to, and Samuel-299 had almost imperceptibly shaken his head, causing Jack to sit back down, resigned.

"Do they think you started the fire?" Althea asked finally.

Jack shrugged. "Probably."

He acted like he didn't care, but she could tell he did by the way he sank farther into his seat. A clock on the wall ticked steadily, punctuating the beeps from the monitors. Althea was warm now, but Jack's shirt clung clammily against his chest. She unwrapped herself from the blanket and offered it to him. He accepted it this time, shrugging it over his shoulders.

"I don't know what happened with Nyla, but I was at the cottage with you last night. I'll tell them."

Jack shifted in his seat. "Thanks," he said.

"She's waking up," a Samuel said, and Althea jumped from her chair.

Nyla moaned and twisted her head away from Samuel-299's penlight as he pried her eyelids open.

"Nyla," Samuel-299 said. "How are you feeling?"

She brushed his hand away and squinted her eyes, seeing Samuel-299, Althea, and the other Samuels in the room.

"Hey," Althea said. "Are you okay?"

Nyla smiled at Althea, reached for her hand. "My head hurts."

When they touched, Althea felt her friend's confusion more strongly.

"There was a fire. Do you know what happened?"

Nyla's smile dropped slightly as she sorted through her memory.

The sound of a chair scraping the floor made Althea turn her head to see Jack making his way to the door. He'd been concerned all morning about Nyla, as anxious as she was to be sure she was okay. Now that Nyla was awake, he didn't want to be in the room with her.

Samuel-299 nodded to another Samuel, indicating that he should follow Jack out.

"Jack?" Althea said. After everything he'd done to save Nyla, she didn't understand why he wanted to leave now.

Then Nyla saw Jack, and her clasp tightened on Althea's hand. Nyla's fear seeped into Althea like a current. Nyla sat up in the bed and Samuel-299 eased her back down.

"What's he doing here?" Nyla said, her voice shaking. "He tried to kill me!"

Jack's eyes widened. Althea saw the surprise there, but she

couldn't help from stepping protectively between him and Nyla. Jack saw her shield Nyla from him, and his shoulders tensed.

Samuel-299 took a quick breath. "What's she talking about, Jack?"

Jack backed away, shaking his head. "I don't know."

"What do you mean, he tried to kill you?" Althea asked Nyla.

"He was so angry," Nyla said. "He started the fire; he locked me in the lab."

Samuel-299 spoke sharply to Jack. "Is that true, Jack?"

"No." Disbelief filled Jack's voice. "When she told me what you did, I was mad, but, Sam, I wouldn't hurt her!"

"Jack," Samuel-299 said, his whole body sagging over the bed.

"Sam, I didn't do this. You have to believe me."

"He was angry," Nyla said, her nails digging into Althea's hand. "Angry at me. There was no one else in the building last night!"

Nyla shuddered at the sight of Jack. Althea could tell she wasn't lying, that she believed what she said was true, but it couldn't be. Jack had saved her.

"I was with Jack last night," Althea said, to Nyla and Samuel-299. "He couldn't have started the fire."

Samuel-299 ignored Althea. Three Samuels converged on Jack at the same time four Viktor brothers came in to take him. They'd been just outside the door the whole time.

His head still bowed, Samuel-299 said softly, "You should have run, Jack. Why didn't you run?"

Jack paled as if Samuel-299's muted words were a blow to his face. The Viktors took his arms, which hung limp at his sides, all the fight drained from them. They led Jack from the room, and Nyla watched him go, still squeezing Althea's hand.

The next day the Council convened about the fire, and Althea was there not as official Council Recorder, but as a witness. One of her sisters sat at Althea's little desk in the corner, taking the minutes.

They'd rearranged the main room of Remembrance Hall in a way Althea had never seen before. The Council was no longer facing each other around their familiar table, but rather in a straight row facing out. Jack stood on a dais behind a wooden railing. As the members explained to the small crowd sitting in the hall, they had convened to discuss the explosion in the labs. They were calling Jack *the defendant,* or sometimes *the subject.* The way the Council members glared at Jack made Althea wonder just how hard they'd investigated. They seemed sure already of his guilt.

Althea had read about court trials in old records. Vispera had no experience with such things. With only nine known and predictable personalities, breaking the law had become a thing of the past. The words *Harmony, Affinity, Kinship* were painted in bright oils on the wall of the hall and embroidered on the badges sewn into the Council members' clothes. Jack stood alone before his accusers.

He'd been led in by a Viktor and a Kate, his wrists clapped in chains they unlocked once he reached the dais. The metal jangled together in a sound that would have seemed almost cheerful if the image of them weren't so disturbing. None of the brothers or sisters had ever been held by chains. It was too horrible to think about.

She tried to make eye contact with Jack as he stood on the dais, but he stared straight ahead with a mask of indifference, as if girding himself against what was to come.

Althea hadn't been allowed to speak with Nyla-313 after the clinic, or to Jack. She'd failed to calm Nyla, or convince her that she couldn't *know* it was Jack who started the fire. She hadn't even figured out how Nyla ended up in the labs that night or what had made Jack so angry. All she knew was that she'd heard the explosion and seen the beginnings of the fire while Jack lay sleeping a few feet away from her.

A Kate opened the meeting by outlining the details of the fire. All fifteen fire alarms in the building had been disabled, and most of the exits had been blocked from the inside. North Lab was in ruins, and all the amniotic tanks had been destroyed. The only person injured had been Nyla-313, although the Kate said three Viktors and a Hassan had been endangered as well. The Viktors had suffered smoke inhalation, and the Hassan had been hit by falling debris.

Nyla-313 was brought in. She walked slowly, leaning heavily on the Samuel escorting her. He helped her into a chair facing the Council, with Jack to her left. The Council asked her a series of questions to establish the events that led to the fire.

An Inga took over the questions. "And when was it you arrived at North Lab?"

"Early in the evening," Nyla said. "Around six."

"And you went straight to the subject's room?"

"Yes."

Althea sat up, listening for the question she was sure was next.

"And when did the subject leave the building?" Inga asked.

"About eight."

Althea couldn't see Nyla's face while she spoke. She saw the back of Nyla's head, and the faces of the Council members, and Jack's hard expression. Why didn't they ask what happened while Nyla-313 was in the labs? What had led to Jack running away? The Council didn't usually tolerate secrets. *Unless*, Althea thought, *they already know what Nyla was doing there*.

"When he left, what did the defendant say to you?" Inga asked.

Nyla paused, ordering the events in her mind. "When we were done with the Pairing, I stayed for a little while, and then Jack —the subject, I mean—he threatened me. He was aggressive and emotional. I was scared of him."

"What did he say?" Inga asked. "What did he actually threaten to do to you?"

"What he said . . ." Nyla paused and closed her eyes, bringing up the scene. "He said he *didn't want to hurt me,* which I took to mean that he was thinking of hurting me."

Inga stole a glance at the other Council members. "Go on," she said.

"Jack—the subject—left the room. I was bored stuck in there, and afraid he'd come back. After a while, I guess I fell asleep. When I woke up, the fire had started. I was trapped. I screamed over and over, and then the smoke came under the lab door. I guess after that, I passed out."

Althea tried to swallow past the tightness blocking her throat. That was what she'd missed. Jack and Nyla had Paired.

While Nyla gave her testimony, Jack never turned to Althea. His eyes were focused, staring at the floor. He remained outwardly impassive, with only the tension in his jaw betraying his intense concentration.

Althea's mind wandered around the question of why she even cared about the Pairing. She gazed almost without seeing at the back of Nyla's head and, before long, realized her hands were clenching the fabric of her scarf and twisting a thread through her fingers. The hem had frayed badly.

Dimly, she heard Inga say, "What was he emotional about?"

"I don't know," Nyla said, her voice raised in confusion. "He kept talking about my sister, Nyla-314, and he seemed upset that she hadn't come to see him. He'd wanted to Pair with her, I guess. There was, I don't know, something he wanted to say to her. But she was home, working on the hybrids for our apprenticeship."

Jack blushed at the mention of Nyla-314.

So it hadn't just been Nyla-313. Of course, that made sense. If Nyla-313 Paired with Jack, other Nylas would have as well. It simply made it awkward that there were only one of Jack and ten of them. If he'd had nine brothers, it could have all been accomplished in one evening, quite a bit more simply. Althea tried to relax her hands again. She smoothed the twisted fabric of her scarf. None of it should mean anything to her, after all. Yet even as she had the thought, an unpleasant warmth crept up her neck that reddened her cheeks like prickly wool just under her skin. With a deep breath, she tried to still her hands. She looked up to find Jack looking back at her. For the first time in the whole proceeding, their eyes met.

He was still so strange, that was the problem. Everyone in the room, all they saw when they looked at Jack were the ways he was unlike them. She stared at his face, examining those things that made him different. The planes of his cheeks, the pale, straight eyebrows, the broad, squared shoulders. The colorless ocean-gray of his eyes.

His eyes, she realized after considering for a moment, weren't as strange as she'd first thought. If she looked closely at them, framed as they were by the foreign lines of his face, they now seemed rather familiar. They were bright and lucid, like the sky on an overcast day, or the mottled shadows along the path to the river, the one she and her sisters took to capture fish in woven baskets. She'd thought he was so different, but he wasn't, not really. She'd never known anyone like him, but with an overwhelming clarity, she found she knew him. She could see inside him, and she *knew* him.

"He tried to kill me," Nyla told the Council, and the Inga nodded as if she sympathized, while Samuel-299 rubbed the skin of his brow.

On the dais, Jack shook his head in frustration. He opened his mouth, thought better of it, and then raised his hand instead, seeking the Council's attention.

Inga turned slowly to him. "What do you want?"

"I'd like to speak," Jack said quietly, apparently striving for calm. The Inga silently consulted the other Council members and then nodded. Jack said, "I never tried to kill Nyla. I'd never do that."

"Well, did you *threaten* to kill her?" Inga said.

"No, never. I just wanted to get out of the room."

"Did you threaten to hurt her?"

Jack hesitated. "No, I didn't."

Inga shuffled some papers on the table and picked one up, read from it. "Did you say to Nyla-313, *I don't want to hurt you*?"

"Yes, but that's not the same—"

"And you did seek to lock her in your room?" The question,

ringing through the meeting hall, sounded to Althea like a decisive statement.

Jack struggled to frame an answer and then sighed. "Yes, I did," he said finally. "I wanted time to get away without the Council knowing. I just wanted to leave, that's all."

After a long moment, the Inga, scowling, turned back to the Council members.

*Well,* Althea thought. *That made things worse.*

The meeting hall closed in on her, stuffy and hot. Sweat trickled down her back, and she thought about what Samuel-299 had said the Council would do when they changed their minds about tolerating Jack. The room was suffocating. A wordless sound escaped her, causing the Council members to pause and look up. They were all looking at her now, the Council, Samuel-299, Nyla-313, Jack. She clung to the bench in front of her and pulled herself to her feet. The Viktor at the door opened it for her. The floor wavered.

From the corner of her eye, she saw Jack take a step in her direction, as if moving to help, despite the guard.

"Althea?" Samuel-299 said from the panel.

She tried to speak, to excuse herself for disrupting their proceedings, but was afraid she'd pass out if she didn't get through the door.

She made it to the hallway and stumbled into one of the Samuels. He caught her arms.

"Are you okay?" he said.

No, she wasn't. She couldn't sit in the meeting hall anymore, couldn't listen to her friend talk about Jack that way. She couldn't watch the faces of the Council members, who were obviously only biding time until they pronounced Jack guilty and then . . . did what? Killed him? She couldn't bring herself to look into Jack's eyes anymore, eyes that seemed to see something in her that made his lips part the slightest bit, as if he was about to say something only she could hear far across the room.

Althea pushed the Samuel away. She sat on the bench outside the meeting hall doors, catching her breath. She longed for her sisters. They would calm her, ease the panic that overwhelmed her.

As the shakiness ebbed, Althea leaned her head back on the wall, wishing she hadn't left the meeting hall. Now she wouldn't know what was happening.

The slam of the entrance door from the Commons jangled her nerves. It was Carson-292. She had noticed he wasn't representing the Carsons in the meeting hall. He led the younger Carson-312 with him, a small device clutched in his hand. It was shiny and silver, with copper wires twisting around it.

Althea stood, worried at their determined strides.

"What are you doing here?" she said to Carson-312.

Carson-292 brushed her aside and strode toward the double doors of the meeting hall. "This doesn't concern you, Althea."

"Wait." Althea scurried in front of them. "Is it about Jack?"

"I saw him, Althea," Carson-312 said. "I saw him start the fire."

Althea pointed her finger in Carson-312's face. "That's a lie, Carson. He was with me when it started."

Carson-292 had walked ahead of them. He turned back to Carson-312 and Althea, his hand resting impatiently on the handle of the door.

Carson-312 smiled at Althea, an ugly smile, shrewd and calculating. Pointing to the device held by Carson-292, he said, "See that thing? It's a timer. It was found in the rubble this morning. It was stolen from the tanks in the lab. He was with you when the fire started, because he made sure of it. He's using you as an alibi."

She shook her head. "You're setting him up. You hate him, you always have."

"Carson!" Carson-292 said sharply.

Althea followed them into the meeting hall; the proceeding was disrupted with the entrance of the Carsons. Still standing on the dais, Jack glanced uncertainly at the Carsons, but seemed relieved to see Althea again. She was supposed to be there to get him out of this mess.

Althea blocked Carson-312 from moving up the aisle of chairs. "You can't lie to the Council."

"Althea." He placed his hand gently on her shoulder. She batted it away, and his eyes hardened. "He's dangerous. You know it as well as I do. We've put up with enough from him, and it's time someone stopped him."

Althea watched helplessly as Carson-292 approached the Council and placed the device on their table, telling them what it was.

"You saw him in the labs?" the Inga asked Carson-312.

"I saw him sneaking toward the labs last night."

"Then why wait until now to say so? Why didn't you tell someone right away?" Althea asked from across the meeting hall.

"Sit down, Althea," the Inga said. She turned back to Carson-312. "And you're sure it was the defendant you saw?"

"Positive. He's been stealing from the labs, things like this timer, and he snuck out last night. Everything going wrong, it's been him the whole time. He ruined our fields, he stole the timers on the tanks, and he destroyed the labs. Who else could it have been? He thinks he can tear down our community, and I'm not going to stand around watching it happen."

"He has no proof!" Althea said, yelling this time.

"Althea, stop," Jack said, in a voice meant only for her.

She didn't stop, though. She pushed past the Viktor and made her way to Carson-312. He stood in front of the Council, smug and arrogant. She wanted to hit him, an urge toward violence she'd never felt before. She stood in front of him to block him from the Council table, making them listen to her. "Jack was with me last night, outside the wall."

The Althea on the Council cast a sharp look at Althea. She wasn't supposed to cross the wall, and doing it to see the human boy certainly wouldn't go over well.

Inga sighed patiently. "Given the timer, that clearly doesn't prove he's innocent of starting the fire."

Carson-312's lip slid into an incredulous smile. "I can't believe you're going to defend him over one of your own. He's nothing, Althea, an animal."

Althea moved toward Carson-312 until her face was right next to his. Up close, his heavy breath brushed her skin. She saw the tiny hairs of his left eyebrow and the way his scar made a smooth, white line between them.

"Don't say that!" she hissed.

Carson-312 pushed her aside with unexpected force. She lost her balance and tumbled against the bench, hitting her head on the wooden rail and falling to the floor. A Viktor tried to grab her arm as she fell. Carson-292 reached down as if to help her up, and half the Council members were yelling, trying to regain order.

Althea saw Jack above the faces crowding her, and in a second knew what would happen next. *No, don't,* she thought. *It was an accident, I'm not hurt.* But it was too late. Jack's eyes already flashed with a rage he'd suppressed for years.

Bracing his hand on the railing of the dais, Jack leapt over it and lunged at Carson-312, easily dodging the Viktor closing in on him. Jack shoved Carson against the wall, pinning him there with his forearm.

"Touch her again, I'll kill you," he said.

"We're not kids anymore. Why don't you try?"

They both swung at each other, with the Viktor struggling to keep them apart. Each landed a blow, but it was Carson-312's head that snapped back.

The Viktor was knocked aside as Jack threw Carson to the floor. Holding Carson's shirt bunched in his fist, Jack hit Carson twice more before he froze and pulled back. As if realizing suddenly that they weren't, in fact, children anymore, he stared at Carson. Jack was seeing what everyone else in the room already had. Even through his anger, Carson suddenly looked no different than the hurt and bloody fifteen-year-old boy he'd been in the schoolyard after Jack had attacked him. Pinned by Jack once again, facing his blows, Carson was terrified.

Jack paused and then, as if he couldn't help himself, gave Carson one last blow, but it was a pulled punch, barely grazing the other boy's chin. Jack shoved off him. Carson sat up, testing his bruised jaw.

"Get up," Jack said. His body radiated a barely contained fury.

When Jack turned his back, Carson made to lunge at him again, but Samuel-299 pressed a hand to his shoulder. "Be still," he said tersely, and Carson reluctantly complied, glaring furiously at Jack.

Three Viktors burst into the room, each holding an electric prod, the kind used to control cattle. They surrounded Jack, aiming the prods at him. Jack swept his hands into the air, surrendering. Even outnumbered and next to all the Viktors, weapons in their hands, he looked strong. Strong enough to kill anyone in the room, if that was what he wanted to do.

The Council members looked on stonily, the Inga especially. It was over, Althea realized. They were going to find him guilty, no matter what she said. Jack had locked Nyla-313 in the labs and then he'd attacked Carson-312. He'd sealed his fate.

"No," Althea said. "He's innocent. Samuel, tell them!"

Samuel-299 only turned away, his face creased in grief, as the Viktors put Jack back in the chains. The Council filed out of the room to make their decision, and Samuel-299 followed.

"Jack," Althea said as he was hauled away, the chains jangling against the floor.

He gave her a small smile, as if to say he was sorry for disappointing her.

It wasn't fair, though. The Carsons were setting him up; they had to be. The Council was too narrow-minded to see it.

Althea dropped onto the bench. Perhaps she was the one too blind to understand who Jack really was. She'd witnessed it more than once, the times he'd resorted to violence, as if a well of anger boiled inside him and lashing out was the only thing he knew how to do. And the evidence of the timer had been damning.

Nyla-313 passed by, close enough to reach out and touch her. "I'm sorry, Althea," she said.

Althea heard the sadness in her friend's voice, and knew if she looked up she'd see tears in Nyla's dark eyes. She didn't look up.

"I know," Althea said, leaning on the bench in front of her, resting her chin on her arms as Nyla-313 walked away.

*Chapter Twelve*

# JACK

Jack once read a story in his mother's journals about something that happened long ago. She'd uncovered the information while digging through years of research on genetics, humans, and the Slow Plague. It wasn't a story Jack had ever seen in the textbooks the clones read in school.

In the early years of Vispera, the clones found evidence that not all humans had died during the Slow Plague, that there were pockets of life scattered here and there around the globe. Most reports turned out to be unfounded, but the clones sent search parties in any case to look for survivors. They collected about 120, mostly from the north, and brought them back. All data and records indicated that these were the only humans who'd survived the Slow Plague, and they were grateful for the prospect of a community, a civilized home. They'd struggled alone for over a decade to live in a dead world. They had seen Vispera, with its protective wall, its thriving population, and orderly rules, and had known, finally, they'd be safe.

The first thing the clones did was separate the humans, putting the women in a cluster of huts on the edge of town, while the men were to live in a barn in one of the far-off grain fields. The clones put them to work building the structures that would become the clone models' dorms.

They didn't allow the humans to have Pairing Ceremonies, even among their own population. If the humans began breeding, the clones knew where that would lead. They'd slowly populate the earth again, even starting with only 120 specimens. They would spread like ants, and in a short time, they would outnumber the orderly and controlled people of Vispera, whose population never increased beyond the capacity and desires of the community. And then the humans would take over, and once again the world would collapse with disease and disorder. So the humans were separated, monitored, and controlled. And they proved useful.

Genetics were complicated, and his mother's journals contained only a quick reckoning of what had happened to the humans, but Jack gathered they had been a convenient resource. When the Viktors needed to work hard to keep up with the others in the scientific breakthroughs being made, the clones borrowed a genetic marker from one of the humans to help future Viktors become quick studies. The Kates seemed to lack self-control, the Meis tended toward irritability, and so on, until these humans had provided the genetic nuances the clones needed. In only a few generations, the clones had what they would need to mold themselves into perfectly balanced specimens, each model complementing the others' particular traits and strengths. Which was good, because the humans had become problematic.

In Vispera and the other communities, violence was virtually unknown, and conflict rare. The clone models communed, reaching peaceful resolution to disagreements, short-circuiting possible dissension. The humans, on the other hand, became increasingly difficult to manage and predict. They began fighting the tests and refusing work. Some ran away, only to be brought back again, as it wouldn't do for a human to go unmonitored. And then there was the difficulty that they kept getting pregnant.

The women were eliminated first. It was unfortunate, the Council members agreed, but the humans had served their purpose. The men were kept in the barn and put to work tending the fields and cattle. But they became violent and dangerous, and the measures in place to control them weren't working. In any case, the clones had devised machines to do the jobs of the men. Within a year, they had been eliminated as well, their water poisoned so they drifted off to sleep. The clones saw nothing to be gained in making them suffer. The only remnants of their existence in Vispera were the vestiges of the women's huts on the edge of a field, now nothing more than piles of thick grass and mud bricks, and also the barn.

Once painted a bright chrome yellow, it stood out against the red barns that held cows, mules, and horses. On the inside, instead of animal stalls, the yellow barn held cages with iron bars, and iron rings poked out from the walls to hold the rusted shackles attached to clusters of manacles. The yellow barn hadn't been used since the last human men had been caged in it over two hundred years ago, and it sloped precariously to the side. The yellow paint was hardly recognizable, the wood rotted, and the roof had caved in, letting in the torrential rains, nesting birds, and ambling rodents.

When Jack was a child, he liked to explore the planted fields, and he'd naturally come across the yellow barn sitting in a barren isolated plot of its own. He would climb the beams, falling to the ground more than once. One time his mother had found him there, and he'd seen the way a veil fell across her eyes when she saw him playing in the open cages. She'd taken his hand and led him away, telling him that the yellow barn was a bad place.

"All creatures are precious, Jack," she'd said. "My people have done terrible things. We need to learn how to do better."

That was the same year she ran away from Vispera. The same year she died.

After the fiasco of the trial, it hadn't taken Jack long to figure out where the clones were taking him when they led him away from town. He'd been confined to the yellow barn, though none of them, not even Sam, had bothered to tell him what that meant. As each hour passed in the barn, however, he became more and more certain that they'd decided he should die.

The rusted bars of the cage cast long shadows across the floor at night. Jack couldn't reach them to see if any were loose. The Viktors had strung shackles through the rings bolted to the far wall of the cell. They were just long enough for Jack to lie down, though even then the cuffs pulled at his wrists and cut into his skin. They'd taken his clothes, and he shivered each night against the wall, hugging his knees. They'd brought him no food, and nothing to drink but a murky bowl of water filled by the rain that streamed through the open roof. He'd been abandoned. He yelled that first day until his voice was hoarse and his throat raw, then he'd given up, exhausted. He felt hollow with hunger, his lips were dry and cracked, and his muscles cramped. If they had decided to kill him, he was beginning to wish they'd just get on with it.

On the first night, he'd been unable to sleep. He was too cold, too constrained by the shackles, and simply too angry. Sleep came on the second night, though it felt more like drifting into a dark abyss than rest. The next morning, he woke with the first beam of sun trickling through the cracks in the barn walls.

The rumble of a man clearing his throat caused Jack to shift position, and he cringed at the jagged needles of pain in his limbs. An older Carson, probably one of the 290s, sat before him on a rough chair on the other side of the bars. A Council badge was sewn into his shirt. His legs were crossed, and one hand was folded over his knee. He ate a cut of meat on torn bread and sipped from a bottle of clear water in his other hand. A small parcel lay by his feet.

Jack eyed the Carson warily, squinting against the bright light from outside. His eyes followed the water to the man's mouth. It wet his lips, and Jack licked his own with a parched tongue.

"The Council argued for a long time," Carson said after swallowing a mouthful of the sandwich. "They decided someone should let you know what we're doing with you. I volunteered." His mouth, shining with moisture and grease, twisted in a half smile.

"Where's Sam?" Jack asked. His voice, dry and unused, came out rough.

"We thought it best someone else deliver the news."

"You're going to kill me."

At first, the coldness in the man's eyes told Jack he was right, but then Carson tore off another piece of bread and shook his head.

Speaking around his mouthful, he said, "That's what most of us wanted. It's simple, and would follow the protocol of a failed experiment. But Samuel-299 wouldn't agree. Certainly it would be much easier at times if one person had clear authority. But that's not how things are done in Vispera. We communed on the matter, and it became clear that Samuel-299 feels you should live more strongly than others feel you shouldn't. We reached a compromise."

"And?"

Jack strained to listen to what Carson was saying, but the water bottle was sweating, and a drop slid down, pooling in the crook of Carson's finger. Unconsciously Jack moved to rub his parched lips with the back of his arm, briefly forgetting about the shackles. He sucked in a breath when the chains sliced into his raw skin. Carson's eyebrows twitched a fraction.

"We'll make use of you in the fields."

"That's dumb. You have the machines for that."

"Indeed. I may have said something similar. But it keeps you away from town, and away from the Gen-310s."

Jack snorted. Their logic was absurd. "How'd Sam talk you into that plan?"

"We don't allow anything to exist with no purpose. As of now, you're about as useful as a plow horse. We'd hoped for more." Carson took a long drink, downing half the water. He shrugged. "Although I've been against using your genetic code from the beginning. You introduce disease to the community."

Jack tried to absorb what Carson was saying, but his mind felt fragile with thirst, hunger, and fatigue. It was like hearing someone through a long tunnel.

"Disease? You mean asthma?"

"One of a million diseases that died with the humans. And Samuel thinks you're worth the risk of bringing it back. I can just imagine where that would lead. Not to mention your emotional instability. I've known for a while it was you sabotaging our fields and tanks. Now I have proof."

"No, you don't," Jack said. "I didn't do those things."

Carson laughed quietly. He reached into his shirt pocket and pulled out a clear, flat slide as wide as his thick fingers. It glittered slightly in the morning sun, a bright sliver of technology in a barn all but reclaimed by dirt and brush. "See this? It's you, Jack. Your cells, your genetic sequence, whatever you want to call it." Carson inspected Jack through the transparent square. "Everything you are is contained in this flimsy piece of glass. We have a fair amount of it—human genetic material. Unpredictable stuff. Our embryos almost always fail, and then every human we do manage has something wrong with it."

When Jack reacted to Carson's words, the man smirked, and Jack realized he'd just been told something he wasn't supposed to know.

"Jack," he said, condescension thickening his voice, "did you honestly think you were the first? The only human we've brought back from extinction?" He gave a bland chuckle. "There've been a number over the years. See, the Council thinks we need a tenth clone to balance out the community, a fifth male for the five females. It was looking good for you until you started breathing like a fish flopping on a hook. Now you're just another failed audition, useful for a few gene markers we might find convenient, but otherwise a waste." Carson leaned toward the cage, elbows on his knees, as if he were passing on a confidence to a friend. "The humans have always been a disaster, you know. Endless war, poverty, genocide, inequality, pollution—to say nothing of an obsession with sex and reproduction. Your kind would have killed the planet if they'd lived. That's the human legacy, all just historical memories now. And your grab bag of genetics, too. Curved spines, seizures, limps, terrible eyesight, flat feet, runaway cancers, chemical, psychological, or emotional instability. It's a wonder your species existed as long as it did."

"Maybe the problem wasn't your test subjects. Maybe the problem was you."

Carson paused and looked at Jack as if he really were a specimen under glass. "There's a reason humans are gone." He leaned forward and peered into the cage. "Honestly, not a single one of you has been any good." He shook his head. "You certainly are some animal."

Jack knew what Carson was seeing. He was filthy, naked, chained to the wall, and staring desperately at the pathetic few inches of water left in Carson's bottle. He supposed he didn't make such a great representative of humanity right then.

Carson stood and slid the glass square into his pocket. He wiped his greasy hands on his shirt and scrutinized the barn with distaste. He lifted the parcel from the ground and threw it into the cell where it landed near Jack, just out of reach. Then he drank again from the water, leaving a small bit splashing at the bottom.

"Here," he said, tossing that too between the bars of the cell. It rolled to Jack's feet, spilling what little was left inside. "Samuel-299 wanted you to have this."

Carson turned his back and strolled past the empty cells toward the entrance. Jack watched the spilled water seep into the floor of the barn, leaving a damp outline in the dirt.

"Right. Some animal," Jack said, just loud enough for Carson to hear.

That night, Jack didn't even have the energy left to shiver. He drifted in and out of sleep. His tongue felt swollen, his mouth dry. The drops of water he'd gotten from Carson's bottle were gone in seconds, and he was only left wanting more. Streams of blood dried down to his elbow from where the shackles' metal edge had cut his skin when he'd tried and failed to reach the parcel.

Jack felt half dead, but he could see the cornfields through the barn door that Carson had left open. They swayed with the gentle wind as if they were breathing. The sound of the breeze mingled with the buzz of insects and croak of frogs. Jack heard the music of it, felt it deep in the earth at the same time as he felt it in the bones and blood of his body.

The Council wanted a tenth clone. Nine was an odd number, and the clones had never been much for odd numbers. Was that what his mother had meant when she said they needed him? That they needed future generations of Jacks, all polished and perfected like the others, refined for useful traits and cleansed of anything undesirable?

No, his mother wouldn't want that. She'd fought the Council, fought the clones. She wanted him to be human, not another one of them.

Whatever the Council may once have planned, Jack found he was glad he'd failed their audition. There was something wrong with the clones. Maybe they didn't have things like bad eyesight, or deformities and diseases, things like his asthma, but three centuries ago they had murdered 120 humans they'd promised to keep safe.

They'd killed his mother for no reason he would ever understand.

Jack drew himself upright on the wall, listening harder for the night's music. The clones would say the night was silent, and perhaps it really was. Perhaps he was still dreaming, and it was only a human dream.

Jack's leg brushed something at his side. The parcel, the one Carson threw into the cage; it was next to him now, several feet closer than where it had landed. Beside that was the water bottle, full and glistening, cool condensation dripping down its side. Jack lifted it, held it in his trembling hands as he pulled the top. He drank until the liquid dripped down his chin, his neck, his chest. He tore his mouth away from the opening, knowing he shouldn't drink it all at once, but relishing the cold sweetness. He put it down, breathing deeply, then searched through the parcel. In it he found a pair of drawstring pants like the scrubs the Samuels wore in the clinic, some bandages, an inhaler, and a long iron key. The key opened the cuffs around his wrists. His numb fingers fumbled with it until it turned and the manacles released. He clenched his teeth to stifle a sob as they dropped, the pain and stiffness stabbing into his joints.

After searching the bag, Jack listened intently to the noises from outside. Someone had been here. They'd filled the water bottle and reached from outside the bars while he slept and pushed the parcel to where he could reach it. Maybe Sam, though surely Sam would have woken him, talked to him. Was it Althea? She would try to help him, he knew, even if it got her in trouble. The thought of her being close gave him the first sense of warmth he'd felt in days.

There was a rustle, and a hint of movement outside. Jack narrowed his eyes into the night, staring at the moonlit shadows through the thin crack between the wooden boards of the barn.

Hidden in the fields of corn, on the edge of the wavering stalks, he saw motion, then stillness. The crack darkened, and his view of the field was blocked by something—a body, and then a face.

And then, mere inches away on the other side of the wall, Jack saw his own pale eyes, glimmering and laughing in the darkness.

*Chapter Thirteen*

# ALTHEA

There'd been no Council meetings since the disaster of the last one, and Althea hadn't once been able to corner Samuel-299. She'd resorted to planting herself outside the clinic for the past three days, watching the Samuels come and go, the Gen-300s, Gen-290s, 280s, 270s, all of them, including those from Gen-310, but Samuel-299 never appeared. He was avoiding her. Though she knew, when he saw her, he wouldn't be able to hide his reaction. He would know what she wanted. They'd taken Jack away, and she had no idea where he was or what was happening to him. The only other person who would care was Samuel-299. She'd seen his face when the Council had used the word *elimination*. So she waited.

The nights had been cold, but the day was warm, and the space outside the clinic wasn't shaded. In the weed-filled ditch near the path, flowering amaranth drooped low in bright bursts of rosy color, drying in the heat. The red dirt in the clearing seemed to have absorbed the air, and it crunched hot under her feet. She would rather be with her sisters in the cool shade of the wide-leafed trees, chasing the tetras that flickered in Blue River, but she felt helpless. She had to do something.

Nyla-313 came up the path. The hem of her blue dress floated in the hot breeze, brushing the tops of her sandals.

"I thought you might be here again," Nyla said. "You're still trying to find Samuel-299?"

"He knows where they took Jack," Althea said, squinting up at Nyla, a dark silhouette against the sun.

"Why do you care so much?" Nyla said, sitting down.

"The Carsons were lying. It's not right."

"Do you think I'm lying?"

Althea took Nyla's hand, and in touching her for the first time since everything had happened, she felt a stir of doubt in Nyla.

"No, not lying," Althea said. "But I don't think you know what happened, not really."

"He did lock me in the lab that night," Nyla said.

"I know. He shouldn't have done that."

They both fell silent for a moment, sitting in the remorseless sun. Then Nyla grinned and dug into the bag on her shoulder. "I have something for you." She pulled out a pear, and when she turned it to Althea, Althea saw her own face looking back, molded into the round base of the fruit.

Althea laughed, as much at the pear as the pleased look on Nyla's face.

"The Kates are hosting the next Pairing, and they're making these for each model. What do you think?"

The pear cupped in her palm felt cool, the skin coarse and freckled. The Kates had captured the Altheas' features. The wide eyes, straight mouth, and arched brows. *It looks just like us,* Althea thought, her smile fading.

Still studying the pear, Althea said, "Nyla?"

"Hmm?"

Althea considered what she wanted to ask about the night of the fire, the same night she had been with Jack in the cottage while he slept. Images had nagged her, muddling her thoughts. She kept thinking about how the air between them that night had seemed alive, like it had weight and shape. It had compelled her to want to touch him. Nyla already had touched him, and if Althea knew more, perhaps the images of him, and of him and Nyla together, would stop keeping her up at night.

"What was it like?" she finally said.

Nyla laughed. "Being stuck in the lab while it burned to the ground? Not great."

"No, not that. What was it like Pairing with him?"

Nyla bit her lip. Part of Althea didn't want to hear what she would say, but another part of her needed to know.

"You know what it's like with the others," Nyla said. "It's fun, and nice. They know what they're doing, right? They follow the rituals, and you can predict how they'll touch you, where and when, all that. But sometimes, well . . . you know how sometimes it feels like the Hassans are distracted during the Pairing, like by their new red bean hybrid or something?"

Althea smiled. "Maybe we should let the boys choose us sometimes."

"Right." Nyla laughed. "Why do we have to choose a boy at all?"

It had always been the girls choosing the boys, and the Pairings were always one female and one male. The traditions never changed. Just like the rituals of the actual Pairing itself, it was always the same. The customs went all the way back to the Original Nine, or at least that's what they learned in their history lessons. The first Gens had designed all the males to be sterile, so Pairing was more civilized than what had come before, but it still connected them all to their human ancestry, and reminded them where they'd come from. Also, as Nyla said, it was fun.

"So it was different with Jack?" Althea said, trying to steer the conversation back.

Nyla considered. "It was different. Samuel-299 gave us a pill, like a little candy, beforehand. Isn't that strange?" Watching Althea's reaction, Nyla's eyes widened as if something had just occurred to her. "Do you suppose, because he's human, he can . . ." She shook her head. "Ugh, never mind."

"He can what?"

Nyla leaned close and whispered, "*Reproduce.*"

"Oh," Althea said. "You mean like the humans did?"

"I can't think about that." Nyla shuddered dramatically. "Anyway, he really had no idea what he was doing. Nyla-314 was the first one with him, and she said it was like he didn't even think about the protocols of the Ceremonies. She said he just kind of . . . took over. By the time I was with him, he knew the routines, but . . ." Nyla made a frustrated noise in her throat.

"But what?" Althea asked, wondering if she thought it had been horrible.

"I don't know. It was . . . surprising, I guess." Nyla giggled, covering her mouth.

"Was it nice?" Althea asked.

"Yes," Nyla said. "And now, ever since, being with the others . . . it's not the same. I don't know. I keep thinking about Jack and how . . . unexpected it was."

Althea propped her chin in her hands and stared into the yellow grass.

"I'm sorry, is that what you wanted to hear?" Nyla asked.

"It's okay," Althea said. "I just need to talk to Samuel-299."

Nyla stood, taking Althea's hand again and squeezing it. She grinned. "Only six of us Paired with him, you know. The others are pretty mad about it."

"Really?" Althea said.

"Really. You should Pair with him, if you want to. You and your sisters. It's just too bad there's only one of him."

Althea nodded without looking up. Was that what she wanted? The idea of him with one of her sisters made her stomach twist in knots, though it shouldn't. She *was* her sisters, and they were her. She felt more confused than ever.

"By the way," Nyla said, "Samuel-299 isn't in the clinic. He's sick."

"What do you mean?" He'd been fine the other day at the Council Meeting. And anyway, no one ever got sick.

"I heard he was sent to work in the nursery."

Althea glanced in the direction of the building where the youngest Gen would be.

"They won't like it if you go there," Nyla said, following Althea's gaze.

"They don't have to know."

Samuel-299 sat on a bench on the nursery playground with little Gen-320s running around him. His feet were planted flat, and his eyes were far away despite the bedlam of the bright outdoors, alive with the chatter of rambunctious seven-year-olds.

Samuel was a doctor, not one of the caretakers. Usually the nursery was staffed with the Gens who had retired from their jobs in the community. It was unusual to see a Gen-290 Samuel there. He looked ill at ease and out of place.

The nursery sat alongside the school in the south part of town. Inside, it had nine different stations. Every child could play in any station they chose, as they often did, but they'd been designed specifically to hone the inborn skills of the individual models. In one corner, paints and easels had been set up, and the Ingas liked to play there. Samuels chose the dolls and toy doctors' kits. Althea remembered the nursery as a child, and she could still clearly recall the smell of old books and records, and the brittle paper of faded maps.

She briefly considered turning around, walking away from the playground, and leaving Samuel-299 be. But she needed to see Jack. She needed to know he was still alive.

She sat on the bench next to Samuel and touched his hand. It was cold, even in the bright sun. His skin had a grayish pallor.

"Althea," he said, unsurprised at seeing her. "You want to know where they took Jack."

"You know, don't you?"

He nodded, but didn't tell her. "I'm off the Council."

"I'm sorry," she said.

His hand clutched hers, pressing her fingers together. His eyes sharpened. "Go to him! He needs help."

When she'd first touched Samuel, she'd felt only a dim sense of anxiety, something faded and weak. When he mentioned Jack, however, the feeling that had been no more troubling to her than a slight headache burst forward, a sharp, stabbing pain directly between her eyes.

*He's fracturing,* she thought. He was losing control of his emotions, and his ability to commune with others had become erratic, weak at times but then sudden and strong. This was why the other Samuels in his Gen had sent him off to the nursery. They either felt nothing from him or they felt too much. Althea pulled her hand free of his, not wanting to feel his pain again.

The children played in the yard. It was some game where they raced after each other, one group of siblings chasing another. One of the little Ingas tripped and fell, scraping her knees on the gravel. She cried as blood oozed from the broken skin. Samuel's gaze flickered toward the commotion, but he didn't react. The Inga's sisters had already converged around her, their red-ribboned braids hanging in their faces as they comforted the girl on the ground.

"Samuel, where's Jack?" Althea asked.

His eyes drifted away from her. She saw the struggle in them, and then watched a light die inside him as all his calculations failed him. Pain was etched clearly on his face.

"He's locked up, in the yellow barn by the east field," he said. "But, Althea, you should leave it, let the Council do what's best." He seemed at war with himself, and she'd disrupted whatever intense concentration it was taking him to forget. "He'll only bring you heartbreak. And then you'll fracture, too."

It had occurred to Althea that she was courting trouble. By helping Jack, what if she ended up fracturing, like Samuel-299? She would have to be careful.

Samuel's gaze bore into her. "I'm weak," he said. "I've been so weak. He needed me, and what have I done? Let the others be cruel to him. That's what Inga-296 said would happen, and I didn't listen. After Copan, I thought I could protect him. But he needed protection from us. What's wrong with us?"

"Copan?" Althea asked. But he wasn't looking at her anymore.

His words, gravelly and low, rumbled in his chest. "There's something wrong with us, Althea."

Althea leaned toward him. "What do you mean?"

"We're clones, Althea. I know we don't like the word, but that's what we are. We're copies of copies of copies of manipulated genes. And those genes are degrading, eroding those parts of us we think we don't need. The human parts. The Council thinks I'm exaggerating the problem. But we're broken."

"I don't understand. What are you talking about?"

He pointed to the children. "Look," he said.

Althea followed where his finger pointed to the little Ingas. They weren't crying anymore. They were communing, their hands held in a circle, placid smiles on their faces as they waited for the last Inga sitting on the ground to join them. Althea stood to leave. The Samuel had become too confused to make sense, and she didn't know anymore how to talk to him.

Then she saw the blood.

The girl on the ground had stood to join her sisters. Dropping a rock, she took hold of their hands. The rock fell to the ground, smeared in red from where she'd rubbed the skin of her knees raw until it matched the cuts of the first Ingas. It was impossible to tell which Inga was the one who fell, as now every one of their knees was scraped and bleeding. Red lines dripped down their shins in a garish reflection of the red ribbons in their hair.

"You didn't even notice, did you?" Samuel said. "Those girls

passed that rock around, one by one, and you didn't even notice."

"What are they doing?" Althea asked. She couldn't comprehend what would make the Ingas act like that. They looked
happy now, despite the blood seeping into their lace-trimmed
socks.

"Your generation is bad, but the 320s are worse." The Samuel
spoke in a detached monotone, like he'd been thinking about
how to explain it for a long time. "We don't feel things like sympathy. Not the way humans did. We *feel* what our brothers and
sisters feel. It should be better, really, than relying on a flawed
thing like imagination." A bleak laugh hitched in his chest. "I
tried to imagine being a father, and look what's happened to me.
But you see," he said, nodding toward the Ingas, still holding
hands. "Communing's not enough anymore."

Samuel-299's emotions shimmered in Althea as his eyes met
hers. She winced with that sharp stab in her head again, and then
she felt nothing at all. The Samuel was blank, and communing
with him was suddenly like staring into a deep black chasm.

"They need the blood," he said.

A chill went down Althea's back, contrasting starkly with the
heated air.

"It will only get worse with each copy we make," Samuel
continued. "And what will happen? What does it mean if we can
understand pain only by feeling it ourselves? Not all pain is as
simple as a scraped knee. What does it mean for someone like
Jack, whose pain we'll never understand?"

Althea had so many questions. She wanted to stop Samuel, to
shake him until that glazed look left his eyes, and make him tell
her what to do, but he turned away, retreating inside himself,

empty and distant. When she realized she'd lost him, she wanted to get as far from the nursery as possible, from the Ingas bleeding serenely into their shoes, and from Samuel, who was beyond help. She reached out to stroke his arm, but then thought better of it. He was no longer aware of her. She backed slowly away.

Althea was supposed to head back to the dorms and meet with her sisters. They were expecting her, and if she didn't show up, they'd be angry, and also concerned. But she didn't want to go back to her dorm right then. The things Samuel had said had scared her, but what she'd seen had scared her more. What other strange behaviors had she missed in her own people, things her eyes had passed over without even seeing? Her brothers and sisters were her entire world, and she was beginning to think she no longer understood them.

The way to the dorms and her sisters lay to the left. Althea went right, down the path that led through the grove of banana trees, to where she could be alone and think.

Bananas hung by the thousands above her. They'd been modified to be sweeter, to drip clear juice with flavors of oranges and strawberries, and to grow in bunches three times the size of early banana trees. The trunks were two feet thick to accommodate the extra weight. Shaggy bark peeled from them and fell, carpeting the ground in papery ribbons.

The ranks of treetops created a cover from the dazzling sunlight, and the air quieted in the dense canopy. After several moments, however, the silence was broken by footsteps behind her. She turned to find Carson-312. He leaned against the trunk of a tree. He must have followed her from the nursery. The shadow of a bruise lingered on his jaw from where Jack had hit him, and his cut lip had scabbed over.

"What do you want?" she said.

"Stay away from him, Althea."

Whether he meant she should stay away from Jack or Samuel-299 didn't matter to her. She didn't want to hear anything Carson-312 had to say. She headed deeper into the trees. He followed her.

"Samuel-299's fracturing," he said from behind her. "This business with the monkey boy is destroying him."

Althea spun on Carson so abruptly he nearly ran into her. "Stop calling Jack a monkey."

Carson stepped back. "You *do* like him."

Althea kept walking. The banana trees closed in, darkening the path with their fanlike leaves.

"I didn't really believe it, but it's true." Carson said. "He doesn't belong here, Althea. He knows it as well as you do. The Council should have eliminated him when they had the chance. The only reason they didn't was to try to keep Samuel-299 from fracturing, but you saw him. It's too late."

She hurried along the path, wanting to get away from Carson, yet he continued behind her.

"You're going to choose him over your own friends, your own people? How can you defend him? He would have killed Nyla."

"Leave Nyla out of it."

Carson grabbed her wrist, yanking her around to face him. "You know what they did together, don't you? What he did to her?"

"Shut up, Carson, or I swear—"

"You swear what?" He pinned her hand and held her waist, keeping her from getting away. The leaves above rustled violently. "You wish it had been you, is that it? Are you jealous, thinking of him kissing her, and touching her, like this? I can't understand you." His fingers tightened as he glared. Althea felt his confusion; he truly wanted to figure her out. He shook his head, pleading with her. "Why do you have to be different?"

"I'm not different. Get off me."

He shifted her trapped hand so it was between them, as if he was showing it to her. His fingers circled her scar, his thumb pressing the raised skin. "You're not like your sisters; you never have been. I have a scar too, I know what it's like to feel different. I'll show you how to make yourself fit." He leaned into her. "It'll be okay. I can make you fit."

"Carson—"

He was falling into her now, and she felt his desperation—he wanted to possess her in some way. His grip bruised. She was about to call for help when the trees above them shook and a form dropped from the heavy branches, landing in a crouch behind Carson.

"Jack!" Althea said with a surge of relief. Carson whipped around to face him.

"Get away from her," Jack said, his voice gentle, even as a sharp, knowing smile played across his lips.

"You've got to be kidding," Carson growled.

Carson charged, but Jack dodged him with a nimble step. Althea scurried out of the way as Carson snarled and leveled a punch at Jack's face. This time instead of dodging, Jack seized Carson's fist as it came at him and at the same time slammed the heel of his palm into Carson's throat, knocking him down. Carson rolled onto his back and gasped for air. Jack slid an arrow from a sheath on his back that Althea hadn't noticed before.

He nocked it in a bow that had been slung around his shoulder faster than Althea's eyes could follow. It was pointed at Carson, who was looking up from the ground, the razor-sharp tip inches from his nose.

"Jack, what are you doing?" she said.

He paid no attention. With the tip of the arrow, he indicated the scar bisecting Carson's eyebrow, his mouth twitching up. "Where'd you get this?"

"You know, you bastard," Carson wheezed, holding his throat and glaring at Jack. "I should have killed you that day. It'd save the Council the trouble of putting you down now."

Jack gave him a grin. "Wouldn't have helped."

"Jack, let him go," Althea said. "They'll kill you! Samuel won't be able to stop them, not if you hurt Carson again."

Jack's narrowed eyes darted to Althea.

To Carson, Jack said, "I want you to tell the Council something. Think you can handle that, *clone?*"

"Screw you," Carson spat.

Jack's smile remained fixed as he flicked the point of the arrow up, cutting across Carson's unscarred eyebrow. Carson gave a shrill cry, pressing his hand to the sliced skin. Blood oozed between his fingers. Jack cocked his head to the side as if considering his craftsmanship.

"A matching pair," he said.

Althea was frozen in place, trapped in a nightmare. Carson's blood glazed the stones in the path.

"You're so dead," Carson said, swiping blood from his eyes.

The laughter left Jack's face. It had never reached his eyes anyway. He kicked Carson's nose with the heel of his boot. Carson screamed in pain, and Althea reeled back.

Jack kicked again, this time hitting Carson's ribs. "Tell the Council I'm not in a cage anymore," he said. "I can hurt them as easily as I hurt you. Got that, clone?"

On his hands and knees, Carson retched onto the dirt path, blood pouring from his nose, and saliva from his mouth.

"Tell them—" He gasped wetly. "Tell them yourself, freak."

Jack lazily shoved him over with his boot so Carson fell sideways, grunting heavily and clutching his side.

Dismissing Carson as useless, Jack acknowledged Althea for the first time. "What about you? Tell the Council what I said."

"Jack, I . . . What are you doing? How could you?" Tears burned her eyes, and she blinked them back. What had they done to him?

His clothes were wrong. He wore a leather vest and dark, narrow boots. She was used to seeing him in the same clothes as the rest of them, the soft colors and loose cottons. A fierce, unfamiliar light shone in his eyes, wild and brutal.

"You," he said, considering her. "An Althea."

Althea could only nod. Tears streamed down her face.

"You're scaring me, Jack." Saying the words made her think of Nyla, and she felt a throb of guilt that perhaps her friend had been right about Jack and she hadn't listened.

The dangerous smile played again on his lips.

He came close to her, his movements swift and lithe. He buried his hand in her hair and grasped the back of her neck so she couldn't move. "The Carson was right. You do like him," he said.

"Who?" she asked stupidly, and then he was kissing her. Thinking to push him away, she pressed her palms on his shirt and felt the control beneath, his muscles tense and strong. He wrapped his arm around her waist and crushed her against him, lifted her until her feet grazed the ground. With his other hand, he caressed her face, a feather-light finger trailing down her ear, playful and mocking.

Althea couldn't breathe, couldn't think. Her own fingers reached up in numb reaction, touching his hand as it slid down the side of her neck. Something wasn't right. The skin of his hand was gnarled and leathery. It twisted up his arm, unnaturally smooth, scarred as if from a long ago burn. He smelled of wood ash and skinned animals. She sucked in a breath and pulled away, staring into his ocean-gray eyes, Jack's eyes, but feral and feverishly bright.

"Who are you?" she said in a tremulous voice.

"Don't you know?" His breath was hot in her ear. "I'm the snake in the garden."

He winked, and his hand slipped into the pocket of her dress. The heat of his skin against her thigh burned through the fabric and she closed her eyes, catching her breath at the intimate contact.

As she struggled to make sense of what was happening, a yell came from behind of Carson attacking again. She felt herself thrust away, shoved to the ground. She heard the whistle of an arrow, a deadened *thunk* as it hit its mark, and then footsteps racing into the trees. When she looked up, she was alone but for an enraged, screaming Carson, his shoulder pierced by the still-quivering arrow.

Her fingers trembling, she reached into the folds of her dress, seeking the strange weight in her pocket. Her hand emerged holding the pear Nyla had given her, bruised and speckled with dirt from when, earlier, it must have fallen from her pocket.

White and sticky with juice, the mark of a bite sank into the contours of her own face looking back at her.

With brittle laughter still ringing in her ears, she dropped it on the ground as if it had teeth.


Althea had no idea who to tell about the boy who looked like Jack but couldn't possibly be Jack. None of it made sense. In the end she didn't have time to work it out, because Carson shouted Jack's name to anyone who would listen while the Samuels tended to his injured shoulder and broken nose in the clinic.

She'd half dragged Carson to the clinic while he cradled his arm, crying with rage, pain, and humiliation. As he'd leaned against her, his emotions roared into her, threatening to overwhelm her. It was a relief to hand him off to the Samuels.

Carson hadn't been lying then about the night of the fire. He'd seen someone he believed was Jack sneaking into the labs. It was the same boy who'd found them in the banana grove, the same boy who'd kissed her. But that boy wasn't Jack. They both were quick and strong, but this boy was wild, with a ferocity in him, a cold determination she couldn't imagine in Jack, no matter how much the Carsons pushed him.

Now Althea stood before the Council. They waited, patient and strangely unreadable, while she told the story of what had happened in the banana grove and encountering the boy who was clearly Jack's brother. She ended by saying, "He looked like Jack, but it wasn't him."

The Council members didn't react. They simply rested their elbows on the table, their hands clasped in front of them.

"You're right," the Inga finally said. "That wasn't Jack." Althea waited, frustrated by their lack of response. The whole way to the Council meeting, she'd been mentally rehearsing arguments, calculating how she could persuade them that the boy with the bow and arrow wasn't Jack. She didn't need confirmation of what she already knew. She wanted more. The Inga seemed to sense this. "The person you saw, it must have been Jonah."

"So you have Jack locked up, and you didn't once consider it could have been someone else who did what you accused him of? That it could have been this Jonah?"

Samuel-294, Samuel-299's replacement on the Council, answered Althea. "Copan said he died over a year ago. We thought he was dead."

"How could you not tell him?"

"Tell who?"

"Jack, of course. How could you not tell him he has a brother?" Inga's mouth turned down as if the thought had never occurred to her. And why would it? Jack wasn't their concern. They'd never cared about him.

"When we created the embryos from Jack's genetic sample, it'd been several years since we'd had any success with survivable embryos. We sent some of them to Copan as well," Inga said. "We had Jack, and they had their own human from the same sample—another Jack. They didn't call him that, of course. They didn't give him a name at all. He named himself Jonah."

"But he's *not* another Jack," Althea said. "He's different. He's dangerous."

Samuel-294 shrugged. "Samuel-299 said Jonah's violence was because of how Copan treated their human subjects, but he was always violent. That's why he was terminated. Or at least he was supposed to have been."

"There've been *others*? How many times have you people done this? What happened to them all?"

"Tread carefully, Althea," the Nyla said. "We don't need to explain ourselves to you. You're still just an apprentice; you've never served on the Council. Maybe one day you will, and you'll understand. We act in the best interest of the community."

It stung to be rebuked in the voice of her friend, even if she was an older Gen.

"Jonah wanted me to tell you *I'm not in a cage anymore*. He was in a cage in Copan?" Althea regarded the Council members. They nodded silently. "And now he's here."

"Now he's here," Inga said. "His message shows he's here to hurt us."

"He's the one who set fire to the labs," Althea said.

The Viktor nodded. "The fire destroyed the tanks. We don't know if we can replace them in time."

"And even if we can rebuild the tanks," the Mei added, "he stole the timers that monitor oxygen for the embryos. The birth of the next generation is at risk."

"He ruined our crops," Hassan said. "We'll have shortages now, and we have no seed grain for next year."

As if speaking to himself, the Samuel said, "We've never faced a threat like this."

"Jack was innocent the whole time," Althea said.

Inga abruptly stacked her notebooks as if she considered the Council meeting at an end. "That's not your concern, Althea. Your concern *should* be the fate of Vispera."

"But he's innocent," Althea said. "You can't punish him for something he didn't do." She looked to Althea-298, the Althea serving on the Council. The woman shook her head. She wouldn't help, not when it had to do with Jack.

"We're all concerned about you," Althea-298 said. "Your sisters have noticed your preoccupation with the human."

Althea-298's gaze traveled the length of her, pausing at her blouse, torn and smeared with Carson's blood, then came to rest on her face. This told Althea that she was being assessed, and she tried to steady her expression, settling her mind into calm neutrality. Althea-298 would see that too, of course, and Althea's effort to hide something from the Council, including one of her own sisters, would be noted.

"Three of your sisters have come to me about you," Althea-298 said.

"Which ones?" Althea asked.

"Does it matter?" Inga said sharply.

"They're worried about you," Althea-298 continued. "You've been quiet. They think you're avoiding communing. I know you had a bad experience with the human boy, and now this episode with Carson-312. This is a dangerous time for you, which makes it doubly important that you connect with your sisters. You need to share your experiences with them."

Althea knew she was supposed to commune with her sisters, so they could understand one another and feel what the others were feeling. An image of the little Ingas and their scraped knees flashed through her mind.

"I'm not fracturing, if that's what you're worried about," she said.

Althea-298's condescending smile told her that it didn't matter how calm she appeared or what she said. To deny fracturing was to suggest she didn't care, and to admit it was dangerous. She couldn't win.

They would hold a Binding Ceremony for Samuel sometime soon. She used to think Binding Ceremonies were beautiful. The fractured brother or sister would finally be able to rest, at peace with the knowledge that the ritual would protect the community. For the first time, however, Althea imagined what a Binding would mean for her, and she didn't feel peaceful at all. She pictured her sisters gathered around her, smiling as they took one another's hands and watched the needle slip under her skin.

When she looked up, the Council were studying her, their eyes watchful and dark. How much had they understood of her thoughts? From the looks on their faces, too much. Althea shivered, and the Inga's eyes narrowed even more.

"You're to have nothing to do with the human from now on," Althea-298 said, the warning clear in her voice. "And you're not to be without the company of at least one of your sisters until we say otherwise. Is that clear?"

She should simply have said yes and left. Instead, she leaned forward, her palms on the table. "But now you know Jack is innocent, you'll let him go."

"He's innocent in what sense, Althea?" the Inga Council member asked. "He and Jonah are the same person. What Jonah does, Jack could also do. This is what we know. It's who we are, and it's how we live our lives together."

"But Jack isn't one of us."

"Exactly," Inga said. "There's never been a murder in Vispera, because no one here is capable of murder. Jonah killed people in Copan. What if Jack is a killer? Jonah is aggressive and violent, which means Jack carries a genetic strain for aggression and violence. We do not." Inga stopped, her mouth set in a thin line. "Althea," she said, "you care about the human, but make no mistake. He's dangerous, just as dangerous as Jonah."

"He wouldn't hurt me."

"You may think so, but he can't care about you the way your sisters do. The way we all do."

As if to prove the point, Althea-298 hovered at her elbow. The meeting was over. Althea allowed the woman to take her arm to escort her back to the dorms and into the hands of her sisters. They walked silently through town, but Althea sensed the dim connection of her thoughts being prodded. Althea let it happen as she tried to work through everything the Council had said.

At fifteen, Althea had gone with her sisters and the Gen-300 Altheas to visit Copan. They'd taken a riverboat, and Althea had shared with her sisters the sun-dried apples that Nyla-313 had made for her. Even dried, the apples were bright red and had petals, like roses. They'd tasted sweet, infused with honey and almonds, and Althea ate them with her sisters under the canopy of the boat listening to the white-headed capuchin monkeys hooting at them.

The Gen-310 Altheas had never left Vispera before, and the trip to Copan was the first time she'd encountered the differences that existed among the three communities of *Homo factus*. Every community maintained the same population of nine hundred, the nine models replicated and forming the ten generations. They all held the same ceremonies and celebrations. The Altheas in Copan cut their hair to their shoulders, and their color of yellow was bright and sunny, not the soft butter yellow she and her sisters wore, but otherwise, at first, they seemed very much alike.

After a few days among the Copan Altheas, however, Althea noticed more differences. A Copan Althea poked an annoying dog with a sewing needle under the table. A Hassan and a Viktor argued in the town square, eventually coming to blows. A physical argument wouldn't be tolerated in Vispera, and Viktors in Vispera were focused on defusing quarrels, not engaging in them. The Kates in Copan had walked around with dim, unfocused eyes. The Altheas there told them it was because one of the Kates had worn the wrong shoes to a dance, and they were worried about fracturing. This reasoning had seemed extreme. Looking back, perhaps these were the kinds of incidents Samuel meant when he talked about being "broken."

On the third day of their visit, they'd been in the fields outside of town and passed a long, low building made of white brick, with thin slats on the roof for ventilation. A Hassan had entered the building carrying a cattle prod. A wild shout soon echoed from inside, followed by the rasping noise of the activated prod and a voice yelling a curse.

Jonah had been in Copan at that time. Thinking of Jack being held in that white-brick warehouse made her shudder.

They approached the Althea dorm, a solid brick building facing east, away from Vispera. Yellow curtains hung from the arched windows, adorning the structure with the Altheas' color.

Althea-298 left after Althea's sisters met her at the door. As soon as she climbed the front steps, they all circled her. The anger burning inside her about Copan and Jonah eased away almost instantly as they stroked her back and hair, leading her inside. At first Althea resisted. Surely anger wasn't always bad. Surely sometimes there was a reason to hang on to it. But it felt good to hear their murmurs of sympathy as they absorbed

Althea's frustration and diffused it throughout their group. The sisters undressed her, and she lifted her arms to let them slip a cotton nightgown over her head. She closed her eyes as they tied the yellow ribbons at her throat and brushed her hair. Sitting on the edge of the bed, she felt them around her so close their breath was on her face.

"Tell us about Jack," they said. It didn't matter that it was Althea-318 speaking. The appeal came from all of them, their voices joined as one in her mind. "Think about him now," they whispered. "And then we'll feel it too."

Most of what Althea felt was confusion. The Inga's words rang in her ears. Her sisters knew her, cared about her. Her secrets had created distance between them, and they wanted to bridge that distance, that was all. Her body relaxed against their stroking hands and their senses wove more deeply with hers.

On the way to school once, Althea had found a caterpillar, a fat, emerald-green thing. She'd cupped it in her palms and carried it with her. It had wriggled, and its feet tickled, sticking dryly to her skin all through class. When recess came, her sisters finally realized she was keeping something from them. They'd opened her hands and sighed and exclaimed over it, passed it around, given it a name, and then kept it in a jar with leaves until it was forgotten about and died. Althea imagined her hands cradling memories of Jack the way they had the caterpillar, her palms cupping them in darkness.

The brush tugged at her hair, and the fingers, caressing softly a moment ago, tightened against her. A longing that had no words seeped into her as her sisters sought to draw her feelings out.

Althea shifted away from them. "I'm tired," she said.

Their faces darkened as their touch and minds pulled away.

Althea breathed in relief even as the emptiness and distance she'd created between them frightened her. But something about the brief times she'd spent with Jack made her want to hang on to those moments and keep them for herself. She'd begun to feel that if she communed, the feeling she had when she was with him wouldn't be hers anymore. It'd change and be lost, like the caterpillar.

Althea noted the significant looks her sisters passed to one another as they drifted off to their own beds, realizing they would get nothing more from her about Jack. Her thoughts went back to him. She ran her finger along the scar on her wrist, relishing the feel of the soft white skin, and it came to her suddenly that she was, in fact, fracturing. She'd denied it to herself as much as to the Council, but she knew. Her sisters were only just beginning to fear it. Despite the lingering anxiety hovering in the room that emanated from them like a heady perfume, they hadn't yet let the word creep into their consciousness. But Althea knew what they didn't.

The night closed in, black and foreboding. Her sisters moaned softly in their sleep, sensing the sudden and chilling disquiet that had come over her. Even in the midst of her fear, however, she knew it was true that she was fracturing. She knew, because she didn't want a cure.

*Chapter Fourteen*

# JACK

J ack had spent the entire day working in the fields, the massive thrashing combines churning on either side of him. They trundled through the rows like great lumbering beetles, their teeth gnashing into the earth, lifting roots and rocks. More than once, he'd been put to work tinkering with a slowed or stalled machine, but mostly he'd been cutting wheat and barley with nothing but a curved blade. It was such a joke that he was out there for six hours doing work that took a machine twenty minutes. Tired and hungry, he returned in the evening to the yellow barn where a meager plate of food awaited him.

The Hassans who supervised the fields kept an eye on him most of the time, and occasionally a Viktor walked past. Jack didn't know why the Council cared whether he ran away or not. The Carson who'd come to the barn had certainly thought he was pretty useless. If they would just give him some supplies, he'd leave, and they'd never have to deal with him again. But he had nothing, only the clothes he wore, and he didn't love the idea of trying to survive in the jungle without food or even a proper knife. Anyway, he couldn't leave. He needed to see Althea.

He sat cross-legged on the floor, eating from a tin plate, and then she was there, standing at the bars. He stood, wiping his blistered, dirt-smeared hands on his pants, but those were filthy as well. It was hopeless. Althea gave no sign of noticing his appearance. She smoothed her hair, which had curled in the humid air, and placed her hand on a bar of the cell.

"I found you," she said. "You okay?"

When he nodded, coming close to her, her grasp on the bars relaxed.

"What took you so long?" he teased.

"My sisters. They won't let me out of their sight."

Althea observed everything with slow deliberation, as if she were forming a puzzle of the minute details surrounding her. Her mouth turned down as she took in his cell. The pile of metal chain in the corner, the filthy pallet he slept on, and the tin platter for food.

He shifted uncomfortably. She chewed her lip. "This is where you sleep?"

Jack could only shrug.

"It's horrible," she said.

"It's not like I can go back to the lab. I burned it down, remember?"

Her eyes darted back to him. "Don't joke about that."

"I just meant, maybe when they figure out I'm innocent, they'll let me out of here."

"They won't," she said decisively. Her eyes focused on him. "I need to tell you something, Jack. You have a brother."

She said it so quickly, so matter-of-factly, it took him a moment to absorb the words. He must've appeared dazed, because Althea's voice sharpened, drawing his attention back to her. "Jack?"

She was watching him, and he wanted to say he was okay, but his thoughts were so jumbled his mouth wouldn't form the right syllables. The word *brother* sounded over and over in his head, blazing and loud.

He sat heavily. "What?" he managed to get out.

"I saw him in the banana grove," she said. "His name is Jonah."

Althea recounted what had happened since Jack had been locked up. While she talked, he didn't ask why she'd been in the grove with Carson-312, of all people.

He tried to hold back a smirk when she described how Jonah had knocked Carson to the ground and taunted him. Carson had it coming. Jack wished it could have been him defending Althea, making the other boy look scared and foolish. But then Althea said Jonah had threatened the Council, and actually shot Carson with an arrow before running away.

"He acted like it was fun, hurting Carson, scaring us. He said he would hurt the Council."

Althea was leaving out some part of the story, but there was already so much information to consider that he didn't press her.

The blue-gray eyes he'd seen outside the barn wall—he hadn't been dreaming.

He had a brother.

He'd brought Jack water, helped him. He'd moved the bag dropped by Carson-292 so Jack could reach it. His brother. *Jonah,* he said the name to himself.

Althea waited for Jack to respond, like she expected something from him, some insight or explanation for the other boy's actions, but Jack didn't know what to say. He didn't mention the water or the parcel. Althea seemed to have already formed an opinion about this other boy, and Jack wasn't ready to form his own.

"I should get back to the dorm," Althea said eventually.

She tucked her dark hair behind her ear, uncertain what to do with her hands. He wanted to ask her to visit him again, but that was what he'd always said to the Nyla before she left, and he didn't want to say the same thing to Althea.

Then she said, "I'll see you tomorrow, Jack."

The next time she came, she brought a clean blanket, and he recognized the soft yellow that was the Altheas' color. The blanket belonged to her, and he could smell the scents of vanilla and lavender on it.

After that, every time she came, she brought some small comfort for him. She gave him a bar of pink, flowery-smelling soap. She brought him his guitar from the cottage, and having it again made the nights alone more bearable.

She also brought food. Jack would have been happy simply with larger portions of the meat, potatoes, and carrots he usually had at the end of the day. She brought exotic creams whipped into icy clouds that tingled on his tongue, and cubes of meat grown like vegetables in gardens. Once she brought a little pod like milkweed. She sat outside the bars with her feet tucked under her and opened it, revealing a ball of golden cotton. She held it out to him.

"Try it," she said.

He held the bit of fluff uncertainly, and then put it on his tongue, where it melted into sugary air, leaving a taste of lemon in his mouth. It was so sweet he wasn't sure he liked it, but he liked the way she leaned forward, waiting for his reaction.

On this night, a breeze blew from the east, and laughter drifted to them from Vispera's Commons. The moon painted the distant mountains silver and blue. Jack wanted to ask her to bring him more useful things—a pack, tools, food for a journey. Then he noticed her yellow dress and the knit shawl bundled in her lap.

"It's a Pairing night," he said. He tipped his chin at her, a question stalled on his lips.

She pulled at the fringe on her shawl before stating the obvious. "I didn't go."

After a long pause, he asked, "Won't they miss you?"

She'd been coming to see him every night. She'd certainly be missed during a Gen-310 Pairing Ceremony. He was indescribably glad she was with him instead of Pairing with one of the clones, but no clone ever missed that ceremony. It would mean trouble for her, and because of him.

She didn't answer, but met his eyes, communicating something he couldn't quite make out.

"I have something for you," he said. He fetched it from his pallet and came back, taking both of her hands and dropping into them a small bead. He'd decorated it with scrolling lines in the outline of a ginger flower and tied it on a leather string as a bracelet.

"It's like the one you wear," she said. He nodded. "Are you giving me this so I look different from my sisters? So you can tell us apart?"

He couldn't tell if she was joking or not, but he flinched anyway, thinking of the many Nylas who'd come to his room. He realized now, however, that he'd been blind with them. He could no more mistake Althea for one of her sisters than one of the Ingas for his dead mother.

"That's not why I made it," he said, pulling the bead back from the bars.

"No," Althea said, grabbing his hands. "I didn't mean that. I'm sorry." She bit her lip. "Can I still have it?"

He'd found the cohune nut on the path to the barn, and he'd wanted her to have something from him that only he could give. She held out her arm through the bars, and he wrapped the ends of the string around her wrist. They were close enough that he could feel her soft breath on his face.

"You can put it on my other wrist if you want," she said. He stopped and looked up. "So it could cover the scar. I know it's ugly."

Jack shook his head. "No," he said simply.

The laughter outside had stilled, though the breeze lingered. The clones were in the midst of their ceremony, selecting those they were going to spend their evening with in the tents. She hadn't answered when he asked if they would miss her, because of course they would. It wasn't as simple as choosing him over some brief evening's entertainment. The choice she'd made was like a stone dropped in water, leaving ripples across a deep pool. She must be aware there'd be repercussions. Jack thought about his mother and was afraid for Althea. If they tried to hurt her . . .

As if to put aside thoughts of what the future would bring, Althea smiled and her hand brushed the line of his jaw, her touch as light as the sugary cotton. She stood and wrapped the shawl around her shoulders. She spun, letting the skirt of her dress undulate in a wide circle. It was the Pairing dance, the same dance the clones were doing at that moment on the Commons in Vispera.

Her movements were light and graceful, and Jack could see without really trying the structure and timing of the dance, and also the story in it, ancient yet alive. Without taking his eyes from her, he took up his guitar. He'd tried for a long time to be one of them, and he'd only suffered for it. He was done pretending he was something he wasn't.

He waited for a quick tap of her toe in the dirt, and then he played. He plucked at the strings, sensing the flow of her body in the vibrations of the instrument. His music settled into the beat of her dance. At first she hesitated as if confused, but she kept dancing until they were each in time with the other, and after a while, her face beamed with realization.

She could hear the music.

He saw the comprehension not just in her face, but in the fluid ease with which she moved. It was in her limbs, in the pulse and twist of her turns, in the joy enfolding her whole being.

When the dance ended, sweat glowed on her skin and her breath was quick. She knelt down, and with tears, she touched his face. They leaned together through the bars and their lips met, warm and slow. The last thrum of the guitar lingered in his body before it grew into something more.

Althea took his hands through the bars. She held them with reverence, like he'd just performed some otherworldly magic. From the pocket of her skirt she pulled a long yellow ribbon. She wrapped the end around his wrist, and then crossed his palm to loop around his fingers. She kissed him again as the silky ribbon glided over his skin. His lips parted from hers to speak, but then he stopped and, wordlessly, he halted her elaborate movements with a hand over hers. He unwound the ribbon and coiled it back into her palm. Her hand closed around it, and he felt a pang at the confusion he was causing her, knew she was thinking he didn't want her.

It was too hard to explain. He didn't want to *Pair* with her. That was what the clones did. They did it ceremonially, as a performance of something human and long past. He didn't think less of them for it. But as often as he'd wished to be a part of their world, he wasn't and never would be. He was human, and he was learning more and more about what that might mean. It was a human longing that made him ache to press his lips against hers again, to feel her skin on his, to get lost in her soft, delicate touch.

He didn't want ribbons and rituals.

He wanted *her*.

The next day, Jack was tired. He'd been unable to sleep during the night and now, working in the fields, he labored in frustrated exhaustion.

He couldn't stop thinking about Althea. Part of him wished he'd just taken the damn ribbon. Althea had known they wouldn't Pair, not while he was locked in a cage. The ribbon had been only a token, a symbol. He should have tried harder to make her understand. She'd left quickly and awkwardly after they'd kissed last night, and what if she didn't visit him again? She must think he was inept and ignorant, a primitive creature who couldn't comprehend their most basic rituals.

Jack hacked at the stalks of wheat with the small sickle. The sunny, cloudless sky was such a contrast to his mood, it made him feel the world existed only to spite him. After all, he wasn't supposed to be here. If the earth noticed his presence at all, it was only to wonder why he was laboring in a field that wasn't his instead of dead with the rest of his kind centuries ago.

Jack hurled the sickle aside in disgust. There was no Hassan in sight, so he lay back with his arms behind his head. On clear days like this, the mountains seemed to stretch on forever, and Jack imagined he could see the curve of the earth in their distant ridges. He closed his eyes, letting the hot air prickle his skin and feeling the energy in the ground beneath him and the rumble of the engines in the distance. He'd almost drifted off when a group of voices came from across the field above the noise of the threshers. Jack sat up, expecting to see the Hassans checking on him, or maybe the Viktors. Now that the Council knew Jonah was alive and in Vispera, they'd ordered patrols of the surrounding fields and jungle. Jack had been looking for Jonah himself, staring into the corn at night trying to see if someone was out there, but he'd seen no one. It was frustrating, knowing Jonah had been right outside the barn, could still be nearby, but was keeping his distance. Jack wanted to see him, talk to him, find out what his life had been like. They were brothers, after all.

Instead of Hassans, it was the Gen-310 Carsons crossing the field in a line and heading straight for him. Carson-312 led the grim-faced group, a cut across his nose and a bandage-wrapped shoulder showing beneath his shirt.

Jack eased himself to his feet, surreptitiously retrieving the discarded sickle as he rose. However dulled from hacking grains, the blade would still cut if propelled with enough force. He held the handle in a loose grip close to his thigh.

"Monkey-boy's gone down in the world, sleeping in a field

like a cow," Carson-312 said as they approached. "I know what'll wake you up."

"Carson, there are things you don't know."

"We know what you did to our brother," one of them said.

Jack had never been good at distinguishing one clone from another. He kept his eyes on Carson-312, who inched closer, concealing something behind his back.

Jack could take one of them easily. Given his strength, he guessed he could handle a few of them. But his odds against all ten were not good.

The Carsons surrounded Jack, trapping him in a circle. Jack held his sights on Carson-312, calculating quickly. If Jack could talk him down, this would end. If they did fight, attacking Jack all at once, Carson-312 was his target. Take down the brother whose eyes glinted with cold resolve, and the rest would fall away.

Or at least, that's what Jack hoped.

He nodded to Carson-312's injured shoulder. "That wasn't me," he said. "I've been locked up. You made sure of that."

"I know what I saw." Carson-312 pointed to his bandages. "You think you can try to kill me? Attack me, attack an Althea, and get away with it?"

"What about Althea?" Jack said, taken aback.

"I know she's been coming to see you. You're trying to turn her against us, her own kind."

"I'm not trying to do anything. She can do what she wants."

"And what she wants is to kiss you?" he said. He saw the surprise on Jack's face. "You think I didn't see? You did it right in front of me. I guess the Nylas weren't enough for you, now you want all the Altheas, too."

It took a moment for Jack to realize that Carson didn't mean last night. But Althea hadn't mentioned kissing Jonah when she'd told Jack about her encounter. That was part of what she'd left out.

Jack's hand slackened on the sickle.

The Carsons saw his distraction and took advantage by moving in. Carson-312 edged closer, confident and aggressive. Jack stepped back and bumped into the Carsons behind him.

Jack's gaze swept the field, hoping for anyone, maybe a Hassan. There was nothing except an untended basket and another mindless thresher churning up the east field.

In the corner of his eye, Jack saw a Carson to his left move uncertainly out of the circle. Despite the solidarity, they didn't all have Carson-312's fiery certainty. They might still back out.

"You don't have to do this," Jack said to the hesitant Carson.

"Yes," Carson-312 said. "We do."

With no warning, a stabbing pain seared through Jack's shoulder and vibrated down his spine, dropping him to his knees. When he opened his eyes again, the pain had stopped, but every limb trembled, and barbed lines shrouded his vision.

Carson-312 held his hand out for Jack, showing him the cattle prod he held. "Like a cow in a field . . ." he said, grinning.

While Jack gasped for air, trying to regain control of his body, the cattle prod hit a second time, immobilizing him. He fell to his side, teeth clenched, pain hammering his body. When the prod released, Carson-312 didn't expect that Jack, ready this time, would recover quickly. From the ground Jack grabbed the device and twisted, wrenching it until he held it himself. Still shaky, he swept the prod at the circle of Carsons and they edged away.

His breath rattling his ribs, he said, "You can still stop."

"Not till you're dead." Carson-312 lunged. Jack dodged the blow and sliced the sickle across Carson-312's arm. He reared away, and Jack hit him with the prod. Carson-312's body shivered in spasms against the current, like Jack's own had. Jack pulled the prod away, wishing he felt more triumphant in the other boy's pain, but feeling only sickened. Blood oozed from the gape on Carson's biceps, and Jack almost tossed the sickle aside. It was sharp enough to kill, and he didn't want that.

Some of the Carsons held back, stunned at the bloodshed. They didn't want to fight either. Jack turned from them to concentrate on the others. One of them grabbed Jack around the neck, and Jack elbowed his ribs. Two more attacked, but Jack rolled clear. He lost the prod, but used his leverage to topple one brother onto the other before Carson-312 lurched to his feet.

Jack still felt the electric shock from before zinging through his nerves, and his muscles were tiring as the Carsons continued their attack. Still, if he conserved his energy, he'd hold them off for a while yet. Half of them were on the ground groaning, and more were inching away. The remaining three were poised, but tentative and afraid, holding their heads as they felt the pain of their brothers.

Carson-312, up and fighting again, stumbled. He was still bleeding from his arm, and he favored the shoulder that had taken the arrow. Jack would outlast him. It wouldn't even be hard if his brothers would only give up.

He braced for Carson-312's approach. Anticipating the punch telegraphed by the other boy, Jack poised to grab Carson-312's arm midswing. At the last second, Carson-312's bloody teeth appeared as his lip curled into the same grin Jack had seen on Carson-292 in the barn. Jack didn't have time to register the smile before an intense pain hit him from behind. It radiated out with a white heat that arched his back as if it could break his bones.

Even as the first shards of pain jerked through his body, too late he realized he should never have dismissed the Carsons who'd backed away from the fight. They had taken up the cattle prod. The sickle fell from Jack's fingers as the prongs on the end of the white stick dug into him and didn't let up. A scream he didn't recognize as his own ripped from his throat. He writhed on the ground, and still it didn't end. Finally the stabbing fire ceased, but by then his lungs were closing. He struggled to take in a breath. An inhaler was in his pocket, but he had no way to reach for it; his hands were useless as bags of sand. The familiar panic settled over him like a suffocating blanket. Then all ten bodies of the Carsons blocked the sun.

Jack twisted in on himself, shielding his face with his arms, and they descended from all directions. Heavy shoes rained down on his back, his arms, his legs and head, until there were so many they were meaningless, an endless haze of pain.

Jack heard their yells, their grunts of loosed energy as they kicked, the high drone of the prod striking blistering flesh, but it all grew faint, replaced by the high-pitched whistle of rasping breath. He fell slowly into a black void, and was grateful at least for the privacy given him by that dark place.

He knew, of course. He'd made a mistake, and it was a bad one. He'd misjudged the force of their bond. Jack may have been stronger than them, and quicker, but they had each other.

Dimly aware that he would lose consciousness and still the blows wouldn't stop, Jack realized how fitting it was. He'd always failed to grasp the essential nature of the clones; he'd never be one of them, he'd never understand them, and now he'd die because of it.

## Chapter Fifteen

# ALTHEA

Althea arrived late for breakfast at the dining hall. Her sisters were already seated and passing platters of eggs, sausage, and pineapple. She had ruined the night of the Pairing, again, and given the way she felt at the moment, she wasn't at all sure slipping away before the ceremony to see Jack had been worth it. None of her sisters said anything as she took her usual chair, and they regarded her with carefully placid expressions.

She'd spent her entire life with her sisters, every waking moment, so it was as natural for her to scan the mosaic of their emotions as it was to braid her hair and brush her teeth. There was no doubt about the aching questions she perceived from them. *Why do you want to be different from us? Why have you stopped trying? Why don't you love us anymore?*

Althea ate silently, barely tasting the food. She touched the bracelet Jack had given her. It was no longer around her wrist, but tucked into the pocket of her dress. She'd taken it off, knowing her sisters would see it right away and ask why she was wearing such a strange trinket.

She was still bewildered by what had happened in the barn. What Jack had done with the guitar had left her dazed. She'd been dancing as if at the Pairing Ceremony, and he'd made the noise with the strings she'd heard before, only this time she hadn't experienced it as a jangling clamor that scoured her nerves. The music coming from the guitar freed something within her, like the sun burning away a heavy mist. The sounds he made reverberated in her chest and stomach, as if coming from somewhere deep inside her, not from Jack.

At first she'd felt weak from it, ready to collapse. It was too much, crushing and heady. Then all of a sudden, the dance felt . . . easy, almost obvious in a way it never had before. She'd never felt anything like it, and she'd wanted to give something back to him.

Which had made it that much more confusing when he'd rejected her ribbon. It didn't seem possible that she could have read him so poorly. While she danced, he had followed her every movement, his eyes clear as water. He desired her, and she wanted him like she'd never wanted a Viktor, Carson, Hassan, or Samuel. But something had gone wrong, and she had no idea what it was.

Carson-312 had accused her of being jealous, saying she wanted Jack to touch her the way he'd touched Nyla. She didn't want to be jealous, certainly not of her friend, but she had no other word for the jagged teeth gnawing at her insides. Breakfast was finally winding up when a murmur rippled through the hall. The sound moved like a living thing, growing steadily louder, until everyone stood, asking what was happening.

A Viktor rushed past the Altheas' table, and then another,

their faces severe. Althea-312 tugged the sleeve of an Inga at the table behind.

"What's going on?" she asked.

"It's Copan," she said. "Something's wrong in Copan."

Kate-280 entered the hall and waited coolly for the crowd to fall silent.

"The Council has received word from Copan," she said with a voice loud enough to carry across the huge dining hall. "It is with great sadness that I bring you terrible news." She paused a moment for that to sink in. "The community in Copan is in ruins."

The crowd in the hall erupted with cries and shouts. Kate-280 raised her hand, calling for silence.

"As far as we can tell, Copan's water supply became contaminated with large amounts of Somnium, and the resulting hallucinations led to panic, violence, and widespread destruction. Their grain mills are destroyed, their food stores burned, and the town itself is rubble. The Council will organize the generations of Vispera to help in the wake of this calamity. We'll load boats with supplies of food and medicine and deliver it to Copan." Kate looked around the Hall. "Some of you will be sent to assist in restoring order. If reconstruction is possible, we will devote our resources to it. If it's not . . . well, I must be honest with you. I don't know if our brothers and sisters in Copan can survive."

With that, Kate-280 left. For several moments, the hall maintained a stunned hush before erupting in exclamations and fear-ridden chatter.

Like all the Gens, the Altheas had linked fingers under the table while Kate-280 spoke, and Althea felt their anxiety alongside her own. She allowed her hand to intertwine with those of the others.

"How could this happen?" Althea-317 asked. "How did Somnium get in their water supply?"

"We have to help," Althea-312 said, and the sisters nodded agreement. No further discussion was needed.

Althea felt herself nod along with them, and the fingers of her sisters tightened around her own. At least for now, they'd forgotten the ruined Pairing and she was back in the fold as the communal rush of distress and excitement overpowered the disconnection they'd been experiencing. Their eyes softened with relief when she murmured, "Yes." She would help in the campaign for Copan.

Someone touched Althea's back, and she turned from her sisters to see Nyla-313 kneeling beside her chair.

"Althea, I've been looking for you. Something's wrong."

"I know. Copan. Kate-280 just said."

"No, not that." Nyla glanced at the other Altheas and lowered her voice. "The Carsons told us they were going to the fields to deal with Jack. Those are the words they used — *deal with*."

Althea's hand dropped out of the linked chain of her sisters' fingers. She clenched Nyla's arm. "When did they leave?"

"Just a few minutes ago. Carson-312 told us because he thought we'd be glad to see Jack punished, because of the fire and everything, but that's not what we want at all, Althea. I'm worried. I think Carson-312 might be fracturing. His brothers can't hold him together anymore. Carson-315 mentioned a Binding Ceremony, but they're scared of what that means."

"I don't care about Carson-312," Althea said. She stood,

ready to race out of the dining hall, but Althea-318 grabbed her wrist.

"You can't go. We need each other right now."

"I have to," Althea said.

Now all her sisters stood and gathered, unsure how to deal with their particular crisis being swept up in the general one.

Althea-316 pushed forward. "You can't come back from this."

The nine of them huddled closer. Their nervous fingers slipped through one another's hair, touched the sleeves of dresses. Their fingers twined. Tears filled all their eyes except those of Althea-316, who glared. They already knew she was going to leave them.

"What is wrong with you?" Althea-316 said.

Althea backed away, grateful for Nyla's hand in hers as she left behind the sensation of her sisters' roiling emotions.

Althea and Nyla ran up the hill toward the fields. They'd just come over a steep ridge when Althea saw the Carsons heading toward them. Far beyond them, at the edge of the trees, lay Jack, still as death on the ground.

"Get Samuel," she said to Nyla. "Samuel-299."

"He won't come," Nyla gasped, her hands on her knees. "His brothers won't let him."

"Tell him Jack needs him. He'll come."

Nyla nodded and turned back to town. Althea ran. She pushed through the Carsons, but Carson-312 grabbed her arm.

"This has nothing to do with you, Althea," Carson-312 said. "Leave it alone. Go back to town." He looked terrible, bloody and bruised.

"What have you done?" she said angrily. Her accusing gaze cut from one Carson to the other until it stopped at Carson-312. "What have you done?" she said again, this time truly mystified.

"You were there. He tried to kill me!" Carson-312 held her stare. When she didn't back down, he cast his eyes away.

"Let go of me. He needs help, he's . . ." Althea stopped, her eyes landing on Jack and then farther up on the threshing machine lumbering through the field, its blades whirling, cutting deep into the ground. It was headed straight for him.

Carson dropped her arm, seeing the same thing she did. Althea ran. It seemed to take forever to get to Jack, and when she did, she fell to her knees. Gashes of blood showed bright against his pale skin and a tinge of blue colored his lips as shallow, rattling breaths lifted his chest. The thresher continued on its path toward both of them now as if in slow motion, sluggish and measured, but inevitable. When it reached them, Jack would be devoured in its blades like so many ripe stalks of corn.

Ignoring that his arm was surely broken, and not concerned about other injuries, she pulled at his body, trying to drag him clear. She couldn't budge him. He was big, and she wasn't strong enough. "No," she cried. "Jack, get up! You have to get up!" She turned her head to the Carsons. "Help me!"

They were already walking away again, heading back toward town. Only Carson-312 turned halfway round when Althea called, but he didn't stop.

"You can't let him die!" she yelled.

Althea tried again and again to move Jack, ignoring the exhaustion overtaking her. The thresher rolled closer. It had no key, no ignition, no driver behind the wheel. The field machines were mindlessly automatic, controlled by Hassans from computers in town. Althea turned her eyes from its onslaught, refused to let it scare her into giving up. But Jack was so heavy, a dead, unmovable weight. The ground vibrated, and the rumble of the engine grew louder. She hit him, her fists beating his insensible body. "Wake up!" she pleaded. The machine was so close now that the whirring blades fanned the hair from his eyes. With her forehead pressed to his chest, she whispered, "Please." The word was lost in the roar of the engine, a torrent of noise louder with each second. "Please, please, please." She closed her eyes and placed her body over his.

All at once, the noise stopped. Althea's breath shuddered into Jack's shirt. A bird chirped in a nearby tree.

She looked up and was met with the tall blades of the thresher, sharp and shiny as knives, mere feet from Jack's leg. Carson-312 was standing beside the hulking box, a metal panel open at the side, a cattle prod still buzzing in his hand from where he'd fried the controls. With a last sizzling pop, the giant engine, so much bigger now that it was practically on top of them, gave a slow, drawn-out whine and settled harmlessly into the dirt.

Carson tossed the prod to the ground as if he was disgusted with himself. "That was for you, not him. Are you trying to get yourself killed?"

"He would have died. Is that what you wanted?"

"It wasn't . . ." Carson shook his head.

"It wasn't what?" Althea said.

"It wasn't supposed to go that far."

"Really?" She tilted her chin at the cattle prod on the ground, the one the brothers had used against Jack. "How far was it *supposed* to go?"

Carson blinked at her, and Althea remembered what Nyla-

313 had said, that Carson-312 was fracturing. His brothers had followed him to the fields, but they weren't with him now. Only Carson-312 had come back. He was at risk, just like her. Althea couldn't help Carson however, not now, not when Jack was bleeding next to her. She turned away from him. "Go home. Tell the Council what you've done. Let them deal with you."

In the silence after Carson left, Althea sat on the ground next to Jack and waited. She didn't know what else to do. When Samuel-299 finally arrived, he came with Nyla and two more Samuels from the clinic carrying a stretcher. A Hassan also came to repair the broken thresher.

Samuel's hand shook as he checked Jack's pulse.

"How did this happen?"

"Ask the Council," Althea said bitterly. "They're the ones who caused all this, with their secrets and experiments."

"It was the Carsons," Nyla said, her hand coming to rest on Althea's arm, pulling her close.

Althea's anger began to drift away as her friend's calm seeped into her. She jerked her arm back, needing the anger if only to keep from crying.

The Samuels grasped Jack and lifted him onto the stretcher with no more care than if they were loading a cart with logs. Jack struggled unconsciously as they lifted him, as if he were still in the middle of a fight. Samuel-299 placed a hand on Jack's chest and murmured to him. Althea couldn't hear what he said, but Jack settled down again.

They carried him across the field and into the town. Althea watched them go, wondering if the feeling consuming her was what Jack felt all the time, this feeling of being alone. She remained crouched in the dirt, his blood drying on her arms, not trusting her legs to carry her back to town. Nyla knelt beside her then, and this time Althea let herself be taken in her friend's arms. She leaned into Nyla, searching for anything to ease the pain before it swallowed her as completely as the storm clouds swallowed the Novomundo Mountains in the distance.

*Chapter Sixteen*

# JACK

Jack remembered pain. He remembered the swerve of the sky as he was lifted from dirt. He remembered numbing cold, rough hands, and Sam's voice as it had been years ago when he was a child. But mostly he recalled pain in every part of his body, pain that made him want to escape the world. And he held an image of Althea bending over him, her hair curtaining her face. *You'll be fine,* she said, over and over.

He was in the clinic, in clean scrubs and pressed white sheets. Someone had washed away the blood and dirt. He wasn't sure how long he'd been here. Two, maybe three days?

He licked his lips, feeling the cuts there, and when he shifted position, a sharp stab tore through his side. Gingerly he felt his ribs. They weren't broken, but he knew he'd find dark, ugly bruises when he lifted his shirt.

His head pounded, and his wrist was in a cast. His back, where most of the blows from the Carsons had landed, throbbed with an ache that radiated into his limbs.

All in all, he was surprised it wasn't worse.

The room was dark, and there was no clock to tell time. Sam

and Althea had visited earlier. They'd visited often while he was hovering in and out of consciousness.

A form outlined by the moon perched on the windowsill across the room. Jack sat up in bed, avoiding leaning on his broken arm.

"Who's there?" he said.

The figure pulled a banana from a bag on his shoulder and peeled it with showy deliberation. "Hello, brother," he said, taking a bite.

All the aches in Jack's body vanished at once. He took a long breath, steadying his pulse. Still his heart hammered in his ears.

"I've wondered where you were," Jack managed to get out.

Jonah hopped down from the window, landing soundlessly on the tiled floors. His gray eyes, familiar yet unreadable, raked over Jack's face.

"They sure did a number on you," he said. "Sorry I wasn't around. I had some things to take care of in Copan." He finished the banana in two quick bites, then threw the peel out the window.

Althea had said her sisters were leaving for Copan in the morning to help the clones there. She said someone attacked them. She'd also told him she wasn't going.

"That was you," Jack said, his voice level. "You destroyed Copan."

"They destroyed it themselves. I just helped them along." Jonah wandered the room, opening a closet and peeking in the bathroom. He pulled out the drawer of a cabinet on the far wall and rifled through its contents. "Do they keep any Somnium here?"

"I don't know." Jack's head throbbed. Seeing Jonah felt surreal, like he was in a dream. He looked just like Jack, his hair and eyes, his build. Jonah had a scar at his hairline, and the skin on one arm was twisted by old burns, but in every other way, they were identical.

Jonah moved on to another drawer. "The clones don't dream, did you know that?" he said conversationally. "They kept altering their genetic code, and I guess they lost some things along the way. Somnium gives them hallucinations, like dreams while they're awake. In small doses, I guess they find it pleasant, but give them enough, and it's all weird visions and nightmares." Jonah turned toward Jack with a genial smile. "They sure can wreck a place." He returned to searching the cabinet, pulling out another drawer. "I tried Somnium once. Didn't do anything for me. Turns out, it doesn't work on humans because we already dream. That's crazy, right? Not being able to dream."

"I guess," Jack said.

"Hey, there's something I've been looking for. You ever hear them talk about something called the *Ark*?"

Jack shook his head. "What is it?"

Jonah shrugged. "A human thing. Doesn't matter." He found some tape and bandages in another drawer, and some vials of gold liquid that he opened and sniffed, trying to figure out what they were. He tucked it all inside his bag, then came to the foot of Jack's bed. "I'm glad I found you," he said. "I knew about you, but it took forever to finally get here. But this is good. We can work together. We have each other now."

Jonah's ease and confidence was an advantage. He'd clearly had time to plan this meeting, knew what it was he wanted. Jonah's head wasn't swirling with countless questions. Jack, bleary with pain and drugged sleep, had no idea where to start.

"Work together doing what?" he said thickly.

"Destroying them, of course."

Jack shook his head. "Destroy who? The clones?"

"Yeah, who do you think? Look at you!" Jack's cuts and bruises stung anew under Jonah's sneer. He thought of the yellow barn, the cage and shackles, laboring in the fields, the Carsons stalking toward him. "You're nothing here," Jonah said. "They think they want a tenth clone, but it'll never work for them. No, we're too *human* for them. They forgot they've had three hundred years to change themselves, and now they think they're perfect. They look at you—at us—and they're terrified."

"They're not terrified of me."

"Listen, Jack, I've thought about this. In us, they see everything they've lost, things they didn't even *know* they lost. Sure, their mental tricks make them feel connected or whatever. But they don't love each other. You know that, at least. When one of them dies, they burn the body and move on like it was nothing. And why shouldn't they? They have countless replacements. If they don't even value their own lives, how are we supposed to? They're just . . . cheap copies."

"It's not like that," Jack said. "They're not all like that."

Jonah shook his head. "I get it. You have that Althea clone. I'll show you, she's just like all the others."

"Don't go near her!"

"Hey, take it easy," Jonah said, hands up in surrender. "I'm your brother, I care about you. Nobody else here does, including the Althea."

"She does care," Jack said, though his voice didn't rise above a whisper.

Jonah contemplated Jack for several moments.

Lying in bed and seeing his own eyes squinting back at him, evaluating him, Jack felt as if his brother knew all his doubts, hopes, and fears.

"At the barn, I heard the old Carson talking to you about how there was something wrong with you. They think we're defective, but they're the ones that are defective. We're better than them."

"I am defective," Jack said. "In that field, I almost died because I couldn't breathe. I'd call that a defect." Something occurred to Jack. "Do you have asthma?"

Jonah shook his head. "Genes are complicated. The clones think it's all so simple, that they can manipulate everything until it's exactly how they want it. But maybe there's a reason you have asthma and I don't."

"That makes no sense."

"It's evolution, Jack. Back when there were humans everywhere, a lot of them had diseases. And sometimes, with certain diseases, those who had them were the only people in the whole world immune from things that could maybe kill everyone else. I read about it."

"Yeah, well. The humans are all dead now."

"Listen, it wasn't asthma that almost got you killed. It was the clones. Come with me, Jack. We'll get them back for what they did to you, what they've done to *us*."

"What are we supposed to do? There are only two of us, and hundreds of them."

"Try telling that to Copan," Jonah said. He settled himself on the edge of Jack's bed and pulled from his pocket a little feather. It was bright and iridescent, with streaks of turquoise, green, and orange. He handed the feather to Jack. "There's this bird that lives in the jungle, a kind of bird of paradise. You've probably seen it. It lays these eggs on heliconia plants. The eggs are really small and sort of purple, and the thing is, they have these shells like paper. They're thin, like they could break if you just breathe on them. No kidding, I once saw a butterfly put its leg through a shell." He leaned toward Jack to make his point, and his eyes narrowed. "Vispera is like that. Strike the clones in the right way, and they'll fracture as easy as those bird eggs."

Jack dropped his head into his hands.

"You okay?" Jonah asked. "You don't look so good."

When Jack looked up, he found Jonah watching him, worry in his face, and then voices came from the hallway. Jonah leaned over the bed. He grabbed Jack's good hand and thumped it against his own chest.

"You feel that, Jack? It's blood, mine and yours." He bent down and pressed his lips roughly to Jack's forehead. Pulling his bag onto his shoulder, he went to the window. "Blood doesn't lie. You'll change your mind. And believe me"—he winked— "they'll pay for what they did to you."

Jack swung his legs over the side of the bed, forgetting to be careful of his arm. "Don't hurt them, Jonah," he said.

"Oh, I'm not going to hurt them, brother." He looked at Jack over his shoulder. "I'm going to kill them." Jonah sprang outside and disappeared into the dark.

The air coming through the window, thick and wet, blanketed the room with an oppressive heat. Jack's fist crumpled the sheet. He wondered if his brother might be crazy.

Yet still . . . Jack lay back, the room spinning around him. He breathed in, trying to calm his racing pulse, and fought the call in his blood, vast and deafening, to follow Jonah into the night.

By the time Althea came into the room, Jack had already hauled himself from bed and was struggling to tie his shoelaces one-handed.

"You shouldn't be up, Jack," she said.

"I'm fine," he said, though when he straightened, he gasped with the pain. "I have to go."

"What's happened?"

"Jonah was here. He's plotting something."

Althea took his arm and turned him to face her. "Jack, slow down. What's he going to do?"

"I don't know," Jack said. "He wanted me to come with him, to help do . . . whatever he's going to do. Maybe the same thing he did in Copan."

"Why would he do that?" Althea paled.

"Why do you think?" Jack ran his hand through his hair, a rush of resentment building in him. "Look what happened to me. They were going to kill me. And I don't mean the Carsons, I mean the Council."

"Calm down, Jack," she said, trying to make him sit. "Even if you can find him, you're in no condition to stop him. We need help."

"Anyone who helps us will kill him."

"Maybe you should consider what—"

"Don't," Jack said, turning on her. "Don't say it."

He wouldn't let them kill Jonah, not when they'd only just found each other. He'd be damned if he'd let the clones take his own brother from him. If Althea said Jonah should die, Jack didn't know if he could take it.

"I was just going to say, maybe you should consider what you plan to do before running off."

What *was* he planning to do? Jack had no idea. He sat on the bed, his body shuddering with frustration and pain.

Althea sat beside him. "I know he's your brother. I understand that."

Jack struggled to concentrate. Something fluttered in the back of his mind, light as insect wings. "Jonah said he was trying to find something called the Ark. Do you know what that is?"

Althea shook her head.

"He said it was human."

"Samuel-299 would know. He's spent lots of time in the Tunnels, and that's where everything human is stored."

"I can't trust Sam," Jack said.

"Then what do we do?"

Jack suddenly heard his mother's voice in his head, saying, *These things are for you. They belong to you.* She'd been talking about the guitars he'd collected from the Tunnels, and the boxes full of papers and books she'd stolen, things she'd taken for him. Or it would have been stealing if anyone had cared that they were gone.

"Not everything is stored in the Tunnels," Jack said. "I know where we need to go."

*Chapter Seventeen*

# ALTHEA

The cottage was dusty, and Althea felt cold in the damp room that had been Inga-296's office. She wished she'd brought a sweater.

Althea would have been seven when they held the Binding Ceremony for the Inga. She'd heard the stories. That the Inga was crazy, that she'd locked herself away from the community, away from her sisters, surrounding herself with relics from the Tunnels. Jack had never been part of the story, and the image the other children conjured was terrifying—a woman with tangled hair and wild eyes, cut off from everyone, her mind lost. Nobody liked going in the Tunnels, and the idea of someone fracturing from spending so much time there only reinforced the pall of superstition that hung over the place.

What was called the Tunnels was actually a cavern running deep underground, entered through a cave to the north of Blue River.

Even as their time was ending, humans had poured their energy and resources into preserving the relics of human history. Althea admired their resolve and courage, if not their attachment to what amounted to little more than junk. In the face of not just their own individual deaths, but the end of all humanity, they wanted the world to survive. Years ago an earthquake had collapsed all but one wing of the Tunnels. Althea supposed her people could have excavated the buried items, but little of the faraway past interested them anymore. All that was left of the Tunnels was the section marked *Art and Literature*. The other sections listed in the catalogue — *History, Science, Engineering,* and *Recreation,* each with over a hundred subcategories — were entombed close by under mountains of pulverized rock. The electronics, transportation machines, reels of microfilm, government documents, weapons from long-dead wars, seeds of extinct plants, tissue from extinct animals, clay objects from the Stone Age and Mesopotamia, and a matchless treasury of other things, all gone. Except for the Sample Room, Vispera had no use for what survived.

Or at least, most of Vispera. From walls of boxes and piles of paper in disarray in the Inga's office, it seemed she'd been consumed by the past. They'd come here to search for some clue of what Jonah was looking for, but it seemed an impossible task.

Althea worried Jack had left the hospital too soon. His pale face shone with sweat as he attempted to hide his discomfort, and his bruises had turned a dark, garish purple. Now they were hidden under the cotton of his shirt, but she'd seen them at the hospital while Samuel, with dazed eyes and methodical hands, had tended an unconscious Jack in the clinic.

Althea picked up another of the boxes and riffled through it, looking for anything that might refer to the *Ark*. None of the debris Inga-296 had collected from the Tunnels helped Althea understand the woman's fascination with what the humans had left behind. From the things she was finding—old teacups, post-cards, cartoon drawings, small ceramic statues and trinkets—it was all nonsense, a massive waste of human effort. If they'd focused on survival, on the real world instead of imagined stories—maybe they'd be alive now. She picked up a wooden box with a tiny latch, glanced inside, and set it aside.

"Wait," Jack said, retrieving it from the floor. "I haven't seen this in years." He turned it around, holding it awkwardly in his cast-bound hand. With his good hand, he wound a key on the back, and then opened it again. A cylinder inside spun slowly, hitting tines. Sound spilled out, jangling Althea's nerves. She covered her ears and almost told him to make it stop, but then she saw the way he was holding the box like what it contained was so important, even though she could see herself it was a trivial thing. The satin-smooth wood, maybe rosewood, was inlaid with mother-of-pearl in a pretty scroll design. The noise was altogether different. What she heard initially was a sharp trill. She closed her eyes and concentrated, remembering the way the music had changed when Jack played his guitar. In a few moments, a melody fell into place. She heard the way the notes melded together, spoke to each other, turned into something strange and pretty. The cylinder slowed, a note or two ushering forth, and then it stopped.

Althea thought the music might have made Jack sad. His head was down and the box had slid from his fingers to rest on his lap. But then he grinned at her unexpectedly, wound the key again, and offered his hand.

"What are you doing?" she said.

"Dance with me."

Althea let him pull her up.

Jack was clumsy, with his broken arm and a stiffness that suggested the pain he was in. And the music didn't transport Althea in the same way Jack's guitar had. It plunked along with a repetitive, childish strain. Also, in the dances she knew, she and the Carsons, Hassans, or whoever, were generally side by side. Jack held her waist and her hand, pulling her close to him in a kind of dance Althea had never experienced.

As they moved together, his muscles eased and warmed around her. She breathed in, smelling the stale dusty air of the room but also his skin, like bamboo wood and rain. She lifted her eyes to him. This close, she had to look up to see his face, which was bent over hers. There were no bars between them, nothing keeping them apart. She hesitated. She wouldn't kiss him again, not after he'd given back her ribbon in the barn. If he rejected her a second time, she didn't think she could stand it.

Unexpectedly, however, something flickered in his eyes, and his hand slid down her back, past her hair cascading down, and he drew her close. The edge of his cast dug into her spine. And then, as if he could read her mind, he tipped his head down and his lips pressed to hers, not practiced and ceremonial like all the other boys, not bruising and forced like Jonah, but like a storm breaking in the jungle—sudden and torrential, walls of rain closing them in until they were the only two left in the world.

Jack pulled back from the kiss before she was ready for it to end, before she could focus enough to realize his lips were no longer on hers. His forehead touched hers, and her eyes remained closed, though she didn't remember closing them. The last notes from the music box slowed and petered out.

"I . . ." Her tongue couldn't find words.

"We have to keep looking," he said softly. He hadn't yet let go of her.

She breathed, and wondered if he could hear the shakiness in her breath. This was what Nyla had tried to tell her about being with him. Had it been like this with Nyla? The thought of them together broke Althea from her stupor. She stepped from his arms.

"Right," she said.

He tilted his head at her. "You okay?"

"Like you said, we have to keep looking."

Althea tried to collect herself. She skimmed through a box before realizing she'd already looked through it an hour ago. They were finding nothing, and didn't even know what it was they were looking for. In the corner of her eye, she noticed Jack wasn't moving, hadn't opened another box. She looked over at him. His mouth was turned up in an amused smile.

"What's funny?" she said.

He shook his head, still with that smile playing on his lips. "Nothing."

"You're laughing at me."

"I'm not laughing at you." He leaned toward her and touched her hand. His eyes held hers in a deliberate gaze. "I like kissing you. But there's no hurry, Althea. We have time."

She tried not to smile back at him, or let him know what a jumble her thoughts were from the lightest touch of his hand. She cleared her throat.

"There are so many boxes left. We'll never get through them all."

"We don't have to. I found this." Jack showed her a damp,

dented cardboard box. Inside were two books. One was blank, but written on the other, in peeling gold letters, were the words *The Ark Project*.

"Is this what Jonah is looking for?"

"I don't know. But if we know what the Ark Project is, then we'll know what the Ark is."

When Althea picked up the book, a paper fell out. It was a color photograph, faded yellow and soft in the crease from having been folded into the pages of the book for what appeared to be a very long time.

It was a picture of the Original Nine, the same representation displayed everywhere in Vispera. She'd seen it a million times. The figures were lined up in the same order, held the same stance, wore the same clothes. The difference was that this was a photograph, not a reproduction. Althea could scarcely believe her eyes.

It was so strange to see their faces unaltered by the lines of a brush. Changes had been made in the countless renderings. The faces were all familiar, of course, like those she'd seen her whole life. But the men were more broad-chested, like Jack, and some had the stubble of hair on their faces. Many of them wore glasses over their eyes, but those had been left out of the paintings. The women were mostly shorter than the men in the photo, so that had changed too. The Original Althea wore her hair short, like a boy, and the color was almost black, not the deep brown of Althea and her sisters. As in the painting, Althea recognized the hope in their eyes, as if they were looking toward a bright, promising future. The photo would have been taken in the early days of the Plague, when Vispera was new. The Original scientists were brilliant, forward thinkers, planning a beautiful new world. Someone had written, in a spidery script, in the white border, *The Originals.*

"I've never seen this before," Althea said. "I didn't know it existed. What's it doing folded away in a book?"

Jack bent over her, studying the photograph. He was so close she thought he was going to rest a hand on her shoulder, or stroke her hair. Instead, he pointed to the picture.

"Who's that?" he said.

Althea's gaze followed to where his finger touched the image. The difference she'd missed, the one Jack pointed to, was another face behind the Original Samuel and Original Kate, a tenth face among the Nine, one she'd never seen before.

The face of a man, hidden behind the others and in slight shadow, looked back at Althea.

A chill ran down her back.

Now that she saw this new person, it seemed absurd that she'd missed him, but the painting was so familiar, so much a part of her everyday life, that she'd been blind to the glaring change. Her hand was shaking, so Jack took the picture from her and peered at it intently. The man was pale-haired, like Jack, but otherwise they looked nothing alike. He was slender, with a pointed chin and close-set eyes. His tie was askew, and his hair was mussed, as if he'd just run his fingers through it in quick preparation for the photo. His smile was cheerfully crooked, like he was laughing at something one of the others had said right before the picture was taken.

"He's not in any of the paintings," Jack said.

"No." She blinked at the faces, trying to reconcile the history she'd been taught her entire life with the image in front of her. "Was there an Original Ten? You think they made him, too?"

"It would explain why they've wanted a tenth clone so badly. That's how they started out. Haven't you ever wondered why everything is in tens except the number of models?"

"No," she said, annoyed at the question. "That's how it's always been."

"Not according to this."

"Maybe he died." Althea took the picture back. "Maybe they never had a chance to make more of him." She turned the picture over. "There's writing on the back."

They both leaned over to read. The words were in a tight, cursive script, a list down the page. The ink had faded to a pale gray with age.

*Viktor*
*Inga*
*Samuel*
*Kate*
*Carson*
*Althea*
*Hassan*
*Mei*
*Elan*
*Nyla*

"*Elan*," Jack murmured, struck by the realization. "They didn't just want a tenth clone. They wanted me as a replacement for *him*."

If Elan was indeed one of the Originals, for whatever reason, they'd stopped making that model. It would have been centuries ago. And he'd been erased from the records and histories, erased from the painting, just as he'd been erased from the memory of Vispera. Was it possible?

"Jack . . . you were supposed to be a tenth model?" Althea said, imagining what he must be thinking.

"It doesn't matter," Jack said brusquely, hearing the pity in her voice. He took the picture from her and folded it back where it came from. "Let's try to figure out what the Ark Project is."

"Maybe Sam can help."

"No, he'll tell the Council."

"I don't think so. He's fracturing. Jack, they'll have a Binding Ceremony soon."

Jack looked at her, his face a frustrating mask. The Inga that raised him had fractured, and now Samuel had too. And what would happen when it was her turn? Even now, she was supposed to be with her sisters, bonding with them, and instead she was here, helping Jack.

In one movement, Jack grabbed her, suddenly alert. He blew out the candle lighting the room.

"What is it?"

He shushed her, his hand covering her mouth, then peered out the window, straining to see in the dark. She was against the wall next to the window. His body was pressed into her, holding her still.

"Did you hear that?" he whispered.

"No, I—" And then she heard it. A sound outside, twigs breaking, hushed voices giving orders.

"Come on," Jack said, grabbing her hand. "We have to go."

*Chapter Eighteen*

# JACK

The cottage was surrounded. There were at least five clones. Jack cursed himself for getting distracted. He should have heard them sooner.

He led Althea down the short hallway. She clutched the box with the books inside close to her chest. They would have to go out the back. The cottage was small, but it was dark outside, and Jack knew the jungle here better than the clones did.

A back window led into an alcove. He opened a window quietly and helped Althea climb through.

"There's a clearing on the right, but to the left the trees are dense. It'll be dark—you'll be hidden there. I'm right behind you."

"Hey!" a deep voice shouted. "Who's there?" A flashlight swept the side of the house.

"Run," Jack said.

Althea disappeared into the dark, the flashlight beam following after her. Jack ducked away, rolling painfully to his side to dodge the beam. He couldn't see the Viktor, but the light flicked over the space where Jack had been.

The Viktor, hearing their scrabbling, yelled again. "Stop!"

Althea changed direction when a Viktor blocked her route to the trees. Jack followed her as she headed in the direction of town. He caught up, and she grabbed his shirt and pulled him into a cove of brush at the base of Vispera's wall. He shielded her from the Viktor, squeezing her against the rough stones. She was breathing hard. The Viktor ran along the edge of the tall grass. They could hear him talking low-voiced to the others who had joined him. Jack waited several moments. He could feel Althea's quick heartbeat against his chest. They were close, huddled together. If they moved, the Viktors would surely hear them.

Althea's fingers settled on his uninjured arm like butterfly wings. They fluttered up and down in an anxious caress. Jack paused, realizing she was barely conscious of what she was doing. He'd seen that sort of thing enough times to know she was trying to commune with him the way she would with a clone. She looked confused as some distant part of her became aware that her touch wasn't working. That it never would with him.

Althea stiffened. "They're coming back," she whispered, her lip against his ear.

Jack peered out. "Come on," he said, giving Althea a boost over the six feet of stone. He followed, grasping the top and hauling himself up, something he'd done plenty of times as a kid.

On the other side, they worked their way through the trees parallel to the path that headed toward Vispera. At first they went slowly, and then Jack heard the grunts of a Viktor clambering over the wall after them.

He took Althea's hand and veered them left, away from the path.

"Jack, the box!" Althea yelled.

He hardly slowed as he saw it tumbling to the ground.

"Leave it," he said, but she wrenched away. "Althea, don't!"

She turned back. Jack almost went after her, but then the Viktor rushed forward. Althea backed away. The Viktor raised his flashlight.

"Who's with you?" he said.

"No one. I'm by myself."

The Viktor was a Gen-310, the same age as them. The others hadn't caught up yet, and he wasn't carrying a weapon. Jack wasn't about to let a clone take Althea. He moved closer to them, ready to act, just as the ground shivered. A boom shook the trees. The air compressed around them. Birds squawked and scattered into the sky.

There was no time to react before a second distant roar followed, and a third. A mounting glow filtered through the leaves, casting vermillion shadows on the ground and foliage. The faces of Althea and Viktor reflected the glow before the light waned as quickly as it'd appeared. The chase forgotten, the Viktor sprinted for the clearing of the path. Althea glanced at Jack and then ran after, leaving Jack with no choice but to follow them both.

They stopped in a glade looking down toward Vispera, on a path that ended at the bank of Blue River. In the sky far above the trees, blooms of orange and red folded into the night air and merged, resolving in the end to thick black smoke. Watching the explosion, Althea's expression was a mirror image of the Viktor's next to her. It was as if they were concentrating intently, as if distant sounds called to them, voices Jack couldn't hear.

The Viktor reached out his hand, and instinctively Althea took it. Their fingers wove together. Her eyes met the Viktor's, and an understanding seemed to pass between them, a current of energy, fleeting and intense.

"They're hurt," the Viktor said, his tone dipping low as if saying something already understood.

Jack said nothing as Althea nodded. He watched their shoulders touch, their bodies connecting along the length of their arms. The Viktor's thumb brushed the back of her hand, drawing a small circle on her skin. Without another word, they reached a silent agreement. Althea released the Viktor's hand, and he hurried down the path toward the billowing midnight smoke. Althea leaned slightly, her body poised to follow, to race with him to the river's edge.

The remaining security guards emerged from the trees and stared into the distance in a daze. They paid no attention to Jack, simply walked on toward the river. As if they'd materialized in the darkness, even more clones appeared. They came from the direction of town, and they met on the same path. They followed the Viktor, a steady stream of people, toward the explosions, the direction Althea was staring, her grip still tight on the box as though she needed something to hang on to. Althea took a step toward the stream of people before Jack grabbed her hand. He felt her draw away.

"It's the boats, Jack. The ones going to Copan. People are hurt. I have to go to them."

Jack was mindful of the silence of the crowd moving collectively toward the river. There were no shouts, no calls to gather or to wake those still sleeping. Hands reached to twine together and eyes met, but no words passed.

The clones didn't need words.

"Come on, then." He moved to join the line on the path.

"No," she said. "Go back to the hospital. I'll meet you there later." When he shook his head, not understanding, she said, "Jonah did this. They won't want your help."

"You can't know it was Jonah."

"Who else? He's the only one capable."

To Jack, the profound silence of the moving crowd became heavy, almost tangible. The faraway look in Althea's eyes was like cold water dashed against his skin.

"That's not what you really mean, though. If he's capable of it, then I am too, right?"

"I didn't say that."

"You didn't have to. Jonah and I, we're the same person, after all. That's what the Council believes. I thought you were different."

With a hoarse whisper, she said, "I am different."

Jack put his hand into hers as she had done with the Viktor. He held the knot of their fingers in her line of sight and said, "What do you feel, Althea?"

Confused, she searched his eyes. She cast her gaze back to the path. The clones' steps had quickened. They moved as one, responding to some imperceptible impulse like a flock of birds, shifting flight instantaneously. She wanted to join them.

She looked back at Jack. "I don't understand," she said quietly.

"You felt something with the Viktor, didn't you? Something you don't feel with me." They both knew it was true. "Is he one of the ones you—"

He didn't need to see the way her mouth tightened to know he shouldn't say it. He pressed his lips against his teeth, keeping himself from completing the question. He didn't care whether she'd Paired with the Viktor, not really. But he'd seen what had passed between them. She had a connection with him, with all of them, that Jack could never share.

They stood on the path to Blue River, ignored by the clones, the distance between them growing with each moment.

"Never mind," he said, releasing her hand. "They're right, you know. I am capable of hurting them. But it's no more than what they've done to me."

"Jack . . ." She was listening to him, but she was far away. He imagined a girl who looked just like her, with the same serious mouth, her smell and voice, the fleeting line between her eyes. He imagined her on the ground, bleeding and alone.

"Go," he said after a moment. "They're your people. Help them."

She hesitated, then joined the others and was enveloped by the crowd. Jack watched them go, keeping his eyes on her until he no longer knew which one she was.

Jack wandered through the trees, empty now, and then into the banana grove, where Jonah was waiting. He hadn't known he'd see Jonah there, but when he did, sitting on a rock with an arm resting on one knee, for some reason Jack wasn't surprised.

"They'll be looking for you," Jack said.

The steady eyes glinted, and the straight nose and smooth brow, brought into relief by the angular shadows of the trees, sharpened darkly.

"They'll be busy for a while yet." Jonah stood from the rock, and his feet sank into the loamy soil, lifting from the ground the aroma of crushed heliconia leaves and fallen fruit tangy with rot.

The sweet smell made Jack's stomach turn. He swallowed stiffly. "What you're doing, Jonah, it isn't right. You have to stop."

"You think I should leave? Is that what you want?"

*Of course he should leave,* Jack thought. If they caught him, for Jonah there'd be no clean lab room or locked barn. He'd be dead within hours. But Jack said nothing.

Jonah's lip moved, twitching as if on a thread, like he could read the conflict on Jack's face. "I'm not going anywhere, brother. I haven't even begun."

"And what happens when you're done? If you destroy Vispera like you did Copan, where will you go then? Crooked Falls? Where's it end?"

"I have supplies. It's all there, waiting for me. It's waiting for us, Jack. We'll get a boat and go together, as soon as we're done here."

Again, Jack didn't answer. He had no answer to give. Were those really his choices? Help Jonah destroy the clones, or help the clones destroy Jonah?

"You don't hate them," Jonah said softly, contemplating him. "After everything they've done. Is it because of that Althea?"

"Don't talk about her. You know nothing about her."

"I know a lot, Jack. More than any of the clones realize. I've been watching, and waiting. I'm good at that."

Jack ran his fingers through his hair, damp with sweat. A cloud of bats flitted through the trees, rustling the fanning leaves. Jack looked up, his strained attention on Jonah faltering abruptly, allowing him to realize only then how hot he was. He'd spent two days in a hospital bed, and he'd done too much since then. It was catching up with him. He swayed on his feet.

"You going to faint?" Jonah said. Jack shook his head, but Jonah took his arm anyway and clapped him on the back. "It's a good thing we're not like them, or we'd both be on the ground."

"I just have to sit for a minute," Jack said.

"Sorry, brother. Fall over later. There's something you need to see first."

Jack followed Jonah to the other side of town at the West Lab. The ground where North Lab had stood, the building that held Jack's room, was a charred ruin. They passed the empty space without comment, Jonah leading the way to the second floor of the building next door, with its orderly rows of bright, fluorescent-lit rooms.

"Where are we going?" Jack asked, each step feeling as if he were walking against a current.

Jonah moved easily and silently through the building, crouched low, his body aware of every sound and movement. Observing him, Jack could understand how he'd made his way through town unseen for so long, learning everything about the clones, waiting to make himself known by violence and chaos. Jonah's hair, disordered and sun-bleached, was at the moment lighter than Jack's, which was darkened with sweat and falling in his eyes. Jack brushed it away, aware of the heat radiating from his skin.

Jonah stopped at an unmarked door and produced a key. "Not all the clones went to the river." He unlocked the door and held it open for Jack.

The room was like one of the medical bays in the clinic. It was long and narrow, with cabinets along one wall filled with drug vials, and along the other, hanging from hooks, a row of lab coats like Sam and the other doctors wore. In the center of the room, however, was a ring of chairs connected by wires and electrodes emitting a muted electric buzz. In the chairs, reclined back and held down by buckled straps, were Althea's nine sisters. Their eyes were closed, their faces tense but asleep —or more likely unconscious. No blankets covered them, and their yellow medical gowns left their legs and feet uncovered. The pale soles of their bare feet contrasted with the tan skin of their legs, and that sight alone made them seem pitifully vulnerable.

Jack crossed the room and placed his hand on an Althea's shoulder, then jerked it back quickly. Something had shocked him. A current coming from the girl's skin. He realized then that the chairs weren't connected by wires, the Altheas were. And the wires were embedded in their skin, pulsing electric currents through their bodies.

"What is this?" Jack said, his voice harsh.

"The clone doctors invented it. It's called Bonding. It's what they do when a clone fractures. The siblings are at risk. They figure the bond is made stronger if they all feel pain at the same time. At least I think that's the idea."

Jack's muscles went rigid as Jonah slipped an arrow from the quiver on his back, but then he used the blunt end to lift an Althea's hand and drop it down again, limp and heavy.

"There might be drugs involved," he said.

Jack surveyed the tools and instruments on a nearby table —syringes, vials of liquid, bandages, and a few scalpels.

"It's torture."

"Your Althea was supposed to be here, you know. She didn't show, so I guess they went ahead anyway."

It was then Jack saw the tenth chair shoved into a corner, cords and wires dangling off the edge.

"This is wrong. We have to help them."

Jonah propped himself on one of the countertops, one knee casually pulled up. "By all means, play the hero."

Jack looked up sharply, but the lazy amusement that colored Jonah's voice didn't reach the ice in his eyes.

Jack turned to the chair nearest him. The girl in it looked identical to the others; the flat, serious mouth, slightly parted, the creased brow, the smooth skin. It took his breath away, to be so close to her and know she wasn't Althea. That she wasn't *his* Althea.

He searched the sides and underneath the chair, looking for a power source feeding the current. Not seeing one, he clenched his teeth and gripped the main cord leading to the cluster of wires under the Althea's skin. A searing jolt shot through him as he ripped it from the other wires. That Althea's sisters should suffer in this way—it was unbearable.

As gently as he could, he plucked each humming wire from her arms. Pinpricks of blood seeped from where they'd been. As a group, the nine girls let out a half sigh, half moan when the current broke. With some difficulty because of his cast, Jack lifted the girl he'd unhooked and settled with her on the floor. Her skin was too warm, and her head dropped lifelessly from his arm. He glanced up at Jonah, who watched with impassive eyes.

"She's not waking up." With effort, Jack steadied his hand as it passed through the girl's hair. "What do I do? She's not waking up."

Jonah shrugged, running the arrow tip under his fingernails. "Give it a minute."

Even as Jonah spoke, her head lolled to the side and she groaned softly.

"Althea?" Jack said. He didn't know what number she was, but it didn't matter. He felt as if he were holding his own Althea in his arms.

The girl's eyes fluttered open, and her gaze traveled questioningly over him.

"What's wrong with your eyes?" she murmured drowsily. Then something sharpened in her face. She gasped, and every muscle in her body stiffened against him as she fought the hold of his arms. She scrambled across the floor, ending in a crouch against the wall. Her hands rubbed her skin where he'd held her, as if she'd been touched by something cold and unpleasant. "What's happening?"

"It's okay," Jack said, his palms held out placatingly. "It's going to be okay. I'm going to help."

"You?" She looked frantically over the room, taking in Jonah and her still-unconscious sisters, and then her gaze settled back to Jack. "What have you done?"

"It's okay," he said again, hoping to calm her.

"You said you're going to help?" Her eyes narrowed, suddenly less scared. "You can't *help* me. We're here because of you. This is your fault!"

Jack shook his head. "What?"

"You're the reason our sister fractured. You made Inga-296

fracture, and the Samuel too. You're why we're here, and now you want to ruin the Bonding?"

"Ruin? I thought—"

"Get away from me. Get away from all of us," she yelled, standing on shaky legs and moving protectively between her sisters and Jack.

"But . . ." Jack stammered. Jonah was behind him then, lifting him up from where he knelt.

"Come on, brother. Time to go."

The other Altheas were stirring, moaning in their sleep, communing and picking up the emotion of the Althea who stood glaring at him.

"Get out," she said viciously, the echo of her words muttered on the half-sleeping tongues of the other eight Altheas. The chorus of their voices surrounded him, suffocated him. He heard them still while Jonah dragged him down the stairs and outside, until he realized finally he was only hearing them in his head. *Get out, get out, get out.*

Jack looked up at the sky, breathing heavily, instinctively searching his lungs for any sign they were about to betray him. Jonah stood next to him, his light head flung back.

"You needed to see that, Jack," he said coolly. "They'll have a Binding Ceremony for the Althea. Your Althea. They'll kill her. They want her dead—even her sisters do. They have to be stopped. We can take them down, all of them. Help me, and then we'll leave this place together."

Jack stared into the night sky and felt it closing in on him. "Do what you want," he said finally. "I won't stop you. I won't help, but I won't stop you."

Jack couldn't face Jonah. He couldn't bear to see in his brother's eyes the same hatred he felt. He stumbled away, then braced his hands against the side of West Lab and was sick in the squat juniper shrubs at the base of the building. By the time that was finished, Jonah was gone.

*Chapter Nineteen*

# ALTHEA

The night had been terrifying, but they were safe now.

Althea could still feel the heat from the flames on her face. She could smell the burning wood and chemicals on her skin. The boats were lost. The initial blast had destroyed them, polluting the water and leaving burning debris strewn everywhere. They'd tried to salvage the supplies that were to go to Copan that very day at dawn. Vispera was already facing shortages from the ruined fields, and they couldn't afford to lose more, but what few boxes they were able to pull from the wreckage had already been rifled through, the contents taken. Althea knew by whom.

Those who'd been at the boats, preparing last-minute supplies when the explosion erupted, made up the injured who now filled the clinic. It was mostly Gen-300s and 290s. Althea herself had pulled Althea-307 from the banks of Blue River. She'd been face-down in the mud. Althea couldn't tell how badly she was injured, but blood covered the front of her dress. The other Gen-300 Altheas stood to the side, their faces white as paper. They didn't move to touch Althea-307, making Althea wonder if their connection with Althea-307 had already been broken by death.

Althea's sisters hadn't been at the explosion, but when she returned from the wreckage, they'd all climbed from their beds, and now they were sitting up together in a circle, holding hands. After the horrifying night and her last conversation with Jack, the comfort of her sisters was like a warm, familiar blanket.

Sitting in a circle in the dorms, her hands twined with those of her sisters, she felt calm. Like the other times she communed with them, the warm liquid filled her limbs. She'd been close, but she wouldn't fracture. They welcomed her back, and they were here, together, out of harm's way. They needed her. Vispera needed her. She was one of them, and nothing else mattered.

The Altheas had put on the necklaces that had been a gift from the Gen-300 Altheas on the occasion of the Gen-310s' first Pairing Ceremony. With Althea-307 in the clinic and close to death, it seemed fitting to wear them. They were made of pale, lustrous pearls that glistened in the light of the candles next to each Althea's bed. The pearls warmed against Althea's skin. If they had a Ceremony of Loss, which they would hold for Althea-307's accidental death, as they did for any untimely death, they would wear them to that, too. The pearls had been collected from oysters off the coast a day's journey away. Smooth and iridescent, they shivered along her sisters' necks, picking up different colors from the candlelight; silver and gold, pink and blue. Althea focused her eyes on the colors. They came and went in the flickering light, swimming on the creamy surface of the beads like shimmering, silver-lipped oyster shells and the ocean from which they'd come.

Althea could picture the ocean. The colorless gray mingled with the warm liquid calm from communing with her sisters, until that calm retreated slightly, a tide going out. Then, like rustling pebbles pulled by a receding wave, the ocean gray she'd imagined turned into the gray of Jack's eyes.

Althea's eyes snapped open at the same moment all nine faces of her sisters turned toward her. Their sharp anger engulfed her, and she dropped their hands with a gasp.

"It's been a long night," Althea-316 said tersely. "We should go to bed."

With weighty tension in the room, they changed silently into their nightgowns, and Althea climbed into her bed, the last in the row of ten Althea beds.

Althea waited until her sisters' breathing deepened, and then dressed and slipped quietly out, clutching the box holding the two books she and Jack had found.

She needed to escape the suffocating room, her sisters, and the frightening accusation she'd seen in their eyes. She didn't know if they were already planning a Bonding Ceremony for her, but even if they were, she had some time before it happened. She'd get away before then somehow. She just wasn't sure how yet.

Jack was probably asleep at the clinic. He'd looked ready to collapse before, worn down with exhaustion and also, she knew, with the strain that had developed between them. She crept down the stairs of the Althea dorm to the common sitting room in the foyer. She found a chair in the corner and settled into the soft cushions. She'd been unable to look at the books until now. When she touched the cover of book titled *The Ark Project,* shreds of cloth sprinkled onto her hand. She flipped through it. The type inside was minuscule, and none of it looked like it would be useful in figuring out what Jonah had planned. It was a sort of textbook compiled by something called the *Global Health Initiative,* and it was full of lists and numbers, all of them mystifying. The book actually referred to the Original Ten. She turned the pages quickly.

Most of what she found in the book was familiar. It told the story of the scientists who created the original models. It related how those scientists traveled from places all over the globe, forgotten places with names like *Bali, Saint Petersburg, Patagonia, Sweden,* and *the Marquesas Islands,* and how they'd gathered together for the final phase of their work in what would eventually be known as *Vispera.*

The book also narrated the advance of the Slow Plague over three decades, from the time the scientists had seen the first hints of something wrong, the first clues that pointed to the inescapable deterioration of the human immune system. The Plague manifested in myriad diseases, lethal allergies, and physiological disorders that made the human species unable to carry on. The world itself had turned deadly, as if the very air they breathed and the food they ate had turned to poison.

The book set forth tables and charts that displayed the death toll. A million here, a billion there. It included lists of hospitals shut down, government budgets for medicine running empty, names of city parks appropriated for cemeteries. Some human interest stories were recounted amid the numbers, lending a living reality to the awful census of doom. By the time twenty years or so had passed, there were just pockets of humans left in remote Pacific islands and out-of-the-way highland regions of Central America.

The scientists had three decades to build a new world, one that wouldn't die out the way their own had. In thirty years, they themselves would be dead, and only their legacy would live on.

The narrative of the Slow Plague came to an end, and the remainder of the book contained a series of words in lists followed by seemingly endless numbers. At first it looked like gibberish to Althea, but then she realized that she didn't recognize the words because they were actually names of people according to the human custom in which everyone had a distinct name rather than the designation and number of a particular Gen model. The humans always had more than one name, and sometimes three or even four. There were thousands of names in the book, running down to the final page.

She closed the volume and sat back. Something niggled at the back of her mind. She felt there was something familiar about the list.

She picked up the second, unmarked book, and was surprised to find close lines of handwriting covering each page. The first page read: *The Journal of Althea Lane, 2068.* Althea had never heard of any journals or diaries from the Original Nine. If they existed, surely they'd have been on display in a special place, maybe in Remembrance Hall. If the date was right, the book was old, but it hadn't disintegrated with age. That meant it must have been in the climate-controlled environment of the Tunnels at some point, and Inga-296 had taken it. Althea turned the pages to read.

## FROM THE JOURNAL OF ALTHEA LANE
### Costa Rica
### 2068–2107

(Excerpts)

*February 3, 2068*

When Hassan and I were flown to San Francisco from Burlington for interviews, the executives at Global Health Initiative showed us the model of the community they were building. The cluster of labs with state-of-the-art technology, vast storage caverns, dining halls, warehouses, residences. They said much of it hadn't been built yet, and that was only five months ago. Now that we've arrived in Costa Rica, I see a whole community risen up as if out of thin air. I walk through this town they've built, and if it weren't for the humidity of Central America, not to mention the toucans and howling monkeys, I'd think we were still in Vermont.

I'm beginning to understand the wealth and resources devoted to this Project—I find myself capitalizing the word, because that's how it sounds when Una Vispa says it. It really is her vision. When she first offered the positions to me and Hassan, I was a bit starstruck, to be honest. Not just the head of Global Health, but the woman who actually conceived of and formed the most important international organization devoted to securing funds for medical research—research that will benefit the whole world. And she was sitting in our living room, drinking that cheap tea Hassan buys!

We'd already been through the countless exams, including blood tests and genetic history. Dr. Vispa wouldn't say exactly what all that was for, but she did volunteer she was collecting the best scientists in the world, the most brilliant, and also those with healthy, strong constitutions and well-documented family histories. I guess to make sure we wouldn't need any extensive medical care while living in such a remote region. We've also been selected for our youth. We've all earned doctorates, and none of us is over thirty, meaning we'll be able to oversee the Project for years to come. She gathered agronomists, cytologists, epidemiologists, geneticists, physicists. The goal of the Project, she said, was to research the spread of the autoimmune disorders we've been seeing in so many children, though I'm not clear what my role as an evolutionary biologist might be. Dr. Vispa assures me I'm important to the team, however.

She really is a visionary. She looks exactly like she did in that documentary Hassan and I just watched, the one where she bought all this land in Costa Rica and then used her wealth and influence to have it declared a semi-independent province, free from the taxes and regulations of either Costa Rica or the United States. She's so elegant, with her flowing white hair, startlingly blue eyes, and perfectly tailored (and extraordinarily expensive) pantsuit. Even drinking out of Hassan's ridiculous BE POSITIVE LIKE A PROTON! mug, she managed to look regal and charismatic.

She explained to us that the financing from the World Commonwealth is far greater even than that provided for the Greenland plantations, the Sahara canals, even the new NASA missions. She took such barefaced pleasure in her project that it was impossible not to be delighted too. But then she turned solemn, saying it was worth every penny, that she'd even devoted a huge portion of her own wealth, because after all, it certainly would be the "last significant investment made in our epoch of humanity." I'm not sure what she meant, but it certainly sent a chill down my spine!

It's rather wonderful, I think, though Hassan is concerned. He says all the protocols and political machinations that made this happen are unlike anything he's ever seen, and he thinks Dr. Vispa and the executives at Global Health know something we don't. He's a worrier. In any case, a full community of scientists, engineers, technicians, support staff, and construction workers has sprung up seemingly overnight, and I'm still amazed we've been selected for this project. "This is our destiny!" I said to Hassan. "It's what we were born to do, I can feel it!" He laughed and kissed me, even though I know he thought I was being hopelessly dramatic.

It's so lush and vibrant here, our own little slice of Eden, and when I think of the good we will do in this beautiful place, I can't help but be thankful.


*September 30, 2069*
Today, over a year since we arrived and with the labs finally set up and the construction crews and support staff evacuated, the Project has officially launched. Hassan and I sat in the front row of the auditorium to hear the keynote

address, and it was here that Dr. Vispa revealed the true nature of what we were setting out to do. We had thought we were here to find a cure, but it's now clear that was never the intention.

She started with slides on the huge screen behind her scrolling through, showing human development starting all the way back in the Paleolithic Era.

As the slides reached the Middle Ages, she told us what many of us had already suspected. Global Health has decided confidentially that a cure for the Slow Plague, as we're calling it now, is scientifically not within reach, and perhaps never will be. In other words, it's destined to continue its terrible work of extermination. It isn't just affecting children anymore, either. After it spread to adolescents, it started appearing in adult populations as well and, according to Global Health's data, it's crossing all borders of income, race, and region. Nobody knows any of this yet, however. To forestall planet-wide panic, Global Health will withhold any official announcement for as long as possible.

A palpable sense of doom crept into the room. Dr. Vispa paused for a long moment, head bowed. A shudder rippled through the crowd. The slides continued behind her, showing the Renaissance, the Enlightenment, the Industrial Revolution. They sped by, faster and faster. The eighteenth century, the nineteenth, the twentieth and twenty-first, showing images and faces so quickly it all became a blur. When the slides reached the end of our age and the new century coming upon us, the screen went stark white. We squinted against the light, blindingly bright in the dark hall, and then Dr. Vispa spread her arms wide, bestowing a kind of benediction on us all, and she smiled.

"Now," she said. "Now is when we shape the future."


*March 24, 2070*

Dr. Vispa designated the first phase of the Project "Enhancing Development," which is a stage of intense genetic engineering that will ultimately send an improved adaptation of humanity into the future, a version free from the effects of the Slow Plague. Even in the midst of working nonstop, night and day, I still can barely grasp the enormity of what we're doing here and the magnitude of Dr. Vispa's vision. This is no five-year research grant like we thought. This is the work of decades, the work of a lifetime.

With political instability spreading in South America, travel has become more difficult, but my visit home to see my family is still scheduled for next month. We're sworn to secrecy, both on the advance of the Slow Plague and on our Project in Costa Rica, so when Mother asks why I've been kept away for so long already, I won't be able to convey how important our work truly is. They don't know that, at this point, we really are the only hope. When it comes time to say goodbye, I don't know how I'll manage it. How can I not warn them of what's coming? I keep waking up at night drenched in sweat, tears streaming down my face, feeling in my heart that this visit will be the last time I ever see them.

Dr. Vispa spoke at the last assembly about the coming second phase, which she said is as complex as the first, inasmuch as it involves laying down the moral and social foundations of the future community. She pointed to the slide on the presentation, "Enhancing Genetics & Establishing Culture." I've gotten to know Dr. Vispa more since coming here. I've always recognized her passion, but I've seen more lately how she has a flair for the theatrical. She slapped her hand on the podium, saying, "Ladies and gentlemen, this is not arrogance! For the first time in human history, this is something we can do. Why build a world that will simply survive? We must build a better world. Harmony with one's fellows, stewardship of nature, no war, no poverty, no racism, sexism, or class warfare. We will reconstruct and atone for our sins of the past. That is the visionary future that will be carried forward by the descendants of these young people!"

The fifty of us who'd been selected by Dr. Vispa (the "genetic seeds," as we're called) stood at that point and endured the applause that seemed to last forever. Dr. Vispa stood before us, beaming at all she'd accomplished. She's an amazing woman.


*January 10, 2077*
We have our first success!

Finally, after all our work, all our failures, we've created the first entirely viable clone generation. Hassan has been calling them *Homo factus*—the Made Man—and it's true, they were indeed made by us. Now here they are, healthy and whole!

Only ten of the gene models have ever shown viability,

so it seems we're limited to those samples as we move forward, rather than the fifty we'd hoped for. We have five females and five males. Dr. Vispa especially was disappointed that her own sample never worked, though we tried countless times, and she poured so many of our resources into that one effort. She jokes that she's lost her chance at immortality.

It was only late last year that the rest of the world became aware of the devastating impact the Slow Plague will inevitably have. The scientists here estimate another thirty years of human life before there's nothing left. Panic has been kept at bay for now, with reports of countless research outfits still working on a cure, giving people hope that humanity will be saved. Only we at Global Health know that those pathways are already dead ends.

We can't make ourselves immune from the Slow Plague but, as the results of the blood tests prove, at least we know the clones won't fall victim to it. We're hoping that when they eventually sexually reproduce, they'll be a population free of this awful disease. It'll be a long time, however, before we can rely on sexual reproduction with a limit of only ten individual gene types. As we move forward, I'm sure we'll find a way to develop more, and if we refine their scientific inclinations and educate them accordingly, they can continue the work of creating a more diverse gene pool after we're gone.

After such a long time, and with so much happening in the world, it's indescribable to see these tiny babies finally with us. I was thrilled that both the Althea clones and the Hassan clones were among the survivors. The Althea babies look exactly like me, right down to the birthmarks on their cheeks. My grandmother used to say it reminded her of a rose, so I've chosen one of the little Althea clones to call Rose. She is darling.

The new babies are a welcome distraction, and everyone is delighted with them. I've been too committed to my research to want my own children, and Hassan questioned bringing them into the world when they're sure to suffer from the Slow Plague and we're facing a planetary epidemic. He said their birth would be equivalent to "a death sentence in an empty world." These clones, though. I feel such affection for them. I love seeing ourselves in their faces.

We held a celebration in the assembly hall, and after the speeches were over, Dr. Vispa called us—those whose genes now represent the survival of humankind—outside to have our picture taken. I have the photo now on our bookshelf, and it inspires me every morning when I go off to the labs. When I look at the ten of us lined up on the steps of the residence hall and think of our work guiding the Project, I whisper Dr. Vispa's words to myself—a better world.

For the first time, I have hope for what's to come.


The next several entries detailed the early lives of the first generation of cloned children. The Original Ten cared about them enormously, according to the Original Althea's journal. They played with them and lived with them in some facsimile of family life that Althea couldn't quite figure out. While reading, Althea thought for the first time about who this woman really was. Her Original had always been larger than life, a woman in a painting Althea saw every day, and now here she could read about her eating lunch in the dining halls and getting lost on the trails to Blue River. Althea found herself wondering what kind of place the Original Althea had grown up in, and what her life had been like. What had she done when she was Althea's age? Had she enjoyed the same things, or had this woman, like Jack, read books of poetry and played baseball?

A number of details about life in early Vispera surprised Althea. For some reason, she had always imagined the Original Nine—Original Ten, she corrected herself—as living and working alone for all those years, but she realized now that was absurd. The community had teemed with countless others, whole families, and people the Original Althea talked about as friends, acquaintances, rivals, sometimes annoyances. A janitor named Chris cleaned her offices every day and complained of a pain in his back. Althea had the sense of many daily conversations like this. Was this what the humans talked about with each other? Aches, illnesses, poor eyesight, and other structural defects? As time went on in the journal, the effects of the Slow Plague appeared in virulent form. All of them, the Original Althea included—Althea Lane, Althea reminded herself, thinking how strange it was to see her own name with no number after it—suffered from rashes, blood diseases, things with complicated names like rheumatoid arthritis, diabetes, celiac disease, vasculitis, and Sjögren's syndrome. All manner of aches, pains, and allergies that were manifestations of their dying immune systems. They were diseases that had always existed, but they'd become more dire, more difficult to treat, and more widespread. The Slow Plague killed them young, and it killed their children.

Although they were dying, their troubles and pain didn't consume their day-to-day lives. Althea Lane wrote about food, families, animals they lived with and inexplicably gave names to, parties they held to commemorate the day each individual was born. And they talked about weather, always and relentlessly, and the weather of Vispera especially seemed to preoccupy them. Most of the residents of early Vispera, she gathered, had come from elsewhere, places with very different climates, places called San Diego, New York, London, Tokyo, New Delhi, Burlington, Edinburgh.

The humans had spent evenings staring at *televisions,* appliances Althea had never really understood until she read about them in Althea Lane's journal. A "show" would unfold elaborate tales pantomimed by humans pretending to be someone else. They watched the television often, and Althea Lane especially liked a television story called *Family Days,* about a human family, a mother and father, three children, grandparents, neighbors, and pets.

The television also showed real stories, things happening to people on continents thousands of miles away. Many of the stories were about money, another concept hard to grasp. Althea knew from the histories that money was coins and slips of paper, and those became plastic cards, and then those eventually turned into electronic abstractions, but nevertheless one the humans would compete over and trade for things they wanted. They didn't work together as a collective, like Althea's people in Vispera, but fought one another for resources, sometimes viciously.

Money seemed to have a lot to do with the collapse unfolding far away from early Vispera. Those with lots of money seemed to live longer, but not by much; they died too, and their children died with them. Althea Lane didn't write very much about the collapse. It was as if she didn't want to face it, as if writing it in stark lines in a journal would make it more real. Althea knew the history, however. From the point the Plague became public knowledge, it had taken thirty years for humans and human civilization to become sick and die, thirty years for it all to disintegrate into ashes. The telephones and televisions; the intangible money they valued so much; the particles of information floating through the air like dust motes, appearing suddenly and miraculously on glowing screens; the machines flying over the earth, carrying people to bodies of land all over the world, even carrying people to the moon. The families and birthdays, the mothers, fathers, children, and pets. All of it gone.

In 2090, Althea Lane received word that her mother had died four months before, and *Family Days* aired its last episode. She wrote about the Originals gathering around a glowing communal television with the surviving cooks, janitors, medical personnel, and lab assistants of Vispera. They watched the end of the story of a family that had never really existed. They grieved the loss of the story and the people in it as if they'd been real, but Althea understood it was not just the made-up family they were mourning, but the familiar world they had always known that was now coming to an end, a world that wouldn't be making any more television stories. Their world was falling apart, and their own families, their real families, were dying. When the show ended, they held each other and wept.

Althea turned the pages, and read.

# FROM THE JOURNAL OF ALTHEA LANE

(Excerpts)

*April 15, 2091*

Word came today that Dr. Una Vispa died a week ago, on
April 8, Easter Sunday, during the siege on the U.S. Global
Health headquarters in San Francisco. She was there to
fight for the continuation of the Project, which the new
government's administration was threatening to shut
down, calling it an abomination and a drain on resources
desperately needed in the States. Before she left, I heard her
speaking to the president of the World Commonwealth on
the phone.

"You have no authority over Global Health!" she said.
"In any case, what use is it to feed your children? They'll
be dead before the decade ends! The work Global Health
is doing in Costa Rica is not for something as insignificant
as individual existence. We are working for human
existence."

To the end she was silver-tongued, authoritative, and
relentlessly single-minded. She was eighty-nine, an age
none of us can hope to reach anymore. She'll never see
the world she built come to fruition, though none of us
really will, not with the Plague sweeping through us as it
is. Half of our community is gone now, but we carry on.
This Project was her passion. Samuel said she was like
a gardener who plants a seed but never sees the garden
fully grown, never reaps the harvest. We've changed the
name of the community to Vispera, in her honor. It means,

appropriately, "eve," and we surely are in those last dark hours before a new beginning.

The first clones are fourteen now. They stared at us with blank eyes when we told them about the death of the woman responsible for their existence, a woman who'd sat with them in lessons, teaching them almost every day of their lives about everything from history to morality to science. "You should just make more of her," one of the Kate clones said. I guess they're too young to really understand. They're a strange little group.


*May 31, 2094*
The riots in Brazil have spread into Peru and Argentina. The news out of India is even worse, and the World Commonwealth is saying they've lost contact with China. That's what they said: "We've lost contact with China." How is that possible? We're so secluded here, closed in by the mountains, these images of disaster we see on television seem unreal.

The first clones are seventeen now and they assist us in the labs. They're learning as much about genetics as we can teach them, surpassing us at times in knowledge and research.

I wish we hadn't fixed the eyesight of Hassan's clones. I realize our genetic manipulation of the clones is only in the best interest of the project. But it's so strange to see these young versions of Hassan working in the labs, whispering among one another, looking so much like him years ago when we were in school, only they're without glasses. I remember him only a little older than the first generation is now, before we'd heard anything about the Slow Plague. His brow would furrow, and he'd tilt his glasses on top of his head and peer into the microscope, a pinched indentation on his nose. These clones of Hassan seem to be missing something when I look at them, and I've decided it's the glasses. Hassan laughs when I say this, telling me they aren't missing anything. The glasses, he says, are tiresome, and he constantly cleans them. Why should these new versions of him be subjected to bad eyes? But still. Without them, they will never be Hassan to me.

*August 19, 2097*
Viktor died today while rock climbing in the mountains. It was such a shock to us all. What was he doing rock climbing anyway, with his arthritis? It makes no sense. Such a waste!

*December 2, 2099*
It's been three months since Hassan died from the Slow Plague, a plague that takes so many forms. In Hassan's case, it was the celiac disease, though it could have been the arthiritis. It's hard to tell at this point, we're all afflicted with so many problems.

They didn't seem to care. The Hassans, I mean, although more and more, I find I can't call them that. They're not

Hassan. The more I miss him, the angrier I become with them for not being him.

That's strange, isn't it? That they nod and go about their work when the person who made them, whom they were made from, is dead. He died, and they skulk around the same as they always do, muttering in soft voices, discussing their secret plans. I don't know who these clones made from Hassan are, but they are not him. They lack his warmth, his life, his brilliant mind. They are like reptiles, cold and passionless. They don't trust us, either, those of us still living. They don't want us in the labs anymore, that much is clear. One of the Inga clones told me I had to speak to one of Samuel's clones if I wanted access to the labs. "These are my labs!" I said. "I'm the senior analyst." She told me I should have a nap, then closed the door in my face. They treat us like aging grandparents, slow-witted and senile. I suppose they keep us around out of some sense of obligation.

Perhaps it was arrogance to think we had any control to begin with. We may have created them, but like all children, they grow up and make their own lives. They reject the life we wanted for them.

They refuse to collaborate on our planned shift from cloning to sexual reproduction. They say they like things the way they are! To me especially, as an evolutionary biologist, this is extremely bizarre. You can't simply keep cloning—it won't work. You can't disregard a billion years of evolution! It seems they think they can, however. They'll outgrow this outlandish notion. After all, <u>almost every</u>

species that's ever existed has, consciously or not, been committed to propagation by sexual mating and to the goal of passing genes through one's offspring. That's how evolution works!

Mei's attempt to pair them romantically has turned into something of a joke. I told her it would never work. She was hoping they would embrace sexual reproduction instead of maintaining this now unnecessary reliance on the cloning, but that's clearly failed. She suspects they have perhaps made the males infertile, but the clones won't allow us to examine them.

It's been four years since we lost contact with Honduras, and six since we heard anything from the States. Almost certainly Global Health is completely defunct, and the World Commonwealth is an empty shell, its top leadership decimated years ago. There are other survivors out there, I'm sure, but we have no way to contact them. It's been a long time since we've seen jet contrails passing overhead. Our last long-distance link to the outside has sputtered and died. We are truly alone in this.

Mei now thinks the clones need a religion. They've rejected any of our ideologies, of course, as they've rejected everything else thousands of years of humanity has to offer. For some reason, we thought we'd have more time, and she thinks we need to work harder to provide them a compass in this empty world we're leaving them.

Sometimes I wonder if we made a mistake. We're coming up on the new century, and we don't have much longer. Perhaps humanity was not meant to continue. If man is made in God's image and we fall so short of His perfection, what is this creature we've made? They have our faces, but something is missing. Elan says it's their souls. Perhaps he's right.

How foolish we were, to act as gods.


*April 21, 2102*
Nyla died today. The Slow Plague, as usual.


*July 8, 2104*
Carson and I snuck into the labs and found their notes. It's as we suspected. From the beginning, the clones have been manipulating the genetic codes of the new generations they're creating. It's one thing to fix eyesight, but what they've done . . . changing eye color, skin color, erasing the most inconsequential physical differences. They've taken minor traits present in each of us and either eliminated them or enhanced them somehow. From what we could decipher, they seem to be altering even the way they think. The notes called it Empathic Communal Bonding, though we couldn't figure out what this means.

The changes are so fundamental. They've become alien to me, less and less human every year, with each iteration. It scares me.

This morning I found them in the church, about fifty of the clones standing in a circle holding hands. Their eyes were closed, and they swayed back and forth as if responding to a silent, unimaginable rhythm. I asked if they were praying. They smiled secretly to each other and turned away. A Viktor clone took me by the arm and led me out.

What is going on? What are they up to?

*October 17, 2105*

Carson found Elan and Miranda dead in their bedroom this morning. There's been some talk about an autopsy, but no one seems to have the heart for it. Perhaps we're afraid of what we might find?

I went to speak to the Althea clones again, but they refused to see me. I've been an irritant to them, it seems. They don't like that I've disapproved of their plans, argued with them about sexual reproduction. As I was leaving the labs, though, an Elan clone followed me out. He spoke quietly, as if he didn't want the others to hear.

"We're thinking of leaving," he said, leaning toward me conspiratorially. "We need your help collecting supplies. They won't suspect you of planning an escape."

I smiled grimly at that. Most of the original residents are too weak to walk, let alone plan an escape. I see the way the clones look at us, watch us. They are horrified by our physical deterioration, and I worry it has only galvanized their efforts to erase all variety in their genetic code. They'll never survive that way.

The clones take care of us, though, in our afflictions. They revere us in their own cold, detached way.

I asked Elan why he wanted to leave—the clones always seem content with each other. I had no idea the Elans were unhappy. He told me about a disagreement among the clone groups.

"You know how we play music at the dances," he said. "The others want to erase music from the genetic code of the new Elan generations. They say it's a waste. They think they've isolated the trait, and in its place they want to implant something useful for work in the labs. That's not what we want, and the disagreement has become intolerable. Some of us have decided to leave and make our own way."

I told him I'd help in any way I could.

I hope the Elans do get away and start something new. I hope they make a better world than we did—this stagnant, rigid community full of these alien creatures, a mockery of everything human.

*November 13, 2106*
They are monsters.

They've killed their own. Hundreds at once. Last year's babies, all dead. The Elan clone, the one who told me he was leaving, his whole generation is dead. And the new Althea clones, because of the birthmarks . . .

Inga and Kate tried to stop them. They were in the nursery when it happened, and they threw themselves in the path of the clones, desperately trying to shield the babies, and now they're dead too. The clones killed them both.

They keep us locked in the residences now, but one of

the first generation finally showed up after I'd requested to meet with them countless times. It could have been the one I used to call Rose, but who can tell? They don't want us to be able to tell them apart. They're disturbed by the very notion.

When she arrived, I asked her how the clones could have done such a thing.

"They failed to meet our genetic standards," she said. "We want only to improve upon ourselves. You're the one who taught us about natural selection."

"This isn't natural!" I said.

She took down the photograph I keep on my bookshelf, the one from '77 of me and Hassan and everyone else on the project so long ago, after the first generation was born.

"Una Vispa taught us that humanity should be enhanced, that we should create a suitable culture," she said. "Well, we've done exactly that. These are our <u>enhancements</u>, this is our <u>culture</u>. What made you think they'd be the same ones you wanted?"

She handed the picture back to me, and I gazed down at it. Tears came to my eyes. So long ago. We looked so happy, so hopeful.

"We will always honor you," she said. "You gave us our start. But we will shape the future in our own way."

They threw the bodies in a pit and set fire to them, as if they were no more than cut logs. They don't care. We can make more, they say. A new batch. The cookies are burned, let's start again. Plenty of eggs, ha ha.

The smell lingers. It won't wash out of the curtains.

I never imagined, with so many of them now, they would end up seeing these lives they've created as disposable.

I'm surprised they tried to explain at all. The horror on our faces meant nothing to them.

*January 29, 2107*

There are just the three of us now, myself, Mei, and Carson.

We found a note tacked to Samuel's door this morning: "Gone rock climbing." We know he won't be back.

I've decided I have to stop them.

The last straw was when a Nyla clone asked me yesterday how many human samples are stored in the Ark. I turned away without answering. I've heard them talking; I know what they want. They don't want to repopulate the earth, which they're perfectly capable of doing now if they wanted. They could create more clones, and with enough variation, they could continue toward sexual reproduction the way we wanted them to. But no. They want to use whatever humanity has left to give. They want to use the genetic material in the Ark to integrate it into their own, twisting and shaping it to their own ends.

It doesn't matter. I don't want them to make more of us. The Original Ten will all be dead soon, and the clones should die with us. I'm going to destroy our genetic samples. They're kept in the lab with the tanks, and I think I can destroy those too. I don't know what they'll do to us when they find out. We're too ravaged by the effects of the Plague for our genetic material to be of any use. They need the stored material, from when we were young.

In any case, without the original samples, they're finished. They've altered their genetic code so much that making more clones from their own corrupt cells will be impossible.

I'm the one that has to do it. I don't care if the clones kill me, and Mei and Carson are too weak. It is my own hell, to know my responsibility in their creation.

Mei says what I want to do is cruel, but I can't understand how she thinks that while the stench of more burning bodies permeates the air out our window. I refuse to let this continue.

I talked to Carson last night. If I don't succeed, he's promised to destroy the Ark if it's the last thing he does. Without the original samples, they might turn to the stored human samples to survive, and I can't let them do that.

After I destroy the samples, I know I should destroy myself. I've been lucky, I'm not as bad off as the others. But because of that, I worry there's a distant possibility that my skin, my hair, something in my cells might allow them to clone more Altheas. Perhaps turning my body to ashes is the sacrifice I must make for everything that's happened. I think back to who I was when this started, how I thought this project was what I was born to do. I think about what I would say to Hassan if he were here. I would tell him that I finally understand what destiny is. I understand that my destiny is my own and, though I had a role in giving life to the clones, I also have a role in ending them.

I can't bring myself to talk to Carson and Mei about how this will all end. They have so little time, and so little left to them, so I say nothing. I know, whatever happens, all of us will be gone soon anyway.

I'll destroy the samples tomorrow, and that should end it. The sooner they're wiped out, the better.

Let the earth start again. Let it be something new.

Eden.

The word is a drop of poison on my tongue.


The remaining pages of the journal were blank. With unsteady hands, Althea turned the last page, where she found a separate note, in different handwriting. It was written by Inga-296.


Althea Lane's death was recorded as the day after her last entry, but the record says she died from the Plague. She didn't, of course. She killed herself. I don't know exactly when Carson and Mei died, but I think it was at the same time as Althea Lane. Perhaps they were killed when the others learned what Althea did, but I prefer to think they died in the Tunnels, trying to help her.

Through my research, I learned that Althea Lane did manage to destroy the original samples. When the clones discovered this, they came looking for her. She hid in the Tunnels, which back then were so vast it would have taken a long time to find her. They trapped her inside, intending to starve her to death, but they didn't know about the explosives the Original Carson had secretly stored.

The caverns collapsed with the detonation. It wasn't an earthquake after all—that was just the story we've been told. Althea Lane died, buried under a mile of rubble. She thought she would destroy the clones' ability to produce more clones, but that was three hundred years ago, and we've successfully reproduced using the copied, previously cloned genes, mostly with no trouble. At least until now. She did succeed in destroying us, it just took three hundred years to come to fruition. Once we began cloning from our own cells, we deteriorated further with each generation. Without fresh genetic samples, we'll continue to deteriorate.

The clones back then made two more generations of Elans before they finally gave up and stopped making the model entirely. It wasn't just the music; it was that they fractured all the time too, and caused conflicts. Maybe they were right to blame the music. I can hear it now, as I write—Jack is in the other room with his guitar—and I've fractured.

The clones back then never could isolate the gene that allowed the Elans to understand music. I can't isolate it in Jack's cells either, and music comes so naturally to him, like an instinct. It's the most human thing I've ever seen. I've looked, I've seen the ribbons of protein and molecules. Music doesn't live there any more than my love for Jack does. They think we're all contained in strings of code, but we're so much more than what can be seen through the lens of a microscope.

I understand now that we're not what the Originals

wanted. We were supposed to start reproducing the way they did, keep humanity alive, but we didn't do that.

I've heard other stories, about people leaving Vispera, leaving the communities. They slip away in the night like the Elans wanted to do. There's a place—the humans called it Merida. It's north, on the old maps in the Tunnels. That's where I'll go.

I see how you look at him, Sam. You love him, and I think perhaps you love me, too. I hope you'll find this, and if you do, I want to say I'm sorry. I can't risk telling you where I'm going. You're not ready to understand what it means to love someone, or to even recognize it, and you don't want to leave Vispera. It's your home; it's where you belong. But it's not my home, not anymore.

It might be a long time from now, but if I make it out, I think there will come a day when you'll want to find me and then we can be together.

Until then, I hope you'll think of me as not just another Inga, but as the person I've become . . .

Your one and only,

Inga-296

Althea clutched the discolored book to her breast, her heart beating wildly. The poem Jack had shown her popped into her mind, the one that called loss an art. *Even losing you,* the poem said. Had Inga-296 thought of Samuel-299 when she read it? Was that why she kept it, because she knew she would lose him?

She loved him, that was clear, even if the letter didn't say it outright.

What Althea had just read, it went against everything she was taught about her purpose, her people's existence. The Original Althea had hated them all. She'd sought to destroy them. Althea felt dizzy as suddenly every belief she'd ever held became a maelstrom of questions and doubt.

Feeling lost, she looked down at the two books in her trembling hands. She smoothed the cover of *The Ark Project*. She had to find Jack. The Ark was not a book, of course. She knew now what Jonah was looking for. She just didn't know what he wanted with it.

The night air had cooled. Althea could still smell the smoldering remnants of the boats. Even if Jack was asleep, or if he was still upset about what had happened between them, this was vastly more important.

She hadn't walked far when she saw him standing in the shadows on the path to the clinic.

"Althea," he said, keeping his distance. He was still mad.

"I'm sorry about what happened earlier," she said.

"It's nothing," he said. "Don't worry about it."

"Okay." She paused, wishing he'd come out from the shadows. "Listen, we have to go to the Tunnels."

"I know," he said. "We should hurry."

Althea narrowed her eyes, peering into the trees. His hair shone silvery in the dark. "Wait," she said. "The Ark. What should we do with it?"

"Destroy it. If it's something Jonah wants, it must be dangerous. We can't let him get his hands on it."

"Shouldn't we find out what he wants it for?"

"Why does it matter? All that matters is that he doesn't get it."

"But what if he *wants* to destroy it? I'll go find Sam. He can tell us what to do. Jack?"

Althea watched his silhouette lean casually against a tree. She heard soft breaths exhaled, a quiet, mocking laugh.

"You're not quite as dumb as the other Altheas I've known," Jonah said dryly.

"Really? How nice," she said. "Where's Jack?"

"He's got some things to work out. I'm helping him, though."

"You can't help him."

"Neither can you, Althea. He just hasn't figured that out yet."

Jonah moved toward her and she backed away, but in a single, unexpected motion, he was out of the shadows and behind her. He trapped her in the rigid strength of his arm, her back forced against his chest.

"Don't be scared," he said, taunting her. He nestled his face into her hair. "Maybe it's a trick. Can you be so sure I'm not Jack?"

"Jack would never do this," she said.

Jonah's hand, hard and fast, closed over her face. A cloth covered her mouth and nose, suffocating her with a bright, chemical smell.

"You think so?" he said in her ear. "You don't really know him like I do."

His arms braced her as she struggled and the world reeled away. She knew that smell, felt its familiar sting in the back of her throat. The trees swayed above her, suddenly lit as if from within and erupting into colors she'd never seen before. The leaves dropped, spun, and then took off into an ocean of sky, a swimming rainbow of nodding, flickering fish.

Somnium, she thought grimly as, against her will, her eyes dropped closed. She clung to the reality of the world around her, what she could feel and hear—Jonah's solid arms effortlessly lifting her, the crunch of his boots on gravel, and her ear against his shoulder. His breathing was even. She thought she was saying words, talking quite sensibly. *Jack won't like this,* she said to him. *I'm sure he'll be upset with you.* She was reasonable and convincing, but then she understood she'd said nothing at all. The brilliant colors of dancing fish continued, impossibly, to swirl behind her eyelids. They shifted and darkened, turning the sky a fiery orange that dwindled finally to dust and ash, and Althea braced herself for the dreams she knew were still to come.

*Chapter Twenty*

# JACK

J ack had looked everywhere for Althea, and he still hadn't found her. He'd even crept into the dorms, only to find her sisters asleep and Althea's bed empty.

He didn't know what had happened to Jonah either. If the Council found him, they'd kill him, and Jack thought they'd probably do the same to him. Jack had come to understand that what Jonah suffered in Copan was worse, much worse, than the isolation and schoolyard cruelty Jack had experienced in Vispera. Jonah wanted Jack to leave Vispera with him, and Jack was beginning to think he might do just that. But first he had to find Althea.

Jack sat on his heels. His feet sank into the mud and he covered his eyes with the cage of his fingers. His head hurt. Something was wrong. What if the Samuels had Althea? What if they were conducting more of their treatments, trying to cure her and keep her from fracturing? Another wave of nausea gripped him at the thought.

He had to keep her safe.

It didn't take long to find Sam. He was at the clinic, with the other doctors and those injured from the boat explosions. He was still useful when they needed so many doctors, even though his brothers were keeping their distance. When Jack saw him alone in the medics' lounge, he was leaning against a wall, his head tilted back, his eyes closed, and Jack was overwhelmed with a sudden surge of anger. At the same time, Sam looked as tired as Jack felt, and thinner than he'd expected. Angry as he was, he ended up yelling across the room so Sam would at least see him coming before Jack shoved him against the wall. Using the plaster of his cast to pin Sam's chest, Jack faced the man who'd raised him, their noses almost touching.

"Where is she?"

"Jack, what are you doing?"

"Where's Althea?"

"How would I know?" Sam said, but he looked away, hiding something.

"You and the other Samuels, you have her drugged somewhere, tied down." Jack thrust away from Sam. The man slumped against the wall, his knees buckling at the sudden release. "You know where she is."

"Jack!" Sam's voice was unexpectedly loud and authoritative, given his wasted appearance. "Stop this!"

"No!" Jack said with equal strength. And then, "Don't tell me you helped them. That you hooked them up to those . . . wires." He felt the strain of exhaustion and stress settling on his rib cage like a weight. His chest rose with quick breaths. Sam studied him.

"Calm down, Jack. You'll have an attack."

"Please, Sam," he said. "Don't tell me it was you."

"Why not? The Bonding is one of my specialties. I've gone

through it myself. It's not that bad, even if it doesn't always work."

Jack stared at Sam, speechless. Sam only shrugged. He motioned for Jack to sit down. Jack shook his head.

"Fine." Sam sank into a brown couch against the wall. "You stand. I need to sit." He rested his elbows on his knees and looked as if he had a headache he was trying to ignore. A clock ticked on the wall above Sam's head. Jack stared at it, struggling to control the violence of his emotions, waiting for Sam to speak. "I'm sorry you saw that, Jack," he said at last. "I'm sorry about the Altheas."

"What was that, Sam?"

"I can see why it would be hard for you to understand. But they volunteered; it's the only way we do it. They wanted to reinforce their bond. It's a legitimate medical procedure."

"It's cruel."

"Our research has suggested—"

"Everyone around me, I hurt them. Inga, you, Althea. Everyone who comes near me, I seem to hurt." Jack put his head in his hands. His voice came out muffled. "What's wrong with me, Sam?"

Sam stared at his folded fingers dangling between his knees. His fingernails were ragged, the skin along the edges broken. "It's not you, Jack. It's us. It's always been us."

"I don't believe you."

"It's true."

Jack shuddered, feeling a wave of dizziness for the second time that night. He blinked away spots that obscured his vision, focused again on the ticking clock.

"Inga had a theory," Sam continued. "She thought that we'd

changed ourselves so much, we'd left something important behind. She thought you were the answer, that raising you to be more human, more compassionate, would help the rest of us. The Council saw you as a possible tenth clone, but she thought it was your humanity that would save us."

"It didn't work."

"That's not true."

"I don't have any compassion, Sam. I'm angry. All the time, at everyone. At you. I'm no better than Jonah. I can't save anyone. I hurt everyone who comes near me, and sometimes I don't even care."

"Maybe we're not capable of being saved."

Jack slowly crossed the room and settled in the chair facing Sam on the couch.

"What's the Ark?"

Sam blinked at the sudden change of topic. "It's an old term for the Sample Room, in the Tunnels."

"That's where my original genetic material came from. What would happen if the Sample Room was destroyed?"

Sam sighed. "The Council thinks we can integrate your genes into ours."

"Why do they want to do that?"

"Because we're dying. Inga-296 wasn't wrong. We've manipulated the codes so much, we've copied them so many times. The problems we face now will only get worse. We don't have the original samples, so the only answer is new variations from freshly cloned humans. Like the variations they think we can get from you."

"From me, and from other human samples in the Sample Room."

"Yes. If it's destroyed, we have no ability to strengthen genes that have weakened over centuries of replication." Sam narrowed his eyes. "Why are you asking me this, Jack?"

"Jonah's looking for the Ark, and I think he wants to destroy it. I told him I didn't care what he did. But now I can't find Althea, and I've looked everywhere. I'm worried. Jonah said he'd show me she was just like the others. What if he has her?"

Sam looked at Jack and rubbed a hand across his mouth. The only sound between them was the relentless tick of the clock.

## Chapter Twenty-One

# ALTHEA

Althea dreamed.

She dreamed about red apples on low-hanging trees falling like jewels on silk dresses that swirled in firelight. She dreamed of music, and the strings of Jack's guitar that plucked notes so rich and warm they drifted like dust into the air before turning all at once into spices, pungent and rosy—cinnamon, anise, coriander, and pepper.

She dreamed about mountains falling into oceans, rivers melting into earth, and jungle vines creeping over every living and dead thing until there was nothing left but a continent of twisted, choking green.

She dreamed about worlds ending.

The riot of colors resolved slowly. After a time, a row of letters became visible, and she found by focusing on one, she could concentrate on dissolving the fog in her head. The letters gradually cleared. She was in the Sample Room, in the Tunnels. The walls of the room were stone, like the rest of the caverns of the Tunnels, but these walls glittered with intersecting glass slides carrying thousands of genetic samples. Human genetic samples.

She was in the Ark. Althea had figured it out back in the dorms, reading the book with the list of names of humans who'd left their genetic material to be stored in the vast caverns of the Tunnels. It hurt her eyes, looking at all the brightness, and then Jack's imposing body blocked her view, except it wasn't Jack. It was Jonah. He crouched above her, peering down. Her arms were sore, and she understood that she'd been fighting in her sleep against a slim wire binding her wrists to a post.

"Here," Jonah said. "Drink." He tipped a cup of water to her lips, and she drank. He pulled it away. "You okay?" he asked.

"Do you care?"

His mouth turned down. "No. You were screaming."

"You gave me Somnium."

"I guess you didn't like it. Some do." He stood, and Althea saw behind him a table covered in wires, plastic, and metal bits. She also saw the book, Althea Lane's journal. She wondered if he'd read it. He went to a chair and picked up one of the devices, twisting wires together. "That's the thing about dreams," he said. "They can also be nightmares."

"Like for the people in Copan?"

"It's not hard to scare someone on Somnium, to put thoughts in their heads. But the clones in Copan, they made their own nightmares. There was something rotten in them, worse than here, even. The Somnium just brought it to the surface."

"They're no different from us."

His hands continued to fiddle with the wires, but his eyes, veiled by pale lashes, glanced up at her. "You don't think so?"

"You think there's something wrong with us, but you're the one hurting people."

"I'm paying them back for what they did to me."

The materials Jonah had on the table were troubling. He was putting together a series of metal boxes linked with wires.

"Is that what you used to start the fire in North Lab? And to blow up the boats?"

Jonah's closed mouth curled. "You have more useful material here than they do in Copan. Is it because this is the first colony, where they grow all the new clones?" He didn't wait for an answer to his questions. "It's easy—I find what I need, I take it. Is Jack good at building things?"

"Not things like that," Althea said. "He doesn't want to kill people."

Jonah nodded, ignoring her tone. "I was taught to kill." He held up his arm scarred by burns. "I wasn't very good in the beginning. I learned."

"Who taught you?" Althea couldn't imagine who would have taught this boy to be so destructive.

"Oh, it wasn't a clone," Jonah said, seeing her thoughts reflected in her face. "No one built me a cottage on a hill, or brought me books and toys." He lifted a piece of glass and peered through it, magnifying one eye. "I never had a Sam."

"So who?"

"Has it always just been Jack?" Jonah asked, talking past her again.

"As far as I know."

Jonah moved to sit cross-legged in front of Althea. "There were ten of us in Copan."

"Ten Jacks?"

Jonah laughed. "Ten people. Humans. All different." His gaze clouded. "I guess that's why Jack cares what happens to you. The clones are all he's had. But we didn't need a Samuel or an Althea. We had each other."

Althea's chest tightened and she twisted against the ties at her wrists. "What happened to them?" she asked, dreading the answer.

"I'm the only one left." He sat up on his heels and leaned his face close to hers. His eyes glittered. "I watched them spend their lives hungry, in pain, in a filthy box that barely let in sunlight—a box that was freezing at night and an oven in the day. I watched them die, one by one. All because you people, you *clones*, were experimenting."

"The . . . clones in Copan killed them?"

"What do you think? I got away. I went back for them, of course, to get them out. I failed. They were counting on me, and I failed."

She searched his face; the tightness around his mouth, the broad forehead screened by colorless hair, the gray eyes bright and vivid. She exhaled slowly when understanding came over her. She watched his face as he became aware, and then he was halfway across the room, as quick as if he'd been bitten by a snake. As suddenly as it appeared, the fire in his eyes reverted to the cool indifference of before, and his face settled into not quite a smile. It was too late, however. In spite of all his cold control, he'd inadvertently shown Althea a part of himself he'd meant to hide. He hadn't expected her to be able to see beyond what he wanted her to. Perhaps, because she knew Jack so well, she herself had changed. On some level, even without communing, she was able to know more of Jonah as well.

"You loved someone," she said finally.

He stood in the center of the room, a fixed smile on his face. "I loved them all," he said evenly. "They were my family."

"But one of them was special to you, right?"

"Uh-uh," he said. "You don't get to ask me that."

He sat back at the table, picking up a screwdriver and the box device. She watched him work for a few moments. The heels of his palms rested on the tabletop as he worked, and still the screws weren't fitting together.

"Your hands," she said.

He put down his tools and pressed his palms to his eyes. "I'm done talking."

"They're shaking."

The chair legs screeched on the floor. He faced the wall of the Sample Room, his back to her. She watched his shoulders rise and fall.

"What do you want?" he said.

"Let me go. You don't need me."

His back still turned, he shook his head. "I do, though. I underestimated Jack's . . . ties here. When this is done, he has to come with me."

"Why? You don't need him."

Jonah said nothing, his back still turned.

"Oh," Althea said, suddenly understanding. "You don't *need* him. You want his company. You want your brother. That's it, isn't it?"

Again he said, his voice forced, "I'm not letting you go."

"Then untie me at least," she said. "I can't stop you or hurt you."

He stepped toward the post and crouched at her side. From

his belt he pulled a knife and cut away the wire holding her, then stepped back cautiously, arms at his sides.

Althea still wasn't sure in what way he meant he needed her. Did he intend for Althea to leave as well, with them, as a way to convince Jack to go? But no, nothing in the way he acted toward her suggested that. He thought it would be easier to convince Jack to leave if she wasn't around anymore. He wanted her dead.

"Stay out of my way," he said flatly.

Without looking at him, she stood. The effects of the Somnium lingered, making the floor waver like the deck of a boat. She wandered carefully to the table and examined the box he'd made. She picked up a heavy metal tube with a black button in the center.

"What are you going to blow up this time?"

"Don't touch that." He snatched the tube from her. "It's dangerous."

"What's it do?"

"Go ahead, press the button." He grinned. "See what happens."

Althea felt cold. "Where's the timer?"

"I used all I had on the boats. Had to come up with something else."

"I don't understand why you want to destroy the Ark. It was built by the humans, people like you."

"Althea-310, I thought you were the clever one. Do you know how long I've been trying to figure out what the hell the Ark actually is? I knew it was here, in Vispera, but I knew only that it was something the clones needed to keep making humans, and by making humans, make more clones. And I figure, what the hell do we need more clones for? Think about it. Countless cells, like this." He pulled from his pocket the glass slide and tossed it on the table in front of her. "These bits of glass, they line the whole room like wallpaper. I didn't know there were so many." Pressing his finger into the slide, he inched it toward her along the table, his face thoughtful. "How do you think they picked who got stored in the Ark? Two by two, from every city, state, country, continent? Was it a lottery? Maybe they were volunteers, and they hoped it would give them some kind of immortality when their world was dying." Jonah pinched the slide from the table and gazed at it against the light, his eyes unfocused as he looked through it. "Maybe they imagined it would save them."

"You sound sentimental," Althea said. The slide, limned in blue against the light, gleamed like ice.

"Really?" He straightened. "I don't mean to. If they did think it would save them, I guess I'm the one who's going to make sure it doesn't."

"But they're human. You could bring them back, start your own community with your own people."

Jonah propped his booted foot on the table and leaned back. "The Great De-Extinction? To build what, a world of people like me? It didn't go so great last time. No, I don't want that."

"Then what?" she said. "You want to start over and reproduce like the humans did . . . sexually?"

Jonah's forehead lined as his eyebrows rose. "That's an idea." Smooth as a cat, he was beside her again, his fingers wrapped in the ends of her hair. She gazed at him, unflinching. His glance darted from her hair to her lips and then her eyes. She remembered his mouth on hers in the banana grove. "It could be interesting," he said, pretending to consider. "Are you my rib, then?

We go forth and replenish? You can do it if you like, I hear. It's the little boys that can't plant the seed, so to speak. Or wait, are you and Jack already sowing that particular field?"

He talked in riddles, but she knew enough to know he was insulting her. She pushed away from his unyielding body.

"No, little snake charmer," he said, dropping the strands of her hair. "The world's hard enough without a bunch of brats running around."

"So tell me what you want."

"What I want is to be left alone. No more humans, no more clones. We've had our hour." He cocked his head then and, without warning, spun away from her. He pressed his ear to the door and waited, listening. Althea strained to hear what he did, but heard nothing.

"Someone's coming?" she said. "Jonah, what are you planning?"

A trace of a smile still playing on his lips, he took hold of Althea's arm. "Sink the ship, drown them all. Easy," he said. "So, Althea." She looked him in the eyes. "It's been three hundred years. Are you ready to fulfill your destiny?"

Which was when she knew he had read the journal, and she knew how he meant for this to end.

*Chapter Twenty-Two*

# JACK

The mouth of the cave that led to the Tunnels dangled with vines. The ceiling yawned high above, alive with chirping bats. Jack and Sam approached a metal door that slid open with a smooth hydraulic inhalation when Sam pressed his hand to a glass panel. They walked down the narrow stone hallway beyond. The silence that descended within the rock walls made Jack aware of the noises that had surrounded them outside: the swaying trees, nattering insects, and howling monkeys. It was quiet within the confines of the cavern, with only the echo of their footsteps and their rustling breath that fogged in the cold air.

The main cavern was immense. The beehive ceiling arched above, and row upon row of shelves lined the open space. Jack had never been in the Tunnels, he'd seen only what Inga or Sam brought back to him. Shelf after shelf was cluttered with a haphazard array of photographs and paintings, sculptures, pottery, porcelain, and figurines. Incalculable numbers of books and crates of discs sat on shelves that soared up to the ceiling, the farthest ones accessible only from metal walkways and a rolling ladder. Behind it all, the veined granite walls of the cave, treated with a polymer for climate control, glowed with milky light.

The Tunnels contained all that was left of human effort and knowledge, and included cultural objects and relics that went back to the beginning of recorded time. Here was all the poetry and stories, statues and drawings, and the texts on language, science, history, and philosophy. It felt strange to be surrounded by such things. Even if Vispera cared little for them, these were human creations, relics of a time that would have found Jack entirely familiar.

Jack peered around the cave, but could see nothing beyond the constrained rings of light under the faint bulbs ensconced in the stone walls.

"Jack," Sam said, his voice hushed in the dim space, "if Jonah's here, what do you intend to do about it? We should tell the Council Althea's missing. They would help."

"No," Jack said. "Jonah won't end up dead because of me. All I want is Althea back. That's all."

"You can't be sure she's here, or even know what you're getting into."

Jack stopped walking. "Everyone keeps saying Jonah and I are the same. They think everything he does, I'm capable of too. And maybe I am. But it also means I know what he's *not* capable of. He won't hurt her."

"He killed one of the Gen-300 Altheas in the boat explosion just tonight. What makes you think Althea-310 is any different to him?"

Jack looked at his feet. "I know he doesn't care about her. But he won't hurt me, not like that."

"You believe that?"

"We're brothers, and that means something to him. He won't hurt me by hurting her."

Jack sounded more confident than he felt. He didn't think Jonah would hurt him, but Jonah hated the clones. And even if Jack was somehow right and Althea's life wasn't in danger, Jack didn't know if he could say the same for Sam.

They continued on to the far side of the cave, where a clear wall separated a section of the Tunnels that held the Sample Room, or the Ark, as Jonah and the Originals called it. The room was pitch-black inside. The shelves in front of the door were cluttered with more sculptures and figurines piled on top of each other. If the humans had a system of organizing the relics, Jack couldn't figure it out.

A clattering came from behind a painting of a horse.

"Did you hear that?" Sam said.

Jack listened. The cavern didn't feel empty anymore. He felt eyes watching, but couldn't tell from where.

The air in the Tunnels tasted stale and metallic, but Jack caught a scent underneath of earth and tamped fire. Facing Sam, Jack could see at his back rows of framed pictures jutting from the walls. The faint light repeated against the glass throughout the length of the dome, creating a mottled pattern on the floor. The pattern danced, then broke into a long shadow that emerged from behind a row of pictures.

"I know you don't want to hurt her," Jack said, his voice carrying loudly through the cavern.

He waited, hearing only Sam's soft breaths.

Jonah spoke from the darkness. "Sometimes we do things we don't want to," he said. "You know that, Jack."

Jack still couldn't see him, but then a form slipped from between the pictures and, catlike, Jonah climbed the balustrade to the stacks above them. Jack strained to see through the blanket of gloom. A light flickered on, illuminating Jonah's face in yellow. Jack didn't see Althea. Jonah crouched on the low metal walkway. He wore a black jacket and a black cap, hiding his pale hair in the darkness. He pushed a rolling ladder to the side.

"Where's Althea?" Jack said.

"There are nine more in the dorms. Why not get one of those instead?" His face twisted into a wry smile. "Oh, wait. They don't like you much, do they?"

Jack said nothing. Sam stood next to him, his gaze traveling back and forth between the brothers. Sam had never seen Jonah before, Jack realized.

"What do you figure it means, by the way, that her sisters hate you so much? She's the same person as them in every way that matters. But she likes you, and they don't. How's that work?"

"Tell me where she is, and we'll leave," Jack said. "I don't really care what you do with the Sample Room."

Jonah ignored him. "On the other hand, I don't think she likes me very much, and I'm just another version of you. Go figure. This might not bode well for your relationship."

"I didn't come here to talk."

"Fine." Jonah shrugged. "The lights work in the Ark. Turn them on."

Sam approached the glass scanner and placed his palm on the surface. The room beyond hummed to life, and fluorescent brightness filled the Ark, seeping out through the clear walls into the main cave, which was still lit only by faint bulbs. The stark whiteness of the Ark was blinding at first. Jack squinted, making out the tiered samples lining the walls. Then, in the center of the room, trapped behind the glass and standing with her hands at her sides, Althea.

Jack pushed past Sam. "Open the door!" he said, unsure who he was talking to.

"Jack!" Althea's voice was muted by the Ark's glass wall. "He disabled the door panel. It won't open."

Jack pressed his palm against the glass panel. The door didn't move. He slammed his hand into the wall.

Althea placed her own hand next to Jack's, against the thin barrier separating them. Her eyes met his, trying to tell him something. She was wearing what looked like the belts the male clones wore during a Pairing Ceremony. They crisscrossed her shoulders and wrapped her middle in inelegant twists. Looped through the belt, from her shoulder to her waist, was a string of white boxes connected by wires. In the center of each, a red blinking light. Explosives. Jack saw then the device she held in one hand. It was shiny and black, a sort of tube. Her thumb, white with pressure, was on a black button at the end, holding it down.

"Is that a trigger?" Jack said, feeling cold.

"If I let go of the button . . ." she said, her voice fading. "Jonah wants to destroy the Ark."

"But," Jack said, "you're in the Ark." Her eyes were clear, her gaze steady. Her lips, serious and flat, cut a thin, determined line on her face. Jack shook his head. "No," he said. "We'll get you out, we'll figure it out. It's a trick. He won't let you die."

"He will, Jack."

Hot rage smoldered in Jack's stomach.

"It'll be okay." Her mouth tilted up in a pallid smile. "There are other Altheas."

His breath caught in his throat. "No," he said.

He turned from her to where Jonah sat watching them, his eyes narrow, contemplating Jack as if he were piecing together a puzzle.

"You won't," Jack said. "You're just trying to prove something to me. This isn't the way to do it."

"The clones are going to kill her anyway, in one of their ceremonies. You've seen the Bonding, seen what they're capable of. It made you sick. They caused all this, not me."

"I won't go anywhere with you if you kill her."

"That button's already pressed. It'll go off when she lets go, and she has to let go sometime. She's already dead. Just like the clones are already dead. You know they are. They can't change, and they can't survive. It's too late for them."

"If that's true, then just leave! What you're doing is crazy."

"Can you stand by and watch them make more humans like us, humans they'll kill after they've stolen what they want from their genes? If the Ark is what they need to survive, I'm taking it from them."

"I've been protecting you, Jonah, but if she dies, I swear I'll kill you myself."

"Maybe." Jonah uncurled and leaned his arms on the balustrade. "But I don't think you have it in you."

"You don't know what's in me."

"You're just like me . . . if I'd been made weak by the clones."

"I don't want to hurt anyone. That's weakness to you?"

Sounding almost casual, Jonah said, "I'm sorry about this, Jack, but you'll see I'm right. You want to say goodbye or anything?"

Jack's mind felt frozen.

"Jack," Sam said. He spoke quietly. "I can fix the door."

Jonah cocked his head, listening. "And what happens when you get inside, Sam? The bomb's going off no matter what you do. Better one Althea than all of us. She said it herself—there are always more Altheas."

Jack began to think Jonah would talk until Althea's fingers gave out if he let him. He was controlling the situation, and as much as Jack didn't want to believe it, Jonah was his enemy now. Even if he did have a reason to hate the clones, Jack had to stop him. He turned to Sam.

"Hurry," he said.

Sam pried open the panel that controlled the lock and examined the wires inside. Althea's brown eyes watched from behind the glass. He scrambled to connect wires, then cried out triumphantly as the door to the Ark swung open. Jack slammed it wider and held out his hand to Althea.

"Come on," he said. "Sam will disconnect the trigger."

"Jack, I don't think so."

"What?"

"It could go off, and then we all die."

Jack desperately wanted to grab her, do whatever it took to make her safe, but as long as she held the trigger, it was too dangerous.

"Give the trigger and belt to me. I'll hold it until you get outside."

"And then you'd die instead of me. No, Jack."

Jack raked a hand through his hair. A stubborn line had appeared between her eyes, and he knew he wouldn't convince her. Jonah slid down the ladder.

"I never saw a clone do anything for a human before," Jonah said.

"You think they're all the same, but they're not. Some of them are different."

"You know what the Altheas in Copan did while we were being tortured and tested on?"

Jack shook his head, unprepared for the question.

"They took notes." Jonah strode forward, and Jack's stomach sank when he slammed the door to the Ark shut again. "So you see, I don't really care if they can change. You think you need her, Jack, but you don't. We'll destroy the Ark, and then we can leave, together."

"I'm not going anywhere with you."

"It's her!" Jonah said, his voice for the first time losing its cool composure. He pointed to Althea through the glass. "She's the only reason you're saying this. You've never seen what monsters they are. We're brothers, Jack. Don't choose her over your own blood."

"If she dies," Jack said, "we're not brothers anymore."

"Whatever you do here won't matter," Jonah said. "The Ark will still be destroyed, and Althea too."

"Then I'll make sure we all are."

The cool eyes appraised Jack. "I don't want to hurt you, Jack." He took off his jacket and flung it to the floor. "But I will if I have to."

Then Jack and Jonah, in twin explosions of movement, came together, each meeting the other halfway.

*Chapter Twenty-Three*

# ALTHEA

S amuel had unlocked the door. Althea was no longer trapped, but the explosives and the trigger were attached to her. If she left the Sample Room, she'd only put everyone else at risk along with her.

Jonah said her sisters had done the Bonding, that Jack had actually seen it, but she'd felt nothing. A few weeks ago, if Althea-318 had a headache, Althea's head throbbed. If Althea-311 sneezed, her own nose tickled.

Fracturing felt nothing like she'd expected. She'd thought it'd be something terrible, sudden as a falling ax, but this had been gradual, and she didn't feel much different in the end. As she examined this new feeling, she discovered she wasn't sorry about it. She was maybe scared of what was to come, but the world looked new. It seemed clearer somehow, the colors brighter.

In that brightness, the two boys fought.

They met with no weapons, body to body, fist to fist. They reminded Althea of the dogs in the book she'd read that night in Jack's cell, all blind rage and violence.

They both fought well. It was clear the two boys were brothers, and not just because they were mirror images of each other. They were equal in all things—height, strength, cunning, and speed. The outcome would be determined by things less obvious, it seemed to Althea.

Jack struck Jonah, and Jonah spit blood. The splotch of pink with a darker red swirling in the center hit the clear wall and dripped down. It would have hit her foot without the wall to catch it. It dribbled to the floor, thick and slow.

It was human blood. Every ounce of their blood was human. It must be, if they could feel love for each other, as she knew they did, and yet hurt each other this way. As much as Jonah tried to hide it, he couldn't hide from Althea that he needed Jack as much as Jack needed him. Yet still they fought.

Althea carefully switched the trigger to her other hand, being sure to keep the black button continuously pressed down. Once it was secure, she stretched out her freed fingers, her thumb aching with how hard she'd been pressing.

Althea gasped as Jonah slammed Jack into the wall, making it shudder. Jack grabbed him and spun them both, so now Jonah struggled between Jack's fist and the barrier separating Althea from them. Jack stumbled and went down, grimacing when his broken arm hit the floor.

Jonah was reckless, and too often left himself exposed. Even now he stood with his shoulders wide, his shirt torn, leaving Jack a clear opening. Althea was sure Jack saw it too, but then Jack backed away, the opportunity gone.

That's when she knew Jack couldn't win. Because what did Jack have that Jonah didn't? He had the Inga—that was the difference. The Inga's letter had brimmed over with love for Jack. She'd died protecting him. From her, Jack had learned kindness and mercy.

And he had Samuel as well, who could only stand by helplessly, just like her, as the two boys did what they each thought they had to do.

There was something else Jack had, of course. He had her.

She could end this.

The device was strangely cool and heavy in her hand. She'd never held such a thing. It should be more menacing, this object that could end all their lives. The door had clicked shut, though, and the walls were strong. Surely they would contain the blast. It would be quick. One bright, fiery light, and it would be over. There'd be a Binding Ceremony for her, one they would have had anyway now that she was fractured, and her sisters would reach for one another's touch and sigh regretfully about the next Pairing Ceremony's uneven numbers.

The black tube blurred in her cold fingers. Less than a minute had passed, but it felt like forever, like time stretched before her slipping away, time she would have taken to discover who she was, this new, fractured person who read poetry and heard music and felt a burning in her chest that belonged only to her, this *Althea*.

She closed her eyes, and the world became distant and muffled, drained of all sound except the sound of Jack's music in her mind. The sound became more beautiful for the pain of knowing she would miss the next time Jack played and caught her watching him, that crooked smile curling his lips, his fingers thrumming to the beat of her too-fast heart.

No, she couldn't think about that. It made it too hard. It would be easy to just let go. What had the poem said, over and over, about losing everything?

It isn't hard.

It isn't hard.

*It isn't too hard . . .*

A hand closed over hers. Her eyes still shut, she took one breath, and then another, before looking up. Samuel-299 gave a minute shake of his head. His hand drew hers away from the tube, her shaking finger from the depressed black button as his own held it down, and then the device was his.

The fight continued, but the door to the Sample Room swung wide. Plaster and porcelain from broken statues littered the floor. Samuel held the trigger and looked out the glass wall of the Ark. His gaze went to the two boys. Sweat and blood dripped down their faces. Jonah had a wooden spear from a display of art on the wall. He used it as a club, but Jack blocked it with the cast on his arm until he finally grabbed it and snapped it in half. They struggled, rolled, and then came to a stop, each with a jagged spike at the other's throat. If either of them wanted, the other could be dead in an instant. Their chests heaved, and their faces, pale and precisely boned, tightened with determination. Neither boy moved.

"Don't," Jack said.

"Why not?" Jonah said, the words forced through clenched teeth. "You think it matters that a *clone* cares about you? That means nothing. You know nothing. You're so weak, so stupid. God, I can't believe how stupid you are, caring about them, wanting them to care about you. You don't need her, or the Samuel.

I didn't need them! I didn't have them, and I was fine!" Jonah shook Jack. He was so angry, but Althea couldn't tell anymore at who or what. "I was fine!" he said again, his voice breaking.

Althea had had enough. Mindful of the thin wire connecting the explosives to the trigger Samuel held, Althea unbuckled the belt and freed herself. She ran from the Ark, straight for Jack and Jonah, throwing herself between them. Their fists still clutched the makeshift daggers as she pried them apart.

"Stop this!" she cried, feeling the unrelenting press of their bodies as they strained toward each other. The tendons of Jonah's neck corded against his skin.

It was Jack who relented first, and when she felt him give way, she pushed as hard as she could. His startled eyes broke from Jonah and, as if emerging from a dream, he took in Althea, out of the Ark and no longer holding the trigger.

Jonah followed Jack's gaze to Sam. He pushed Althea away from him.

"What are you doing?" Jonah said to Samuel.

Echoing Jonah's confusion, Jack said, "Sam?"

Samuel stood in the open doorway of the Ark. "Get out of here, out of the main cavern if you can."

Jack stared blankly. "What?"

Samuel offered a bleak smile. "I'll close the door, but I don't know if it'll hold."

Althea saw the moment realization hit Jack. He looked down sharply, veiling the riot of emotions that distorted his features.

"There's no time left," Samuel said. "It's morning. The brothers and sisters are awake. The Council will know where we are."

"You don't have to do this," Jack said angrily.

"I know the path we're on," Sam said. "Jonah wants to destroy the Ark for revenge, but I have my own reasons. I understand now that it's the only thing that can save us." He looked at Jonah. "I know what they did to you in Copan. I won't let that happen again, to anyone."

Jonah stepped away, blinking in confusion.

"No," Jack said.

"It shouldn't have come to this," Sam said. "I should have done more. But you have to leave Vispera, Jack. Make your own life. Take Althea and go. Promise me, Jack."

Jack could only shake his head. Samuel came forward and, careful of the explosives, took Jack in a tight embrace.

"No, Sam," Jack said, his voice muffled. "I won't let you."

Samuel looked at Althea from across Jack's shoulder. It was a brief glance, but in that glance, they communed.

She felt from Samuel a prism of emotion; intricate, difficult, but strong enough to take her breath away. Even with both of them fractured, as they surely were now, it filled every limb of her body like bright multicolored light, as if he'd been holding on to this one last connection they shared, letting it build until he could use it for his own purpose before losing it forever.

Communing with Samuel was stronger than anything she'd felt from communing before, even with her sisters. She didn't just feel his emotions, she saw the world through his eyes, and she saw into his mind. In the darkness of the cave she saw all three of them, Jonah, Jack, and herself. They looked so young, and she understood that that's how Samuel saw them, as so terribly young. Then she saw beyond what was in front of Samuel's eyes, to the brothers and sisters now rushing to the Tunnels, knowing something was wrong, to the community of Vispera with an expanse of cloudless blue sky behind it, and farther than that, she saw three centuries of *Homo factus* reaching back through time. Samuel saw their history differently than she ever had. He imagined them in a boat drifting with a current, leaving a long, dark chevron behind them in the water, and in front, a still, glassy surface the boat hadn't yet touched, reflecting like a dark mirror the future ahead.

Althea gasped at what he saw there—not just what he saw, but what he *knew*. If he didn't act now, Vispera and everyone in it would die. Perhaps it was too late already. Samuel showed her the dwindling future generations struggling desperately to survive, crawling and clawing their way over countless twisted, suffering bodies. Bodies they'd made from the glass slides in the Ark. It wasn't just the cruelty to the humans that Samuel feared, it was the damage they did to themselves in enacting such cruelty. The same damage Samuel felt inside himself now.

The image shifted then to Jack. He was an infant smiling in a cradle, and then a child running through tall grass into the Inga's arms. Jack's and Inga's images separated, connected, released and caught like woven fibers of two colors joining into a single vivid picture. Althea felt Samuel's despair, his love, and his all-embracing need to fulfill a promise he'd made a long time ago.

She let the feelings and colors recede, and nodded silently to the question in his eyes.

Although it seemed longer to Althea, it had all taken only a moment, and Jack had sensed nothing of what passed between them.

Samuel pulled away and brushed back the hair on Jack's brow. Jack looked lost.

"Jack," Althea said. "Come with me."

Jack swallowed. "Don't, Althea."

Althea considered him—the filthy shirt, the pallid face framed by sweat-stained hair and blood, the overly bright eyes pleading with her. Even understanding what Samuel needed from her, she hated what it would do to Jack.

"Come with me," she said quietly.

He blanched, aware of what she was doing.

"They're here," Samuel said. "They're outside the door. I can feel them there."

Jack seemed in a trance, like he'd gone numb. Althea pushed him forward, getting him to move through the cavern and toward the entrance. He looked back at Samuel as he left.

Jonah's gaze too was strangely empty.

"This is what you wanted, the Ark gone," she said, letting her anger at Jonah fuel the strength it took to penetrate his vacant stare. "Did you want to stay and watch?"

Jonah flinched from her as if he didn't recognize her. Althea shoved him in the direction Jack had gone.

Samuel was in the doorway, the samples in their numberless glass slides shining behind him. The black tube was clutched in his hand, which was strong and steady. Althea placed her own hand over his, just as he had done earlier to her.

"You're sure this is the right thing?" she said.

"In the end, how can we be sure of anything? I know only that he's my son."

Samuel spoke the word clearly: *son*. Althea thought about Althea Lane, about the families that had built Vispera, the sons and daughters, mothers and fathers. Whatever *son* really meant, to Samuel it was painful, dazzling, and the only thing that mattered.

"Keep them back," Samuel said. "I don't want anyone to get hurt, but if I don't do this now, nothing will ever change."

Althea squeezed his hand one last time, then turned from him and raced to catch up with Jack and Jonah. The two boys in front of her were swallowed by the crowd that had come through the door. Samuel-297 was ahead of them all, and he stopped and clutched Althea's shoulders. His fingers dug into her skin.

"What's he doing?" he said. Her teeth rattled as he shook her.

Althea glanced back, and Samuel-297 followed her gaze. The light was still on in the Ark. Samuel was silhouetted in black against it, his lab coat a stark, square outline.

Samuel-297 yanked her back to face him. "We've felt nothing from him for two days, and then just now . . . What was that? What does he think he's doing?"

"You know what he's doing," she said to Samuel-297. "And you don't want to be here when he does it."

Samuel-297's features contorted in disbelief. He'd seen and felt what Althea had when Samuel communed, but processing it was too much. He wasn't going to budge, and the others were coming quickly behind.

She looked back. Maybe the door would hold some of the explosion back. She'd stalled Samuel-297 at least, and she supposed it was best she could do. She couldn't wait anymore. Flinging herself on the Samuel's arms, she dragged him down behind a huge steel cabinet that jutted from the wall. He didn't resist, because he knew as well as she did what was about to happen. Crouched as low as she could get, she covered her head. There was a rush of muffled noise as her hands closed over her ears, and her fast-beating pulse pounded in her head.

A million things could go wrong. The door to the Ark could

crumple like paper. The wall separating the Ark from the cave could collapse. The entire cave could come down on top of them, killing them and destroying everything inside, leaving them buried like Althea Lane years ago.

Althea counted her breaths as she used to do with her sisters when they counted the seconds before the thunder. There was no thunder, however.

There was silence, and more silence.

And then an explosion.

She perhaps fainted, but she wasn't sure. The cavern was oddly quiet, then sounds filtered in and Althea realized that pandemonium had erupted around her. Her ears were ringing, and the crash of rubble and the screams of those around her were muted as if coming from a great distance. She'd been knocked back and lay looking up at the cavern ceiling in a daze, feeling as if her bones had been shaken inside her. She sat up carefully to see the others, farther away from the blast but still stunned, their arms protecting their heads as if they were taking cover in an earthquake. Samuel-297 lay next to her, stirring confusedly, mumbling something she couldn't hear. Before she could do more to gather herself, Jack was at her side.

"Are you okay?"

She nodded, still dazed. Though he was right in front of her, his voice sounded like it came from far away. The Ark was hidden in layers of flame, smoke, and debris. Althea couldn't see the door, but it was apparent the explosion had not been contained. She reached for Jack, but he was staring at Samuel-297.

Jack bent over the man and shook him. He moaned.

"Is he dead?" Jack demanded. "Come on! Aren't you supposed to know?"

"Stop!" Althea said. "You're hurting him."

Jack, getting nothing from Samuel-297, stormed in the direction of the blast. Althea pulled herself to her feet and caught up to him, grabbing his arm.

"What are you doing?"

"What if he survived?" he said, his eyes frenzied. "What if he needs help?"

"Jack, he's gone."

Just as she spoke, a tower of bookshelves fell before her with a crash. Volumes landed flaming to the ground, crackling and releasing snowy ash into the air. One landed at her feet and the pages contracted, wrinkling the words into a knot of flame.

Residue of the explosion—burnt cloth, particles of canvas, scraps of paper—showered them from above like rain. It floated and drifted lazily about their heads, bits of it glowing inside with smoldering ash. The ceiling heaved.

"Jack," Althea said. "The cave."

Jack looked up, bewildered, as if he'd forgotten they were inside the earth and it was preparing to swallow them whole. He looked back down at her, his eyes glancing to her forehead. "You're hurt," he said.

She reached up and felt blood.

"Jack, Samuel's dead." Her voice echoed in her ears. A piece of the cavern wall crumbled to the floor. Samuel-297 must have come to at some point, because she didn't see him anymore. "We have to get out."

Jack nodded curtly. He took her arm, and they hurried toward the entrance of the cave. The sounds of fire, shattering porcelain, and screeching metal emanated from within the murky fumes. The blast in the Ark had shaken the whole cave, and the initial damage was causing more, like the fall of titanic dominoes. Statues skittered along the floor, knocked over by a slab of buckling concrete. Hunks of rock fell like hail, breaking away from the wall and ceiling. A haze of dust and ash obscured her vision, and a thin, gritty powder sifted into her hair and eyes.

Althea looked back. The section of the cave from where they'd come had disappeared, lost in a collapse of ceiling, and the remaining cave felt like it was sagging, like it'd held on for too many centuries and now it had let go into crumbling fissures spreading throughout the floor and walls. The seams patterned the ground in twisting ribbons.

They stumbled from the cave and gasped in clean air while towering plumes of dust rose from the door to the Tunnels. Carson-312 stood nearby with the older generation of Altheas and Viktors. Althea searched the crowd for Jonah, but saw no sign of him.

Low thunder rumbled beneath their feet, and people screamed at the ground tumbling into itself. Althea staggered as Jack's grip tightened on her arm, and she became aware that he was using her to hold himself up. When he folded, she went down with him. His forehead pressed to his knees. Under the open sky, beneath a blazing sun shadowed by sooty smoke, Althea wrapped her arms around Jack's shoulders and rested her cheek on his smooth, dusty hair. She waited for the shudder of earth and bone to slow, finally, and cease.

*Chapter Twenty-Four*

# JACK

Go, Sam had said.

He'd said it again as he held Jack in the Tunnels, an insistent whisper in his ear before Jack had left him to die. It was the voice Jack had known since he was child, a voice he heard while racing through trees into the jungle, trying to get away from the world Sam had made for him. A voice that read to him from textbooks and medical journals in unsure and halting efforts to be a father. It was a voice that, even when he'd failed to listen, he could never ignore.

Jack remembered how he used to think Sam was somehow taller than the other Samuels. It wasn't true, of course, but Jack had felt the truth of it. Sam had always seemed large and imposing, and also safe. With his arms around Jack in the cave, Sam's head had barely reached Jack's shoulder, and the boy had felt Sam's thin bones and narrow rib cage against his own.

Sam held him and whispered in his ear, *Go,* and followed that with another word, a word that flooded into Jack's chest and sucked out all the oxygen.

*Son,* he'd said.

*Son.*

It was early evening. It'd been two days since the destruction of the Ark, two days since Sam was lost in a smoldering pile of rubble and ash. Two days since Jonah had disappeared, slipping away unnoticed by everyone in the ensuing chaos. Jack had found himself outside, a cool breeze on his face and Althea's watchful eyes on him while the Tunnels caved in behind them, and he'd understood that two of the people he cared about most, regardless of what they'd done before, were gone. One he'd probably never see again, the other dead. He'd collapsed then, as completely as the walls of the Tunnels.

Now he was in a windowless room in the clinic, not a patient but a prisoner. He didn't know where Althea was, didn't know what was happening out in Vispera, and he'd exhausted any possibility of escape. When a clone came to bring food, five Viktors followed after, guarding the exit. None of them answered his questions or even spoke to him. The room was sealed tight, the lock unbreakable. He eventually broke down and slammed his fist into the door, which of course only resulted in bruised knuckles.

Jack crouched on his heels in the sterile room, all his energy focused on keeping still. He felt antsy, wanting to fidget and pace the floor. The clinic reminded him of the labs—cold and bleached, with speckled laminate floors and bright lights. But here he had no book to read or instrument to play. Once the futility of trying to escape was clear, there was no distraction but the frustration and worry gnawing at him. Images of the Binding Ceremony where they'd killed his mother flashed constantly through his mind, his mother's screams replaced by Althea's.

The door to the room opened, and a Samuel came in pushing

a metal cart. He peered at Jack with a mixture of confusion and suspicion. It was the Samuel from the Tunnels, Samuel-297. A bandage on his forehead covered the wound he'd suffered in the explosion. Jack watched for the Viktors to enter as well, but they didn't appear. It was just the Samuel. Jack remained still, but inside he was alert and calculating.

The doctor continued to eye Jack as he readied a needle.

"What's that for?" Jack asked.

The man's fingers fumbled with the syringe. The skin around his nails was torn and raw.

"I'm taking a blood sample."

"The hell you are."

The Samuel didn't pause in his task. "Take a seat." He indicated a chair next to the bed. When Jack didn't move, he said, "If you'd rather, I can bring the Viktors in. They'd be happy to hold you down."

Jack glared at the man, but moved from the floor to the chair and held out his arm. He needed to find Althea, and this was the best opportunity he'd gotten to fight his way out. He couldn't afford to have the Viktors showing up.

The needle punctured his skin, and the Samuel attached a tube to the syringe. Jack watched his blood stream into it.

"Samuel-299 said we needed new DNA to fill in the weaknesses of ours. With the Sample Room gone, yours is all we have now."

The vial filled. The Samuel plugged the cap and attached another tube.

"Tell me where Althea is," Jack said.

The man frowned uncertainly.

"Althea-310," Jack clarified.

"Ah. I don't know. Gone, I think."

Jack grasped the Samuel's lab coat, and the needle twisted sickeningly in his arm as he wrenched the man toward him.

"What do you mean, *gone?*"

"Calm down, Jack," the man said. "You'll have an attack."

Jack dropped his hold on the coat. He slumped back in the chair, feeling as if he'd been punched in the gut. It wasn't only that the man's voice was familiar, or even the words, which Jack must have heard a thousand times before. There was something in the man's expression, too. Jack shook his head. It didn't mean anything. He was just missing Sam.

"I suggest you hold still now." Samuel-297 detached the second full vial and connected a third.

Jack could barely shape the words. "Was there a Binding Ceremony? For Althea-310?"

"There have been a lot of Binding Ceremonies in the past couple days."

"If anyone hurt her—"

"We're almost done here," Samuel said brusquely. "You'll know more soon enough."

"Why? What do you mean?"

The man glanced up, considering Jack. "You must know the Council can't let you leave."

"So what, they'll lock me in a cage? Like Jonah in Copan?"

"Probably."

"It's not what Sam wanted."

Samuel-297 capped the last tube and meticulously collected all three from the metal tray. "Samuel-299 wanted to die, and in the process, he released chaos on us. That's what this is, you realize. Chaos. The Council is split; brothers and sisters are divided. There've been more fractures in the past two days than in the past ten years. We're falling apart."

"I won't let them keep me. They can try, but I'll escape."

"I know," the man said.

He slid the tubes of blood into the pocket of his lab coat. They clinked together, the noise muffled by the fabric of the coat. His gaze rested for a long moment on Jack before he turned his back and wordlessly left, leaving the door behind him unlocked and swinging wide on its hinges.

It took only a second for Jack to get over his shock at the Samuel letting him go. He cautiously entered the hallway and edged down its length, still prepared to fight his way out, but every clone he saw was a Samuel, and they all turned their backs when they sighted him, suddenly focused on whatever task they had in hand.

He'd barely taken a breath of fresh air outside when a hand slipped into his and pulled him into a cluster of bushes. Thinking it was Althea, a tight coil inside him released.

"You—"

A finger pressed to his lips, and a Gen-310 Nyla's deep brown eyes held his.

"Hush," she said.

"Nyla," Jack whispered, "where's Althea? Is she okay?"

"We have to hurry," she said, exasperated. "Keep up."

Nyla peered through the branches. There was no one on the lawn in front of the clinic, and Remembrance Hall was dark. The sun was all the way down, but the last rays lingered over the spire of the building and the stained glass glowed in the fading light. Nyla's fingers were still twined with his, and crouching low, they ran across the stretch of grass. Remembrance Hall was to their right, but they went straight on until they were covered in the broad branches of the banana grove. They paused behind an enclosure of trees a few yards off the path.

"If we stay away from open spaces we should be okay. The Viktors don't know we left yet, but there are still patrols out searching for Jonah."

"Nyla, please," Jack said, pulling his hand from hers. "I'm not leaving without Althea."

Nyla rolled her eyes. "I'm taking you to her, okay? It's too risky for her to come back over the wall. The Binding is tomorrow morning. That's why we have to leave now."

"We?"

"What, you don't want me to come?"

The bark and leaves crunched under their feet.

"Nyla, I—"

"Nyla-313," she corrected.

Jack stammered. "Okay. It's not . . . I mean, if you want . . ." He stopped, realizing she was laughing at him. He sighed. "You can do what you want."

"I know."

A sound came from behind a fallen log up ahead, and they paused, still hidden by the evening light and the darkness of the grove. Moonlight mottled the path in lacy patterns.

"It's nothing," Jack said. "An animal. Let's go."

"Wait." Nyla took his hand again, stilling his movement forward.

The sounds of the jungle surrounded them—chirping frogs,

monkeys, the electric hum of a million insects. Jack didn't pull away again, but looked down at their fingers wrapped together. She followed his gaze and then let go.

"You're very strange," she said.

"Okay."

He and Nyla climbed the wall. From the top, Jack looked back at the town. It was mostly covered in darkness, though lights still twinkled throughout the leaves of the kapok tree in the Commons, and a few windows in the far-off dorms were lit. He thought perhaps this was the last time he'd be within the walls of Vispera and the last time he'd see the town spread before him or Blue River coursing past the iron gate.

He heard Althea call his name before he saw her. They'd walked only a few more minutes to reach the cottage when Althea was in his arms, her feet lifted of the ground, her face pressed into his neck. For the first time since he'd escaped the clinic, he exhaled a long, slow breath.

Althea leaned away and held his face in her hands, inspecting him, making sure he'd made it out of the clinic with no new injuries. When she was satisfied, she rose onto her toes, her hands flat against his chest. She leaned close, and they kissed. He smiled against her lips, drifting into her nearness.

Nyla cleared her throat. Jack pulled away, but Althea stopped him from getting too far.

"Let's go, Althea," Nyla said. "We don't have much time before they figure out what's happening."

"I know," Althea answered. "We'll be right there."

Nyla nodded to Jack with a grin.

Jack gave a short nod in reply. Once the Nyla had disappeared into the trees, he turned to Althea.

"I was afraid the Samuels wouldn't go through with it," she said.

"Why did they? The Samuels have never liked me."

Althea led him into the trees, following Nyla. She talked while the last glimpse of the white cottage was covered by dense jungle.

"Samuel-299 communed in the Tunnels. Somehow he did it with everyone at once, but his brothers felt it most strongly. I've never experienced anything like it. So they know how he felt about you." Althea stopped, and her eyes met his. He wanted to look down but couldn't. "Jack, Sam loved you."

"I know," Jack said. And he did know, even if he hadn't always believed it.

Althea watched him from the corner of her eye. She watched him in that way she had, like she was trying and failing to read his mind. She missed communing, and he would never be able to give that to her. Once they left Vispera, they'd be gone forever. Would he be enough for her?

"What happens when we leave, Althea? It won't be easy."

"It'll be okay," Althea said, squeezing his hand. "We won't be alone."

They'd come upon a clearing. In the middle of it were a couple of wagons filled with supplies, and four mules to pull them. A group of clones clustered together nearby. They all looked up as Althea and Jack arrived. Jack took them in, too stunned to grasp what it meant.

"They're coming with us too? How did this happen?"

"I told you, Samuel communed with everyone. When he said you should go, leave Vispera, he wasn't just saying it to you." She gestured to the small group. "They're the ones who listened."

. . .

They walked through the night, getting as much distance between themselves and Vispera as possible. The clones in town would be confused and disorganized for a little while yet, but once they realized that Jack and so many others were gone, they'd come after them.

While they traveled, the clones seemed to keep their distance from Jack. It was a bigger group than Jack could have imagined. It'd never occurred to him that others would want to leave. Everyone was so happy in Vispera. They belonged. They had what he used to always want, why would they give that up?

There were almost fifty of them, divided among the generations and models. Three Gen-290 Samuels had come. They avoided meeting his eyes as much as possible, remaining wary and watchful. Even knowing Sam's feeling, it'd be a while before they had any idea how to act around Jack, and there was nothing he could do to help. The loss of Sam was too recent, and their faces too familiar.

There were Meis, Ingas, some of the older Hassans, four of the Gen-310 Nylas, some Kates, even Viktors.

After walking all night and a day, they stopped to set up camp and cook food. Jack wanted to go farther, but the clones were scared now that they were miles from the safe walls of Vispera, and anyway, they couldn't keep pace with him. He tried not to get frustrated.

"I thought it would just be us," he said to Althea. "I don't even know where we're going."

"Don't worry," she said. "I have some ideas."

A Nyla seized Althea by the arm.

"Come on," the girl said. "Help us organize our dresses in the wagon."

Jack scanned the crowd. There were too many Nylas to keep track of. And exactly how many dresses did they think they'd need? None of them had any idea what they were getting into.

In their first real moment of rest, he had a lot to absorb. Jack turned away from the two girls, needing to comprehend what was happening. He started searching through the wagons, realizing how well organized they were. Occasionally someone came over and murmured a soft hello, or simply nodded to him, or even sometimes clapped him on the back. It was beginning to sink in that they really had left their home to go with him. He'd been an outcast for as long as he could remember, and now they were all following him to God knew where.

He climbed into a wagon and was pleased to find many of his books there, stored with his guitar and clothes. He was still poking through the boxes of supplies when Althea came up behind him. He turned toward her with a smile, and then he saw Carson-312.

"No," he said between clenched teeth. The Samuels and Nylas were one thing, but this? "No way. I don't want any of the Carsons. Especially not him."

"Forget it," Carson said to Althea. "You think I want to deal with him either?"

Carson stalked away, leaving Althea calling after him, but he wouldn't come back. From the thin purse of her lips, Jack could tell she was suppressing irritation.

"Believe me, I get why you wouldn't want him here," she said. "But Carson has no place in Vispera anymore. I think it's been a long time since he felt as though he did."

"I don't care. He's going back." They'd ambushed him, waiting until they were a full day's distance before telling him.

"The people who came with us, they've left their homes, their sisters and brothers. Some of them have fractured. I don't even think all of them know it yet. You don't understand fracturing, but you must know what it feels like to lose everything. You lost Sam, and your brother."

"It's not the same," Jack said.

"It's not the same, but it connects you to them. They're scared and alone. Some of them have never been in a different room from their siblings, and now they're sleeping on the ground in the jungle, far from everything they've ever known. They feel like their hearts are being ripped out. That doesn't sound familiar to you? I know everyone here is looking at you like you're in charge, but you're not. It's not up to you who leaves and who stays. What is up to you is whether you help these people or not. That includes Carson."

"He could have killed me."

"He didn't."

"He would have."

"But he *didn't*. He knows what he did was wrong, and that's something. He helped me escape Vispera before the Binding Ceremony."

She eyed him crookedly, waiting to see what he'd say. Carson hadn't gone far. He leaned against a tree, kicking his feet in the dry dirt. It looked like none of his brothers had come.

The air was still, and the heat of the morning had settled into a mild warmth that lingered in the slow-moving clouds. It'd been a good day for traveling, and Jack was feeling safer with each mile they covered. Not all their days would be like this.

It was going to be difficult, and Jack had no idea how he was going to manage it, especially now that there were so many of them. Althea might not think he was in charge, but they were all watching him. They were looking at him to lead them. They'd need food, they'd need rest and sleep. The entire Gen-230 Altheas were spreading woven blankets on the ground around the camp. They moved slowly but good-naturedly, maybe because they were the only generation that had left together as a fully intact group. But they were ninety-seven years old. Would he be able to get them over the mountains safely? Could they handle the changing temperatures and rough ground? Could the clones even build a fire? They grew half their food in labs. They seemed so delicate sometimes. How would they survive?

Jack went to the tree where Carson stood with folded arms, grimacing at the activity surrounding him.

They were two feet apart, though neither of them spoke until Jack finally said, "Why do you want to come anyway?"

Carson shrugged, irritated at having to answer questions from Jack. "I don't know. I don't feel like I fit anymore."

"I guess now you know what it feels like."

Carson shrugged again, and in the other boy's silence Jack understood that Carson had always known what it felt like not to belong. It was probably why he'd hated Jack so much.

"It'll be hard," Jack said. "Everyone's going to have to work together and help. I won't let you order anyone around."

"I know," Carson said.

Jack grudgingly held out his hand, and Carson shook it. Althea watched them from across the camp, a Nyla by her side.

"I'm keeping my eye on you," Jack said as Carson gave his hand a terse shake, his grip slightly too hard.

"You too, monkey-boy," Carson answered.

Their hands fell away and they looked at each other for a long moment, neither smiling. Althea's optimism aside, Jack figured that was the best they were going to manage today.

Jack went to Althea and pulled her away from the crowd so they were hidden. He drew her close and kissed her.

"Hi, Jack," a Nyla said cheerfully as she walked right past them, even hidden as they were. It was a different Nyla from before, he guessed, but he couldn't tell. Maybe someday he'd get them all straight.

"They keep doing that," he said to Althea. "Saying hello to me."

"They're being friendly."

"That's fine," he said. "But you know I'm yours, right? Only yours. Do you understand?"

Althea gave him a small, pleased smile. "I think so," she said.

After the second day, thirteen of the clones who'd left with them turned around again, returning to Vispera. On the third day, they lost four more. By the fifth day, the remaining clones weren't clinging to each other so desperately, and the crying Jack heard during the night had dissolved into occasional soft sobs.

They crossed the mountains, finding the store of things Jonah had left for himself along with the boat. Jack looked for some sign that Jonah had come back to this place, but found none. He considered Jonah might have collected his supplies intending Jack to find them. The thought was comforting. It told him that, wherever Jonah was, he'd be okay.

In her search, Althea uncovered a package of inhalers tossed in with other medical equipment, and Jack tucked it in his bag. Jonah had brought the inhalers to this place with the hope that they'd be together. Jack held one of the slim gray tubes, realizing it was a gift from his brother. He wondered how long they'd last. He wouldn't be able to get more.

The boat was too small for everyone, so they took what they could from the stockpile and waded across the river on foot, the mules pulling the wagons against the current. After a lifetime of questioning, Jack finally saw what was beyond the Novomundo Mountains, and his heart sank when it turned out to be more mountains. Althea seemed to know where they were going, however. She told him about a place called Merida. She said there might be others there, and whether she was right or not, it was a relief to have a place to go, a destination to aim at.

They passed crumbling stone temples, older than anything that'd been stored in the Tunnels. They headed north and saw a hundred more decrepit buildings, their naked metal beams reaching into the sky like broken fingers. Where the buildings rose from the earth in dense clusters, with silent agreement the group gave them a wide berth, and not just because they seemed about to topple over and crush anyone nearby. They weren't like the stone pyramids in the jungle, ancient and untouched for millennia. These tumbledown buildings were pitch-black and forbidding, and a damp rot seeped from every corner of their cast-iron skeletons. Jack felt no affinity for the people who'd built these things. They were long dead, and what they'd left behind was of no use to him.

For a number of days, a pair of jaguars kept pace with them, their orange-speckled coats glimmering through the green forest. They heard muted roars at night and glimpsed cat eyes reflecting the flare of fires ringing their encampment. The group drew close and encircled their camp armed with pointed sticks and cattle prods jammed on extended staffs. Then the animals disappeared and, with a collective sigh of relief, the group continued on.

After several weeks, they reached a low sloping valley. Jack climbed a steep rise that overlooked the expanse of land below where the mist rose off the distant hills colored with flowers—the purple and red, green and gold—that looked like amaranth in Vispera. Althea came over and sat beside him. They leaned close, sitting together quietly.

"You think we might not make it, don't you? You're worried no one here is strong enough to survive outside Vispera," she said.

Althea had grown thinner since they'd left, and Jack supposed he had as well. Everyone looked tired and hungry. They had blisters on their feet, and their muscles ached. A Kate had broken her wrist, and two weeks ago half of the group had come down with a sudden and dangerous fever. They'd never been sick before, and it terrified them. But Jack had begun to notice the clones' legs and arms were harder now, and there was a determination in their faces that was new. They were stronger than they'd been when they left.

"I don't know if we're strong enough to survive," Jack said. "But everyone at least deserves a chance to try. Isn't that what matters?"

The clones had changed in other ways, too. A Hassan told a story at the campfire one night. It wasn't a very good story—mostly about losing his knife while trying to catch a large snake. But Jack noticed the embellishments he added, the ways the story wasn't entirely what Althea would call *true*. Another night Jack played his guitar, and a few of the clones didn't look quite as disgusted as they usually did. A Mei and Carson-312 even moved together in one of the ritual clone dances as he played. After, the two slipped away to a tent, gazing at each other in a way he hadn't seen before from the clones.

Lying in their sleeping bag at night, Jack said to Althea, "Have you noticed people are talking more than they used to?"

"Their ability to commune is fading. We're a long way from home, separated from our brothers and sisters, and there are fewer of us. It makes the bond weaker." She paused for a long time and then said, "They think when you play music, that's your way of communing with me."

"Huh," Jack said. It was an interesting thought. "Does it feel like communing?"

"No," Althea said, turning toward him with a slow smile. "But we do have our own ways. The others can learn those ways, too."

They moved on day after day. Heavy rains slowed them down sometimes. On a steep cliff, they lost a mule to a broken leg, and a broad rapid-strewn river forced them to make a wide detour for a safe place to cross. The map Althea had brought poked from her pocket, though she'd looked at it so often now, she no longer needed it.

"We should be getting close," she said one night.

And they were.

By the end of the next day, they reached a stretch of land that spread before them, vast and green. The late orange sun warmed Jack's face, while far below, from beyond the foot of a round hill, a score of neat cottages clustered together beside a rushing creek, thin plumes of smoke rising from within, and fields of crops—corn, rice, and bananas—stretched into the distance.

Looking down at this place, Jack didn't know what they'd

find. Would the people here have only one face, or many? Would they be kind? Were they clones, or human, or something else . . . something new?

He'd already lost so much. He didn't know what was to come, and suddenly, after so many days of walking, he couldn't move his feet.

Then Althea stood beside him and her fingers closed over his.

They made their way hand in hand, with steps thoughtful and slow, up and over the green blossoming hill until music, soft and joyful, met them on the wind.

# Acknowledgments

Thank you to my wonderful agent, Adam Schear, at DeFiore and Company. Without him, *Your One & Only* would not exist. From our first conversation, Adam understood my characters and stories, and his insight and attentiveness made this book infinitely better.

I am so grateful to Sarah Landis for choosing this project, and for her knowledge, professionalism, and amazing work in getting my book ready for the world. I loved working with her, and I am proud that she made me part of the HMH team. I am also immensely pleased that her last great service was to put me in the excellent hands of Lily Kessinger, her successor as editor, whose expertise, enthusiasm, and support have been equally invaluable. I am humbled by all the wonderful people at HMH who have dedicated their time to making *Your One & Only* the best it can be, with special thanks to Amanda Acevedo, Harriet Low, Linda Magram, Michelle Triant, Emily Andrukaitis, Mary Wilcox, Catherine Onder, Maire Gorman, Christopher Moisan, Karen Walsh, Mary Magrisso, and Lisa Vega.

I have endless gratitude to my friends and family for their support. Thank you to Caitlin Finlay, Leigh'Ann Andrews, Jordan Andrews, Jill Briggs, Catherine Dent, Ashley Grummel, Peg Keller, Rachel Morgan, Matthew Weedman, Dan and Teresa Schraffenberger, Jonathan Schraffenberger, Carolyn Harlow, Kirsten Faucher-Harlow, and Constance Finlay for offering their thoughts, critique, and excitement. Bill and Rhonda Morgan provided the Powell Mountain roundhouse as a beautiful setting for creative work, and Cup of Joe in Cedar Falls, Iowa, always had a table available and a cup of tea ready.

A special thank-you to Cynthia Bechhold Hawkins, a brilliant writer, reader, friend, and badass unicorn. You are missed.

Many people made this book better than I could have hoped, but if there is a single word in this story that is not the precise right word in the right place, it is only because my father, Robert Finlay, lost a long and contentious argument. He is also the only person a writer could hand an entire book to and get notes back within hours. I'm sorry I didn't always heed them, but I couldn't have asked for a more vigorous and attentive editor.

Ginny and Hattie are my inspiration and joy, my two little people who brighten every single day in their own special ways.

Finally, thank you to the brilliant poet J. D. Schraffenberger for the countless conversations and brainstorms, for the encouragement, and for making me forget why it is we ever needed words for this art. I love you.

## Bio

Adrianne Finlay received her PhD in literature and creative writing from Binghamton University. Originally from Ithaca, New York, she now lives in Cedar Falls, Iowa, with her husband, the poet J. D. Schraffenberger, and their two young daughters. She teaches at Upper Iowa University in Fayette, Iowa, where she is the director of creative writing and an associate professor of English.